THE NIGHT BIRDS

Also by Christopher Golden

The House of Last Resort
All Hallows
Road of Bones
Red Hands
The Pandora Room
Ararat
Dead Ringers
Snowblind
The Ghosts of Who You Were
Baltimore, or, The Steadfast Tin Soldier and the Vampire (with Mike Mignola)
Joe Golem and the Drowning City (with Mike Mignola)
The Boys Are Back in Town
Wildwood Road
The Ferryman
Strangewood
Straight on 'til Morning
Soulless
The Myth Hunters: Book One of The Veil
The Borderkind: Book Two of The Veil
The Lost Ones: Book Three of The Veil
The Ocean Dark

THE SHADOW SAGA
Of Saints and Shadows
Angel Souls and Devil Hearts
Of Masques and Martyrs
The Gathering Dark
Waking Nightmares
The Graves of Saints
King of Hell

THE NIGHT BIRDS

CHRISTOPHER GOLDEN

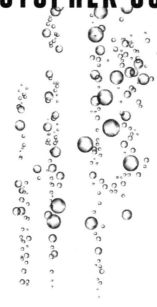

ST. MARTIN'S PRESS
NEW YORK

This is a work of fiction. All of the characters, organizations, and events portrayed in this novel are either products of the author's imagination or are used fictitiously.

First published in the United States by St. Martin's Press, an imprint of St. Martin's Publishing Group

For information, address St. Martin's Publishing Group, 120 Broadway, New York, NY 10271.

www.stmartins.com

The Library of Congress Cataloging-in-Publication Data is available upon request.

ISBN 978-1-250-28591-1 (hardcover)
ISBN 978-1-250-28592-8 (ebook)

First Edition: 2025

10 9 8 7 6 5 4 3 2 1

This one's for Daniel, who was on my mind every day

THE NIGHT BIRDS

1

Out in the dark, the crickets were screaming. It sounded like every cricket on Earth had descended on Ruby's property. There'd been one hell of a lot of rain in the spring, and her grandma always said that meant a mighty swarm of crickets as summer wore on. Now here was evidence that the old lady had known her stuff.

September had sped past, but summer lasted longer these days. It was early October, and the heat and humidity still blasted Texas, forcing her to keep the air-conditioning running at least till sunset. A lot of older folks seemed to thrive in this weather, endured it with a hard-edged pride. Ruby admired their fortitude and considered herself lucky.

Tonight, she sat out on her screen porch, guitar in hand. A warmth pulsed through her, and her muscles melted, thanks to the raspberry-flavored gummy she'd chewed just before she'd come out here. The day had been hot as hell, and after dark, it didn't seem much cooler, but the humidity had withdrawn for a time, and she wanted fresh air. The pregnant blonde who tried to predict the weather on Channel 42 had said to expect a mess blowing in from the Gulf—a tropical storm, maybe a hurricane—but Texas had seen a hundred storms worse than this, so nobody seemed worried. Ruby felt grateful the storm was coming. Its approach had vacuumed all the moisture from the air like the water receding the moment before a big wave crashed onto the sand.

The humidity would come back worse than ever, but tonight,

she could breathe. She strummed a couple of chords she'd been toying with, trying to find the song in her head. At night, it grew so dark she had to rely on the stars to illuminate the patch of yard back there, but she didn't need to see the strings to find the notes.

After a lifetime knowing this house, it felt strange to live alone here. Her grandfather Bill Cahill had died and left it to her, along with his guitars and his vinyl music collection. Ruby had a younger sister named Bella, but she was off in Louisiana somewhere. There'd been the occasional phone call for the first few years after she'd left and one strange postcard from a place called Breaux Bridge that gave them a return address.

When lung cancer had snuck up on Grandma Dot and killed her in a week, Ruby had sent Bella a letter and tried to track down a phone number. She'd even called the police in Breaux Bridge to see if they were willing to make a notification. They were able to confirm Bella was alive and living locally, and they promised to pass on the message. Even so, the wake and funeral came and went without an appearance from Bella. Not so much as a flower or a card. Not even a phone call.

Grandpa Bill never mentioned Bella's name again after that, but when he followed Grandma Dot to the grave, Ruby learned her sister hadn't merely been left out of the will—their grandfather had explicitly disinherited her. *Anyone gives that girl anything of mine, either goods or cash, I'll haunt them to the end of days*, he'd written. *Don't give her so much as a dime from my sofa cushions or a tomato from the garden.*

Not that it mattered. When word reached Bella Cahill that her grandfather had died, she'd written her sister another postcard. *I'm sorry, Rubes*, she had scrawled. *I know you loved him.*

That was that. No call, no visit, no flowers or other remembrance. Just the postcard. Grandpa Bill hadn't left her anything, and it seemed Bella didn't want anything from him. Which left Ruby without family, alone with her music and her memories.

"Ah, hell, old man," she whispered to Grandpa Bill now. She

didn't know whether he'd ended up in heaven or hell, or just turned into a ghost, floating around and keeping an eye on her. That would have been just like him. Whatever had become of his soul, she missed him. Grandpa Bill had left her a house full of memories, including all the records he ever played her and the guitar on which he'd taught little Ruby her first chords.

During a momentary lull in the cricket chorus, she heard a clink of ice shifting in a glass. It was a pleasant sound, a reminder that she'd come out here to do more than tinker with a new song. She'd come out to drink, even taken the time to fix herself a small pitcher of sweet tea margaritas.

Ruby plucked her glass off a little metal table. She twisted the glass around to find the spot with the most salt still on the rim. If a woman troubled herself to mix sweet tea margaritas, she ought to get the most out of it. Of course, that meant finishing her drink before melting ice diluted it any further.

A challenge, but she was up to it.

She took another sip. Shivered with the pleasure of the alcohol's burn. Set the glass down and pondered the chords again, shifting on the cushions, missing the old buzzard as she always did. When Ruby had ditched college halfway through freshman year to pursue music, Grandpa Bill had been the only one who didn't treat her like she'd just stepped out into traffic. He'd had faith in her, and when the rent on her shitty little apartment in Austin was overdue, Grandpa Bill had always paid it.

Times had changed. She'd inherited this house just when she'd started earning enough money from her music that she could've afforded to buy one. The irony hurt.

With the crickets for company, Ruby sipped her sweet tea margarita and enjoyed the solace of loneliness. She'd written a song called "The Gift of Grief" and was surprised by how many people couldn't accept that the pain of losing loved ones could be a gift. It cut deeply, carved out bits of your heart that you could never get back, but that pain meant you had loved deeply and fiercely, and been loved in return. Without love, there was no grief, and despite the pain, that was beautiful.

Her eyelids grew heavy. The sugar in the sweet tea wasn't enough to balance out the alcohol and the gummy and the screaming song of the crickets. It was too loud to be a lullaby, and yet she felt she could nod off easily. The guitar lay across her lap, waiting.

Then the crickets fell silent.

Ruby blinked, suddenly alert. She frowned at the darkness beyond her porch screen. The metal mesh reflected back a bit of the glow from her lamp, which made it even harder to see anything out in her yard. The quiet seemed unnatural. Folks went to sleep early out here, which often meant the only ones awake with her after midnight were hound dogs and horses stabled at least a quarter mile away.

Tonight, she had no company at all. Not a whinny or a bark. Not even the crickets, now.

Ruby ignored the last dregs of her drink. She rose from her chair, set aside her guitar, and went to the screen door, trying to see out into the dark. Nothing made crickets go quiet like that except maybe the roar of thunder or the sudden arrival of an unexpected predator. Not that they were in any danger from predators. They were just crickets.

But they knew when to hold their breaths.

Out in the dark, something moved. Footsteps shushed against the tall grass.

"Ruby," a woman's voice rasped. "You have to hide us."

"Who the hell is that?" Ruby asked, one hand on the handle of the screen door. She peered into the dark and saw a pair of frightened eyes staring back. "Bella?"

"Not Bella," the voice said.

Ruby could make out the shape of her in the dark and the small, squirming bundle in her arms.

A baby.

It began to cry.

Frightened eyes blinked in the dark.

"For his sake and for your own," the dark shape said, "let us in."

And Ruby did.

2

The windows rattled at the front of the Gumbo Diner. When a big gust hit, the plate glass seemed to breathe, straining against the window frames. Galveston had a long history with hurricanes trying to blow the city off the map—just blast across the island and sweep every trace into the Gulf of Mexico. Locals had been worried for a week, but if the latest forecast proved correct, they were in the clear. The hurricane had shifted to the east, expected to ease down to a tropical storm by morning. They were only going to get the outer edges, a lot of rain and bluster.

Even so, there'd be no work tomorrow.

Book felt like the only one unhappy about that.

"Come on, man," Gerald said. "Don't be stupid."

Luisa tapped the table. "That's a little harsh."

"You're right." Gerald raised both hands. "*Stupid*'s the wrong word. But staying out on the *Christabel* during this storm is not smart. I'm not going to say it's irrational, but this decision and irrational are definitely neighbors."

Book smiled. Somehow, Gerald always managed to needle him without making it hurt. It seemed strange that he was an only child, because Gerald Coleman would have been the perfect little brother.

"I'm aware you guys think I'm nuts," Book said. "But I'll be fine."

He felt confident about that. Relaxed, even. Book appreciated the way stress and calamity narrowed options to just a few. He glanced around at the team.

Gerald sighed. "Your funeral, Book."

Luisa Hidalgo hadn't taken her yellow raincoat off throughout the meal, just sat there dripping as she ate. "I know better than to try talking you out of something stupid."

The fourth member of their team sopped up the remainder of his jambalaya with a piece of bread and popped it into his mouth, chewing as if none of this were any of his business. Alan Lebowitz sipped his homemade root beer and then dabbed at the corners of his mouth with a napkin. He behaved as if he were sitting at the next table over.

Book had known and admired all three of them before starting on this project, but he had assembled this team based on more than just their credentials. The project required they spend an awful lot of time together, much of that time in close quarters and isolated from the rest of the world, so he had chosen colleagues whose company he thought he would enjoy. There had been moments of friction in the early days, but time had shown the wisdom of his selections. In a relatively short time, they had become a bit like family, with all the teasing and bickering that word often entailed.

If they were a little like family, then Alan was the lovably grumpy uncle. Book might be the project manager, but Alan had decades on the rest of them, and often a single grumble or sigh from him would set the others laughing, even as he kept them focused. People talked about the wisdom of age as if it were something every senior citizen acquired with time. Book thought that was bullshit—assholes and fools never grew wiser, they just became old assholes and old fools. But as much as they teased him, what Alan had to say always mattered to the rest of the team.

"Alan?" Book said. "You going to chime in here?"

He issued something half grunt and half chuckle. "There any point?"

"Come on," Book replied. "I know you've got something to say."

Alan leaned back in his chair, hands on his belly as if he had a gut worthy of Santa instead of being slim as a fence post. "My view isn't going to change your view, is it? Men my age are known to be stubborn as mules, but I've never met anyone as stubborn as you."

Luisa hugged herself as if the gusting wind outside had blown right through the glass. Her raincoat crinkled loudly. "And if you thought he would listen, what would you say?"

"I'd say Gerald had the right word," Alan replied. "Sleeping out on that old junker is stupid as heck. You don't know how bad this storm's gonna get, but it won't be fun. The docking platform may be welded in place, but there's no telling what a strong-enough storm could do. If it breaks away, getting you off the ship after the storm will be a nightmare. There are too many variables."

Book opened his hands like a preacher, about to explain the research that went into installing the stairs and the docking platform on the hull of the ship, but Alan shook his head.

"No, no, Mr. Book. I'm not trying to persuade you," the old professor said. "Just answering Luisa's question. And now that I have, I'd like to get some coffee in me and go hunker down in my bed until this storm blows over."

Alan glanced around for their waitress and grumbled when he didn't see her. He reached into the pocket of his baggy pants and tugged out his phone. In a moment, he would be lost on Instagram or down some other rabbit hole. At sixty-seven years old, Alan spent more time vanished into his phone than the rest of them put together. Gerald had nicknamed him "the screen-ager."

"I appreciate the concern," Book said, looking around the table. "Whether it comes as questions about my sanity or otherwise, I recognize it, and I'm grateful. But I promise you, I'll be fine.

That freighter has been out there forever. It's been through multiple hurricanes that caused significant damage, and this storm is nothing in comparison."

Luisa nodded. "I know. You're looking forward to it. You've already said."

"I look at it as just more research."

Book spotted the waitress and waved her over. As she approached, he caught Gerald giving him one last admonishing glance.

"I know you're stubborn as hell," Gerald said. "But if you change your mind, you come and sleep on the sofa in my hotel room. I promise not to give you shit about it till the storm blows over."

Book nodded his thanks but wanted to move off the subject, so he was glad when the waitress arrived. The Gumbo Diner's menu offered dessert, but somehow none of them ever ordered anything but coffee after dinner. They ate there nearly every Friday night, after a long week out on the water, and by the time coffee arrived, everyone seemed eager to retreat to their respective corners.

Luisa had rented a tiny apartment outside the city. Alan lived in a B&B patterned after an old-fashioned boardinghouse, where a seventy-five-year-old woman made his bed and gave him breakfast every day. He liked being taken care of but didn't have anyone in his life willing to do the job. Gerald had spent these months in a midrange hotel in the midst of downtown. He liked to be in the middle of things, to eat good food, drink good whiskey, hear live music, and shop for hats and shoes and expensive clothes.

As for Book, he had started out in that same hotel, but soon afterward, he had moved on board the *Christabel.* They all thought he was out of his mind, and Book understood. The freighter had been sitting belly-deep in the water off Pelican Island since the

Big Blow of September 1900, and the ship wasn't going anywhere. You couldn't sink a boat that had already been sunk.

The freighter had run aground way back then and been towed to Pelican's eastern shore not long after. Its dismantling and removal had been planned a dozen times, but there was nothing government did better than steal money from itself. Every time it seemed this eyesore was slated for removal, the funds had been diverted elsewhere.

Over the years, in a stunning example of nature laying claim to something forged by human hands, the ship had been infiltrated by mangrove trees. Roots from the nearby shore grew underwater and up through the rusted iron hull, around broken masts and smokestacks. The trees spread, growing across the still-intact deck, braiding themselves into something beautiful and seemingly impossible—a small mangrove forest that rose forty or fifty feet above the deck. There was something spiritual about it all, but Book didn't dwell on that element of the floating forest. He was here for the science.

Book liked to call it *the floating forest*, but when the Texas Parks and Wildlife Department put together the funding request, someone in the statehouse started referring to it as "the Christabel Project," and it stuck. Book had gotten over it quickly. The beauty of this strange phenomenon brought him serenity—which was the main reason he had been living on board the *Christabel* instead of in a Galveston hotel like the rest of the team.

Peace. Nature. An experience no one else could claim. As a scientist, he didn't believe in magic, but sometimes the world around him offered moments and places and extraordinary experiences that filled him with a sense of wonder and delight, and that was magic enough.

So he would sleep out there tonight, just as he had every night since he had departed the hotel more than three months ago.

The check came, and Book paid. Texas Parks and Wildlife would reimburse him.

Alan stuck his phone back into his pocket. He sipped his café au lait and glanced around at the rest of them. "Weird being here on a Wednesday night."

Gerald smiled thinly. "You're not used to you and Book being the only white people in the place."

Alan shrugged. "There's that. It's also just quieter."

"Might be because of the storm as much as it being a weeknight," Luisa said.

"I don't mind," Alan added. He searched Gerald's face. "I actually prefer it quieter. I also don't mind being one of the only white faces in the joint. Feeling out of place is not new to me."

Gerald gave a knowing look, raised his coffee mug, and the two men clinked cups.

Book's mug was still half-full when he slid his chair back and stood. "You all take your time. I've got a little bit of a drive, so I'm going to head out. Assuming we don't have a miraculous change of weather, just stay home and enjoy the day off tomorrow, and I'll see you out on the wreck on Friday morning."

"Book," Luisa chided him.

He smiled, nodding. "I know. If we want the funding for this thing, I need to stop calling it *the wreck*. I'll see you in the forest, then."

The floating forest. That magical place, on a bed of rusted iron and seagull shit.

As he left the Gumbo Diner, the door blew out of his hand. A bell above the door jangled angrily as he managed to wrestle it closed. The rain pelted him at an angle as he darted across the parking lot toward his decade-old Subaru Forester. It had been a deep green when he'd bought it, but now in the rain and the dark and with the years gone by, it looked like the dusty chalkboard in the old Pennsylvania schoolhouse in the town where he'd grown up. He loved the Forester the way he'd loved that schoolhouse.

The car started right up, reliable as ever. The radio came on, but static grated on him, and he clicked it off. The rain and the windshield wipers kept him company as he backed out of his parking spot, then pulled into the street and headed for the bridge to Pelican Island, happy to be on his own again.

Some people hated isolation, but Book thrived on it. The last thing he'd want tonight would be company.

But the universe had been spoiling Book lately, giving him exactly what he wanted. Tonight, that was going to change.

3

Book drove with the radio off. Despite the rain, he kept the windows down an inch to let in the fresh air. The wipers beat their familiar rhythm while the tires whispered through the slick of water on the road. Somehow those sounds comforted him.

The team worried for him, but he eagerly anticipated the night at sea. The Galveston weather hadn't even reached the strength of an average tropical storm, but it was enough to make him feel wonderfully isolated. How simple the world became for someone at sea with nothing but a yellowed paperback book and a light by which to read. The world had been sliding into darkness for years so that it had become difficult to enjoy literally anything without some kind of mental footnote that tarnished that joy. Out on the *Christabel*, he could focus on work and the water. He could not stop the world from decaying, but in solitude, he could still hold on to the sweetness life had to offer. He would never understand why Alan spent so much time doomscrolling on his phone. The world was ugly enough without seeking out more ugliness.

Book drove north over the causeway that led to Pelican Island and then out toward Seawolf Park. Kids loved the playground there and the opportunity to see the submarine that had been embedded in the ground at the naval museum. Every time he drove out here, Book promised himself he would visit the museum sometime, but he never seemed to manage it.

There were only a few other vehicles on the road, and by the time he reached the small inlet where Parks and Wildlife had their dock, his were the only headlights flashing through the rain. He parked beside a too-large pickup truck belonging to Otis Halstead, the dock manager. Book didn't bother with an umbrella—just locked his car and darted across the lot to the gate, where he tapped his code into the keypad. A loud buzz and a click, and he pushed through, making sure the gate clanged shut behind him.

Then he heard the footsteps. Running in the rain. Splashing across the parking lot.

Someone called his name.

It wasn't Otis. Otis would be in the little shack at the end of the pier that served as both his home and office, and this voice belonged to a woman. Book turned and stepped back to the gate, one hand on the latch. He peered through the chain link, watching the dark figure run, slightly hunched, through the rain. She carried a small black umbrella that hadn't been made to withstand the wind. Spokes jutted out of one side where the fabric had torn. Another few heavy gusts and the thing would be ready for the trash bin.

"Charlie!" she said again.

As she spoke, she lifted the edge of the umbrella. Despite the rain and the dark, the lamp above the gate emitted just enough of a glow to reveal the contours of her face.

Book took half a step back, hand still on the latch. "Ruby?"

She ran to the gate, laced her fingers into the chain link. Beads of water ran down her face as she peered at him from the other side. "I know how crazy this seems, showing up like this after . . . shit, after *everything*. I swear I'll explain it all. But right now, I need your help."

Book stared. Rivulets ran down the back of his shirt. He shivered, though he wasn't at all cold.

Ruby. This was Ruby. He hadn't thought he would ever see her again, but eighteen months later, here she was. Images fluttered in his mind, a deck of cards tossed into the air. When they'd met at that club in Austin, after he'd seen her perform. The first time she had sung to him, alone together in her hotel room. The way they'd laughed after he'd spilled red wine on his favorite chair while celebrating the two of them moving in together.

The look of betrayal in her eyes when he'd let her down.

The way he'd felt his heart carved out on the morning she'd left.

Book twisted the latch. He pushed the gate open. "What's the matter? You look . . ." He was going to say *scared* but didn't want to use the word. Ruby had gone through a lot during their relationship—they both had—but he had never seen her frightened, and he didn't like it.

She took his hand. "Come with me. Five minutes, I swear. Then if you don't want to help, I'll go away."

Book did not want her to go away. He never had. But after things between them had fallen apart, he had figured they had nothing left to say. Yet here she was, and just one look at her brought it all back. The pain still resonated, but all he had ever wanted was to make her feel the way she made him feel. He thought, for a while, he'd achieved that. During those months, when he could see himself through her eyes, he'd never been more content.

Now she needed him.

"Let's go," he said.

She led him across the parking lot, back the way she'd come. He stepped into a puddle. The gate thunked shut behind him, and that was good, because Otis would have been angry at him for leaving it open.

Across the lot, beside an old equipment shed, was a dented Jeep Cherokee that looked at least twenty years old. He wanted to ask who it belonged to and what she was doing driving the old beast, but Ruby hurried to the driver's door and gestured for him to climb into the passenger's side.

The wind blew her umbrella so hard it turned inside out. Ruby flinched as the rain swept her dark hair across her eyes. He saw the resignation in her expression as she released the umbrella. The storm plucked it into the air, and it went over the fence behind the equipment shed and vanished into the bushes on the other side.

She looked so beautiful that his heart broke all over again. Mostly because he knew what they'd lost could never be regained.

Ruby climbed into the driver's seat and slammed the door.

Book got in on the other side. The Jeep creaked as he slid onto the seat. When he hauled the door shut, its hinges squealed, and then they were alone in the confines of the tired old Cherokee, rain drumming on the roof.

Only they weren't alone at all.

Another woman sat behind Ruby. He did not recognize her. She clutched a baby's rattle in one hand, prompting him to crane around and see the infant car seat strapped in beside the stranger.

Book turned to Ruby, testing out a smile. "You can imagine all my questions."

"Charlie Book," she said, "meet Mae Cunningham."

The woman in the back seat, Mae, gave a wary nod as if she might be waiting to see if a bomb would explode. Book said, "Hey," quietly and politely, like they were in church.

"Short version. Mae used to date my little sister. The baby belongs to her—to my sister, Bella—but right now, we believe we're in danger."

Book took that in, focused on the last word. It felt like the world tilted a bit. The fear and worry in Ruby's expression had warned him there was trouble, and though he hadn't taken a moment to ponder it, he had felt pleased that she would come to him in times of trouble. But this was something else.

"What do you mean 'danger'?"

"We need somewhere to crash for a night or two where nobody

would ever look," she replied, ignoring the question. "I thought of you and your project."

"Makes sense," he said. "Unless you find a cabin on a mountaintop, it's hard to get more isolated than out on the *Christabel*."

Had he successfully hidden his disappointment? Hard to tell. In the midst of his surprise at her arrival, he'd let himself wonder if they might not be as finished as he'd believed. Now he put aside such thoughts. Ruby wouldn't have come if she'd thought of a better option, which meant she really did need his help. It saddened him, but clarified things.

"That's it?" he asked.

"The short version, like I said."

Book studied Mae. She had a spray of freckles across her nose and hair a shade of red that looked like it came from a bottle but did not. In the dark, inside the car, it turned nearly black. A copper penny dark with the passage of time.

The baby murmured contentedly in his seat.

"Where's Bella now?" Book said, craning his neck to try to get a better look at the infant. "Why do you have the baby instead of her?"

"Because she's dead. Murdered."

Book whipped his head up and stared at her. "Are you . . ." But of course she wasn't kidding. "Christ, Ruby, I'm so sorry."

He watched her fight to control her emotions. If he pushed sympathy on her, that would only make it more difficult. If Ruby wanted to keep her grief inside, he had no business digging for it.

"The baby have a name?" he asked.

"Aiden," Mae replied. The first time she'd spoken.

"Aiden," Book echoed.

Awkwardness began to fill the inside of the Cherokee like helium inflating a balloon. Book knew he should be speaking but then realized it wasn't really on him to break the silence. He had tried to make things right between them, back when it had all fallen apart. Ruby had made it clear that Book didn't have the words to achieve that miracle, that those words didn't exist. So if someone were going to defuse this moment, it would have to be Ruby.

"The *Christabel*'s not exactly a hotel," he said. "And there definitely isn't anything appropriate for a baby."

"We have what we need for Aiden," Mae said.

Ruby nodded her agreement.

"I didn't expect to see you again," he said, trying to untangle his thoughts. "And I definitely didn't expect you to show up with a baby."

"Don't make it about that," she said. "This is me asking for help. You know I'd never have come if I had another option."

Outside the Cherokee, the wind and rain picked up, gusting hard enough to rock the vehicle.

Mae smashed her fist against the back of Ruby's seat. "Say something! We don't have time to waste on this high school shit." She took a breath and gave him a desperate glare. "You're either going to help us or you're not. If you're not, just say it so we can figure out what's next."

Book couldn't find the words to reply. Ruby showing up would have blindsided him even on his best day. Add in the storm, and this other woman, and baby Aiden, and he could barely gather all the pieces of the puzzle they made, never mind put it together.

"We should go," Ruby said, exhaling.

She sounded disappointed, but Book knew her as well as he'd ever known anyone. This wasn't disappointment. The lines on Ruby's face, the way she exhaled like that—she was frightened.

"We'll go," she repeated as if to convince herself. "Sorry to stir things up."

"I have some questions," Book said.

Ruby and Mae both looked up at him in hopeful surprise.

"You're going to let us stay?" Mae asked.

"Of course I am."

"Then can you ask the questions on the boat, Charlie?" Mae said. "We'd like to get the baby somewhere warm and safe."

So many questions, Book thought. But he nodded. "Fine. But call me *Book*, okay? My first name has old echoes that I don't like."

"Book. You got it."

The baby began to fuss. Book wondered if Aiden needed a diaper change. Then he wondered what the fuck he was thinking, agreeing to take these two women, and this baby who didn't belong to any of them, on board the *Christabel* in the middle of the night. In a storm, after a surreptitious conversation in a car parked as much in the darkness, away from prying eyes, as they could have managed.

"I need you to do something for me," Ruby said.

At which point, he couldn't help but laugh. "Something *more*?"

Ruby didn't share in the laughter. Her gaze locked onto his. "I need you to follow us back a couple of miles to the used car lot we passed. It's across from that taco place with the parrot on the sign."

A chill went through him. "You're planning to ditch the Jeep there?"

"Like I said. We'd like not to be found."

He searched Ruby's eyes, then looked back at Mae again. The baby fussed.

"Fuck," he whispered, closing his eyes.

As far as Book knew, it had been years since Ruby had seen her sister or even heard from her, and somehow that had turned into this shit show. Bella Cahill had been murdered, and these two were on the run with her baby. He should have insisted on calling the police.

And yet.

"Let me get my car. We'll transfer the baby's car seat here," he said. "Mae and the baby can ride with me while you drive this heap to the back of the lot and ditch it. Quicker that way. Less chance of someone spotting you."

Ruby shuddered in relief. She reached out and squeezed his hand. "Thank you."

"Let's just do it fast, before the storm gets any worse," Book said. "And once we're on board, I want answers."

He opened the Cherokee's passenger door, hinges creaking, and slid out. Rain pelted him. When he went to close the door, the wind gusted hard enough to make it slam. Book bent his head against the rain and jogged across the lot toward his Forester.

Inside the car, he started it up. The rain refracted the beams of his headlights as he drove across the lot and pulled up beside the Cherokee. As he jumped out to open the back door and help transfer the baby seat, he thought about that used car lot, wondering how long it would take them to realize there was an extra vehicle in stock.

"This is nuts," he muttered to himself as the rain began to fall harder.

But it was Ruby, and so he would do whatever he could to help her. She was afraid, and the Ruby Cahill he'd known had never been much afraid of anything. If Ruby was scared . . . well, that scared the shit out of him.

He had so many questions.

He felt pretty sure he wouldn't like the answers.

4

As soon as she had driven away from the bright colors of the Gumbo Diner, Luisa had felt more herself. She enjoyed the food and the company, and the routine of gathering with her colleagues away from the Christabel Project, but there were layers to her life—to her self—that only intimacy would reveal. As much as she trusted Book and Alan, there were parts of her they would never see.

Gerald, on the other hand . . . well, she hadn't let him see her deepest self, but he'd certainly seen a lot more of her than the other members of the team.

It wasn't love. In her most honest moments, Luisa didn't see love as even a possibility between them, but she didn't mind. Gerald made her laugh, knew when to be quiet and when to talk, and he always smelled fantastic. A little arrogant at times, but he was smart and eager to experience life. They laughed together in bed, where the sex was hungry and athletic, and he seemed dedicated to finding out how many times she could come before she collapsed. Luisa admired his dedication. They weren't planning on a future, but they were stuck here together for at least two more months. Beyond the immediate release of sex, sleeping together felt good, and convenient, and safe.

Sleepy but happy, she burrowed beneath the clean sheets and heavy duvet of his hotel bed. Humidity had lain heavily on the room when they'd first come in, prompting Gerald to mutter about the hotel maids turning off the air-conditioning. He kept it running just to take some of the moisture out of the air, but the cleaning staff always shut it off. Gerald took it as a personal affront. He had clicked on the AC the moment they entered the room and had wanted to close the windows, but Luisa loved the sound of the storm and the way the wind turned the curtains into swaying, billowing ghosts.

They had showered together, dried each other off, and then Gerald had carried her to the bed, where things had quickly become urgent and loud. Now the only sounds in the room were the storm outside and the ebb and flow of their quiet conversation.

"You really think they don't know?" he asked, running his palm along her belly beneath the covers.

"Not unless you told them."

"I wouldn't do that. I know the consequences." He smiled.

Luisa had been insistent about keeping their arrangement a secret. Any time the four of them were together, she and Gerald drove their own cars.

"You think it's weird, me wanting to keep this to ourselves," she said.

"Not weird. I just wish it weren't necessary. We're both single, consenting adults, and we haven't let anything interfere with the work we're doing. I don't think Book would judge us."

Luisa turned on her side, facing him, and reached up to stroke his face. He looked like a man who did not suffer fools, a man with a hard edge, until you looked into his eyes and saw the gentleness there. She knew he wanted more from this thing between them, but she liked things the way they were, and she wondered how long it could last before that silent push-and-pull became too much for them.

"It's not Book, so much," she admitted.

Gerald cocked an eyebrow. "Alan? I have a feeling we'd have to do a lot more than this to shock him."

"I guess I just look up to him. I can't help thinking he'd disapprove," Luisa confessed. "Not of the sex but that we're being unprofessional or whatever, and the whole team dynamic would change."

"But why Alan and not Book?"

She gave a tiny shrug, the covers rustling along her shoulder. "Daddy issues, probably. Alan's got that grumpy paternal thing going. It makes me not want to disappoint him."

Gerald blinked. "Wow."

"Too honest?"

"Nope. As usual, I'm just impressed by how well you know yourself."

"I thought you'd tease me about it," she said.

"We teased you enough at dinner," Gerald replied.

"True." Luisa poked his chest. "You're lucky I'm such a forgiving woman."

They often teased her for being so tiny a human being. As a teenager, Luisa had been massively self-conscious about being so little, but at the age of thirty-two, she found that she appreciated being different. At dinner tonight, Alan had said her yellow raincoat made her look like a little kid masquerading as an old-time fisherman for Halloween. Luisa had been good-natured about it, mostly because she loved that raincoat. She had purchased it from the children's section at a Dillard's department store in Fort Worth, but she kept that to herself.

He kissed her softly, and she nuzzled against his chest, and they lay together for a time. His breathing evened out, and she thought he must have fallen asleep until she glanced up and saw his eyes were open and his brows knitted.

"What's the matter?" she asked.

"Just thinking about Book taking unnecessary risks."

"He'll be fine."

"I know. He's just stubborn."

Luisa laughed. "And you're not?"

"You don't see me out on that boat tonight, do you?"

"I'd hope you wouldn't choose that over this," she said, wrapping one leg around him. "Anyway, it's creepy out there. You couldn't pay me to stay overnight."

"What, you think it's a ghost ship?"

"Of course not. But at night, with the mangrove forest . . . no thank you."

It was a foolish thought. They were scientists. Luisa had a PhD in plant biology. She knew better than anyone else on the team that, while the floating forest might be strange, there was nothing unnatural about it. Even so, it sometimes unsettled her. She would never understand Book's choice to live out there for the months of their research.

"Well, good thing you're here with me, then," Gerald said.

"Oh, you'll save me from the spooky trees, big man?"

"You're safe with me, honey."

Luisa slid a hand between his legs. "But am I safe from you?"

"Oh, definitely not."

Later, she lay beside Gerald and listened to him breathing. He mumbled sometimes in his sleep, but she could never decipher the words.

Sometimes insomnia would sneak up on her in the middle of the night. Luisa hoped this would not become one of those nights, but for the moment, she didn't mind being awake while he slept. She felt content and comforted, intent upon spending tomorrow in bed with room service meals and British TV murder mysteries. And Gerald, of course.

The wind howled, and she could hear the rain hitting the carpet just inside the windows. Reluctant as she was to get out of bed, Luisa didn't want the rug to get soaked. Slipping from the covers, she crossed the room and slid beneath the curtain on the left, enjoying the way it flapped behind her as if she were the heroine in some gothic novel. The rain that had already fallen on the carpet felt cold beneath her bare feet, and she slid the window shut.

Without the wind, the curtain draped over her, clinging as she peered through the glass. The streets were abandoned. Anyone with sense had gone to bed or taken shelter. A single vehicle passed below, a massive pickup truck. She watched it until it reached a blinking yellow traffic light, and then it turned onto a side street and was gone.

She moved to the other window and was about to lower it when she saw something moving on the road below. She had to crane her neck to one side, trying to get a better vantage. A dark, slender figure darted into the street, like the shadow of a person rather than a person itself. A second emerged from between a bar and a bakery across the street and joined the first, and now she saw they weren't merely shadows. They were women, lithe figures with long, dark hair plastered to their backs and shoulders by the rain. One had her hair covering her face so completely, it seemed impossible that she could see.

The two women were thin as scarecrows, and they spread their arms out behind them as if racing in the rain. The way they ran, so swift and light, she thought they meant to take flight. It seemed whimsical, but Luisa watched them and wondered why instead of delight, the sight caused a wary flutter in her chest.

A third one joined them.

The three women swept through the rainstorm, darting here and there, pausing to look in the windows of parked cars and to lightly touch shop windows with the tips of their fingers as if they were in search of something and they would know it the moment they were near enough.

One of them paused, hung her head, and then turned to look up at the Belmont House Hotel. Luisa held her breath. Through the rain and the dark, there was no way the woman could see her, up in this window, with no lights on in the room. Yet suddenly, it seemed very important to Luisa that she *not* be seen.

Seconds passed, and then the woman joined the other two,

rushing like birds along the street, in search of something or someone. Whatever they sought, Luisa felt glad it wasn't she.

When the women were out of sight, she closed and locked the window and went back to bed. The bottoms of her feet were damp from the wet carpet, but she climbed beneath the covers without hesitation, feeling slightly ridiculous. How many times had she seen videos on social media of fools out in the midst of a hurricane, daring the storm surge or the gale-force winds, feeling wild and courageous instead of stupid? These were just young women playing in the storm, wild and free.

She told herself that.

It took hours for Luisa to fall asleep. She huddled closer to Gerald but didn't want to wake him. If she shared this with him, it would be much harder come morning to tell herself it had all been a dream.

5

Otis Halstead spent most of his time around fishermen. *And fisherwomen*, an inner voice reminded him. At sixty-two, he often found himself being schooled by younger folks about being inclusive with his language. That sort of thing grated on him. He'd spent a lifetime on the Gulf of Mexico, working on and around boats, dragging up nets, cajoling tourists, or carousing with sailors and career fishermen. *And fisherwomen.*

He knew women had a lot of shit to deal with that men never did, and he supported equal pay, women making their own health care decisions, and pretty much anything else the world could do to offset the grim shit. But for fuck's sake, rewiring his brain to speak so as not to offend anyone wasn't easy at his age, especially when the rules kept changing. He just wanted to be kind, have other folks be kind to him, and be left alone to read his mysteries and listen to the waves crash against the pilings on the wharf.

Rain sprayed his face, and the wind plucked back the hood of his coat. Otis didn't bother pulling the hood up again. He kept his hands plunged deep into his pockets and trudged across the parking lot. The wind gusted hard enough to cause him to stumble—at least he told himself it was the wind and not the whiskey. He had spent the past several hours at the Three Sheets Pub, where the fish stew had warmed his insides and a whole lot of Jameson had numbed the rest of him. In weather like this, it wasn't as if anyone would be foolish enough to take a boat out. That hurricane might be losing steam and turning away from Galveston, but the Gulf would still be churning something fierce.

Otis lived in the little shack at the end of the pier, but the Three Sheets served as his home away from home. He ate dinner there most nights, with a discount on his meals that most patrons would have found objectionable. Dianna, the owner of the Three Sheets, was first cousin to Otis's late wife and tended to look after him. But it wasn't the discount or even Dianna that kept him going back to the Three Sheets five times a week. It was the place itself, the atmosphere. The Three Sheets smelled like salt and decades of stale beer soaked into the wide-beamed wood floor. It wasn't a shithole like a lot of dives in a thousand seaports around the world, but it also didn't cater to tourists, and that was the key.

Fuckin' tourists.

He had to be polite to them at the pier. There were harbor cruises and deep-sea fishing charters that operated off the island, and Otis would catch hell if he didn't do his best to make their clientele feel welcome. But the Three Sheets was his after-work spot. There was one light above the door, a few neon beer signs in the windows, and beyond that, nothing to beckon strangers into the place. Most of the patrons were faces he'd known for years, if not decades. Friends and acquaintances and half a dozen pricks he'd gotten into scrapes with during his misspent youth. But they were his people, weathered and scruffy, wrinkled and laughing, voices roughened by various addictions.

Occasionally, some of those tourists and day fishermen would wash up on the shore of the Three Sheets, enjoying what they might call its authentic ambience. Tonight had been one of those nights, with two fortysomething couples who had come in looking for a taste of the maritime life. Otis heard their conversation with the bartender and learned they were the parents of students enrolled at Texas A&M's Galveston satellite, which specialized in maritime programs, but from the sound of things, none of the four strangers had much understanding or appreciation of their children's pursuits.

One of the husbands complained about the way Dianna served red snapper. It came in a chili butter sauce that Otis believed was too good for the likes of himself and the other old salts that frequented the Three Sheets. This newcomer complained it was too spicy.

On his fourth whiskey, Otis had laughed. The husband shot him a look and asked if that laugh had been directed his way.

"No, sir. Just a general commentary on life," Otis had replied. "But as for the snapper, that's just how fishermen down here like it."

Trouble with these two couples was, they were the type who looked at a man like Otis with a total certainty about his character and intellect. They felt superior, and that came through with stark clarity in the way this husband sniffed at him and said, "Don't you mean fishermen and fisherwomen?"

Otis smiled. Knocked back his fifth Jameson. "If I was as out of my element as you are right now, fella, I'd worry less about parsing people's words than understanding their intentions."

The husband smirked at the other man in their group. "I don't think I quite get you."

Otis stood up, grabbing for his raincoat. "Clean out your ears, son. That's what I just said."

He walked out after that, disdain for the assholes only barely blotting out his frustration with his own reaction. Dianna was always kind to him, and he owed her a bit more decorum than he had shown, even with a supercilious prick who was slumming down among the locals.

It wouldn't be that difficult, he supposed, to try to think a little more about twenty-first-century word choice. But he'd be damned if he would do it for the assholes. He'd do it for the young folks who maybe didn't understand that in his mind, they had always been included.

If he'd been sober enough, he might have said something along those lines.

Instead, he trudged through the rain across the pier parking lot. Without his hood up, trickles ran under his collar, down the back of his neck. He barely noticed. In the years he'd been on the water, he had been so wet that his flesh had practically turned to sponge, so having his hair and beard slicked down from the rain felt refreshing instead of being a nuisance.

From his pocket, he produced a jangling key ring and then opened the gate to the pier. He shut it behind him, not so drunk that he would forget to make sure the place was locked up tight. Already, his mind had rushed ahead to the comfort of his recliner, a mug of hot tea, and the James Lee Burke novel he'd started that morning.

He wiped water from his eyes and clutched his keys as he walked toward his little shack at the end of the pier. Office in the front, home in the rear. He had a bedroom, a bathroom, a little galley kitchen, and a living room, all of them small but sufficient for the simplicity of his life. It was all he needed. At this point in his years, it was all he wanted. Dianna worried about him living so isolated, but most nights, he liked it. Most nights, loneliness was a boon companion.

Like tonight. With whiskey and stew in his gut, he didn't have any interest in company.

At the door to the shack, keys in hand, Otis frowned. Something felt different. It took him a moment to realize what had piqued his interest—the lights were on down along the pier and at the slip where Charlie Book kept the boat he had on loan from Parks and Wildlife. The boat wasn't in its slip.

"What the hell?"

Otis clutched his keys and strode down the pier toward the empty slip. Some of the boats had been taken out of the water, but other folks had waited on the forecast and been rewarded for their risk by the shifting trajectory of the storm. Otis hadn't been surprised that Book had left the Parks and Wildlife boat in the water. It was a fairly sturdy craft, but it could have been hoisted out on short notice if necessary.

What he hadn't expected was that Book would roll the dice on taking it out into the Gulf tonight.

"Dumbass," Otis muttered, wiping rain-slicked hair away from his face.

He stood on the dock by the empty slip and looked out over the water, spotting Book's boat immediately. The running lights bobbed on the waves and illuminated the sheets of rain. Squinting, Otis could make out at least one figure on the deck. Book had to be piloting the boat, which meant he had a guest going with him out to the *Christabel.* Otis would never have taken the boat out tonight, but he supposed Book would be all right. The *Christabel* wasn't far offshore, and the surf wouldn't be quite as dangerous unless they went farther out.

Otis worried about the fate of the boat once they got it tied up to the old freighter, but that wasn't his problem. Not drowning was more important than not damaging the boat. They'd be just fine, although any sane person would've been warm and dry in a fluffy hotel room bed tonight.

He chuckled to himself, watching the running lights diminish as the boat traveled onward. *Any sane person wouldn't be out here in this shack when he could be sharing Dianna's bed.* But a paperback and a lonely mug of tea was a lot safer than risking the life he'd built just for the temporary comfort of a night tangled up with a woman who wanted to take care of him, but whom he knew he would disappoint. He couldn't bear the thought of destroying the friendship between them.

Book, though . . . if that fella had a woman sailing out to the *Christabel* with him, Otis would be happy. Charlie Book loved his work a little too much. If anyone needed a romance to lighten him up, it was that guy.

"Better you than me, friend," Otis muttered.

In the rain, he saluted the light off in the distance, then turned and started back for his shack. It took him a few seconds of scraping the key around the lock before he could let himself in, but he got the door open and exhaled in relief as he stepped over his threshold.

When he turned to close the door, he hesitated. Squinting, looking out into the rain, he saw an enormous nighthawk perched on top of a piling. It seemed so unlikely that he blinked, blaming the whiskey, but the bird was still there.

Then the wind gusted, nearly tore the doorknob out of his hand, and he pulled it shut to keep the storm outside. Just before the door closed, the nighthawk spread its wings and took flight, up into the wind and rain. Otis figured it had to be sick somehow, to be out in the storm like that, or so hungry that instead of taking cover, instinct drove it into the air. Sometimes he liked the idea of being a seabird, even daydreamed about it. But tonight, he'd much rather be an old drunk with a full stomach and a warm blanket.

Whatever that nighthawk was hunting, Otis hoped it found its quarry soon.

6

Out on the water, Ruby felt herself calming for the first time since Mae had appeared in her backyard with the baby. She had started the brief voyage on her feet, telling herself it would take a minute to get her sea legs. Now she sat on a bench at the railing, rain soaking through her trousers and plastering her hair against her scalp, thinking sea legs might be a myth. She knew she ought to go inside the cabin, where Mae had taken Aiden and the baby's travel bag, but the last thing she wanted to do was be in an enclosed space with Charlie Book right now.

The irony of the thought was not lost on her. They were about to be cooped up with him on this old freighter, at least until tomorrow. Book had said there wasn't much space for guests, but Ruby's grandfather used to say no matter how small the room, you could always fit more ghosts and plenty of regrets. His scratchy voice came back to her now, echoing in her head. She wished he had been alive to talk to after she and Book had split up. Wished he were alive to talk to right now.

There you go, proving him right. More ghosts, more regrets.

Ruby felt like she and Book had escaped each other's orbit, but now gravity was pulling them together again.

The boat rose on a white-capped swell, changing her view, and out in the dark, she spotted the gargantuan silhouette of the rusted freighter. The mangrove forest thrusting up from the heart of the ship stood black against the storm, somehow foreboding. Ruby staggered to her feet and held on to the railing as she craned her neck to get a better look.

Another swell, and the bow dipped into a trough beside the *Christabel.* Ruby went to her knees on the deck, held on to the railing, and stared up at the side of the rusty freighter. Over the wind, she imagined she could hear it creaking and groaning. The ocean rose again, and she felt certain the next swell would hurl them into the side of the ship. Adrenaline rushed through her, and she turned toward the cabin to search the rain-dark windows for any sign of Book inside. Could he handle bringing this boat in to tie up alongside the freighter?

Yes, she thought. *Of course he can.*

They'd never talked about how much experience he'd had in piloting a boat like this, but Ruby knew him, and she knew he would never have taken them out to the *Christabel* if he didn't have confidence he would get them there safely. Not with Ruby on board. And sure as hell not with a baby on board.

The door to the cabin banged open. The wind snatched it and banged it again. Book stalked out onto the deck, bent against the storm, one hand protecting his eyes from stinging rain. He beckoned Ruby to follow as he raced around the cabin toward the bow. Clutching the railing as she trailed behind him, she shifted her gaze from the rusty freighter to Book's back, and then the cabin. She bent to try to see through the cabin windows but could only make out blurry lights through the glass.

"Charlie!" she shouted. "What the fuck are we doing?"

As she caught up with him, she saw him grab a thick rope with a coil at one end. The boat rose and fell. The starboard side of the hull thumped hard against something, and Book stumbled, went down on one knee, then recovered and tossed the coil of rope over the side onto a thick metal post she had only just noticed.

"Come and hold this!" he shouted as sea spray blasted up to drench them.

Frantic, Ruby obeyed. She grabbed the rope and helped as he

dragged them closer to that metal post. He tied it tightly to a cleat on the bow and turned to rush to the port side.

"Wait!" she called. "Who's at the wheel?"

Despite the urgency of the moment, he smiled. "Who do you think? The baby!"

Ruby grinned, picturing Aiden piloting the boat. The lightness of the moment, the rush of danger, and the confidence Book instilled in her that everything would be all right—all of it should have made her feel happy and safe. Instead, she watched him jump onto the small, floating platform, and her smile bled out.

The events that destroyed their relationship had felt crippling at the time. As the months passed, she had started to form a vision of a future very different from the one she had imagined. Now, a year and a half since the last time they had seen each other, grief thrust its dagger, a weapon in the shape of Charlie Book's smile, honed to razor sharpness by how easily they'd fallen back into the familiar thrill of each other's company.

What the hell was I thinking?

When Mae had told her they needed to hide somewhere, Ruby had thought first of destinations. Nobody would ever look for her in Las Vegas, for instance. She had been there once for a bachelorette weekend and had made it clear ever since—to anyone who would listen—that she had no interest in ever going back. She hated the roving bands of middle-aged men who went to that place to get drunk, screw hookers, and puff up their chests trying to make the world think they were high rollers. Somehow, though, the all-night gamblers were worse. They made her deeply sad. She had gone down early in the morning to get coffee in the lobby of her hotel, and there were people at the slot machines whose red eyes and rumpled clothes made it obvious they had never gone to sleep.

Nobody would ever look for her in Vegas. But Mae had pointed out the obvious mistake in her thought process. Traveling anywhere that required the purchase of a ticket meant a record of that purchase. If she took out enough cash to pay for gas and food, they would still have needed a place to hide out when they arrived. It was simpler to stay with someone Ruby knew, someone who wouldn't turn them away and who could be trusted, but whoever that might be, there couldn't be a public connection. It couldn't be a person anyone would expect Ruby to seek out, and nobody who knew her would ever imagine she might run to Book. Even if somehow the people searching for Aiden learned of her connection to Book and considered him a possibility, they wouldn't know where to find him. The only reason Ruby knew where to look was that she'd run into a mutual friend of theirs in a bar in New Orleans two months before. It had seemed like the perfect solution, and Mae had agreed. Once she'd learned about the *Christabel*, Mae had practically insisted it was their only real chance, and not only because of the isolation.

It feels like fate, Mae had said.

Ruby wasn't so confident. All she knew for sure was that they had bought themselves a little time. But now that she had seen Book again, she regretted not trying for Las Vegas. They'd been so happy, once. Side by side, they had felt like they could build something beautiful in a world that grew grimmer and more terrifying every day. Seeing him now, that familiar face and voice . . . it all hurt.

Jesus, Rubes, she thought. *It was just one smile.*

Things were complicated enough without dredging up the past. She promised herself they would only stay one night, and that as soon as the storm died down, they would figure out another place to seek refuge.

Somehow.

Jesus fucking Christ. Me, Ruby, and a baby.

Fuck's sake.

Fuck.

But even with the tension buzzing in his head, Book was glad to see her. Ruby looked fit and healthy. Better, honestly, as if life without him had been good for her.

The research boat rolled on the waves, tied tightly to the pilings. Rubber bumpers hung all around the boat, keeping it from sustaining too much damage. Quietly intent, Book assisted Ruby as she stepped onto the docking platform, and then they both helped Mae follow, with the baby's bag over one shoulder and Aiden himself in a sling across her chest. Book led the way up the scaffolding bolted to the side of the derelict freighter. The wind whipped along the outer hull, whistling, screaming, breathing as if alive.

They stepped down onto the deck.

Mae grabbed Book by the arm, fingers digging into his bicep. He might have protested, but one look at her face stopped him. Mae had gone pale. Eyes closed, she wavered on her feet, and her grip on Book had been to keep herself upright.

"Hey," he said, "are you okay?"

Ruby replied for her, "She'll be fine. It's just exhaustion."

Mae smiled thinly, painfully, and took a deep breath. She straightened her spine, resettled Aiden in the sling against her chest, and let go of Book's arm. "This thing really is amazing," she said. "It's otherworldly."

Ruby stood beside Mae, looking up in wonder. From the water, the night and the rain had mostly obscured their view of what Book called the floating forest. Now, even in the dark, they could make out the wild, impossibly primeval transformation the *Christabel* had undergone. Mangrove trees grew up through a large hole that rust had eaten into the middle of the deck, as well as up through hatches and vents. A recently added aluminum catwalk bisected the mangrove forest, spanning the gap where the deck had rusted, allowing researchers a closer look. Branches spread outward and upward in a tangle that had swallowed most of the deck. There had been masts, once. It had been common for steamships of its era to utilize both modes of propulsion. Now the masts were broken things, like archaeological relics, and overgrown so that they had become a part of the mangrove forest.

Tiny tree crabs moved along the branches of the mangroves in their hundreds, black and glistening. Something shifted in the dense tangle of branches, followed by a flutter of wings.

"I have so many questions," Mae said, shielding Aiden from the storm as best she could.

"Let's get out of the storm first," Ruby replied.

Book wasn't convinced Mae was as fine as they were both pretending but had no doubt about the sincerity of her reaction to the *Christabel. Otherworldly* was the perfect word.

Mae leaned a bit on Ruby as they crossed the storm-swept deck.

"Don't worry," Book said over the wind and rain. "Dry clothes, coffee, and a reasonably comfortable bed await within."

Something shifted in the branches behind him, but when he turned, he could not spot the origin of the sound. Birds, of course, just trying to survive the night. His gaze shifted, and he looked across the water toward the pier at Pelican Island. There were a few blurry pinpoint lights, but through the rain, he could see nothing else. No boats, nothing but the Gulf of Mexico and the hump of the island. In the storm, with Pelican blocking the view, even the lights of Galveston were gone.

Yet he felt something there in the dark, out in the rain.

The baby let out another cry, which turned into a plaintive wail. Book snapped around to see that Ruby and Mae had stopped at the door to the wheelhouse, and he remembered the door was locked. Whenever they were away from the ship, they kept their workspace locked up tight. Not that he expected pirates or anything, but with the state of the world, you never knew when some asshole might come along and spoil your whole week.

"Sorry!" he said, digging into his pocket for the key.

He opened the door, then stood aside to let them pass. Once

over the threshold and out of the rain, Ruby seemed to let her entire body exhale. Mae took three steps inside and began to cough.

"Shit, shit, shit," she muttered before coughing a bit more.

Book stood with the open door behind him. The wind buffeted him, but the two women were blocking his path. He waited as Ruby dug Aiden out of the baby sling and transferred him to her arms. Relieved of responsibility, Mae stopped holding back and surrendered to a coughing jag so fierce, it seemed to weaken her.

"You said it might be bad—" Ruby began.

"Shut up," Mae snapped.

Book flinched at her curtness. Both women turned to look at him, as if they'd shared something unintended, but he could not imagine what they thought he might have gleaned from that small exchange.

"Are you sick?" Book asked.

Alarms flared in his mind. Goddamn it, *was* she sick? And if so, with what?

"It's just allergies," Mae replied. "Something I ate."

Ruby was ignoring Book, swaying to calm the baby in her arms, even as she stared at Mae as if afraid she might collapse. "Where are the EpiPens?"

EpiPens. Okay, actual allergies, then. But it had to be something serious.

Probably nuts, Book thought.

Mae had trouble breathing. She nodded as she set down the baby bag, unzipped it, and started to dig around. It took only seconds for her to uncap the EpiPen and inject herself, and the moment she set the pen aside, Book felt like a fool.

"I'm an idiot," he said. "Sorry I'm just standing here."

He turned, hauled the door closed, and turned the lock.

"So am I," Ruby said. "There's nothing you can do. She's got it under control."

And she did. Mae slid to the floor and sat with her back against the wall for a minute or two as her color began to improve and her breathing evened out.

"That's terrifying," Book said.

Mae's smile had stories to tell. "You don't know the half of it."

He offered Mae his hand, and she took it. When she had regained her feet, they both turned to find that Ruby had wandered deeper into the wheelhouse.

"This is not what I was expecting," Ruby said.

Book shrugged. "We needed to be able to work here—and sleep here when necessary. If our proposal is approved, we need staff quarters, which will mean overhauling a lot of the interior. But for now, this is my home away from home."

What had once been the wheelhouse—from which the captain or duty officer could pilot the ship—had been turned into an office space. The side windows seemed like they might be original, but the long glass facing out onto the foredeck had definitely been replaced.

"You had the budget for this?" she asked. "If that window's new, this whole space must have been a ruin."

"You'd think," Book replied, unable to disguise his pride. "Oh, it was in rough shape. But when she was first towed in, they weren't sure what they were going to do with her, so somebody bolted a sheet of metal over the window. There was plenty of leakage, but the damage was shockingly minimal. I made the argument that we'd need to be able to observe the floating forest from here and managed to get the state to pay for the new glass."

He gestured around the wheelhouse. "The rest of this I did with the help of my team and a few friends. There's no way to get rid of all the rust. And the smell of it drifts up from below and in from the deck, but all in all, we're pretty happy."

Worktables and small desks were arranged around the space, with two computer terminals, stacks of books, and shelves of potted botanical samples. One wall had been turned into a photo display showcasing birds, insects, and other creatures they had encountered in the floating forest.

Taking off the empty baby sling, Mae tapped one photo in the midst of the others. "Tell me that's not a bobcat."

Book smiled. "We found it in the mangroves. Or, more accurately, it found us. Little bastard attacked Gerald—he's part of my team—and we had to get rid of it."

Ruby stared at him. "You killed it?"

"Of course not," Book replied. "We shot it with a tranquilizer and then transported it to the mainland. I would never intentionally hurt an animal."

"How did it get over here?" Mae asked. "Can those things swim?"

"I guess it must have," Book replied. "Or there's some kind of wildlife vigilante who thought the cat would be safer here in the mangroves than it would be around people. If that's the case, I can't say I disagree."

"Is it the only one?" Ruby asked.

"The only one we found, but I think we're pretty safe."

"You told me about this thing ages ago," Ruby said, "but it's so much stranger than I imagined it."

Mae perched on the edge of a desk. She cleared her throat, the last remnants of her allergic reaction. "How the hell is it even out here? It sank, and they just left it to rot?"

"Yes and no," Book replied. "A hurricane drove it onto rocks back in 1900. The hull suffered so much damage, it wasn't feasible to repair it. They towed it this far, but it took on so much water that it bottomed out right here."

Ruby shook her head in disbelief. "But again, they just left it here?"

The baby gazed up at her while she rocked him back and forth. Aiden seemed locked into the sound of her voice.

Book pointed to a framed photo among the others—this one of the *Christabel* circa 1913, just where she currently sat, only without the mangrove forest growing up from her insides.

"The state intended to dismantle her. First, they tried to get the shipping company to pay the cost. When that didn't work, politicians argued about the expense for decades. Some years, money was included in the state budget but ended up being appropriated for other things. Anyway . . . here she sits."

While they were together, Book had told Ruby about the *Christabel* and his belief that it could be turned into a kind of teaching tool. He had envisioned school groups on field trips, curious tourists, and ecologists making a pilgrimage to understand how nature had claimed the old ship. He hadn't expected her to remember any of that, but he appreciated their reaction to the work he and his team were doing. Maybe his vision would pay off in the long run.

Ruby turned in a slow circle, taking in the whole wheelhouse. "This is so bizarre. It feels like we're hiding from the apocalypse."

"Like the world ended while we were sleeping," Mae added.

Ruby glanced at Mae, and some kind of understanding seemed to pass between them.

"What did I miss?" Book asked.

"Not a thing," Ruby replied. She looked down at Aiden in her arms and spoke to the baby, even though her words were for Book. "Time for a tour, don't you think, little guy? You need to close those eyes."

Book got the message. "Okay. Official tour coming up. Don't expect much. I'm fairly certain the place isn't haunted."

"Only 'fairly certain'?" Ruby asked.

"Well," Mae said with a little laugh, "you can never really be sure, can you?"

7

Book slid off his coat and hung it on the back of the door. Mae took off her jacket, then held Aiden so Ruby could do the same. Book watched as Ruby rocked him in her arms, patting his bottom and whispering soft kindnesses. When she glanced up, he looked away. There was such fragile beauty in that moment, Ruby calming this small, helpless child, that it felt too intimate for him to share.

"You've really been sleeping out here?" Mae asked.

Book smiled. "Not at first. But I got tired of the back-and-forth. It just seemed to make sense. When we finish work for the day, I like to sit and take fresh notes, handle emails, that sort of thing. Cutting out the commute back to town opened up a lot of time."

"It's not creepy being here alone?" Mae said.

"My colleague Gerald always jokes about it being haunted. At least I assume he's joking. But there *are* a lot of creaking noises, and sometimes the way the wind whips through here, it makes a sound that gives me the creeps."

Ruby kissed the baby on his forehead, then glanced up at Book. "But you love every second of it, don't you?"

"You know I do. Isolation. The ocean. It's so peaceful being cut off from all the noise and venom—"

"You mean 'people.'"

Book shrugged. "Same thing. I love it. During the day, it's like my own jungle. I'll show you tomorrow."

Mae had wandered to the starboard window and peered out. She took a deep, slightly wheezy breath as she tilted her head to look up at the storm as if worried that something more than rain might be falling. Seeing her that way, Book realized she had been twitchy all along. Even before her allergy attack, or whatever it was, she had kept looking back the way they'd come like she thought they were being followed. Book wanted to tell her nobody else would be stupid enough to take a boat out tonight, but he didn't know her. Maybe she was just twitchy by nature.

"So, where do we sleep?" Mae asked, turning to him.

Book gestured for her to follow. "There isn't much to this place. Stay near the stairs and you can't get lost."

Mae shadowed him through a hatchway door and down the metal steps to a short corridor. The first room on the left had once been called the map room, where the captain and his officers met to discuss matters of importance and issues of navigation. Book and his team had turned it into a common room, complete with two old, stained sofas, a shelf full of games, and a card table. In one corner were a couple of dozen books that looked well read.

"Not a lot of usable space for such a big ship," Mae said.

"We're slowly reclaiming sections of it," Book explained. "The original steam engine is still there, but the holes in the hull mean the whole engine room is flooded, along with various cargo holds. A lot of the crew quarters and other spaces are still viable. If I have my way, it'll all be museum space, sealed off from the flooded portions."

Mae nodded. "It's unique, that's for sure."

Of the other three rooms they had already made livable, two boasted narrow racks that looked as if they had come from the same supplier who provided beds to state penitentiaries. Prison chic, all around. One of them had two large suitcases open on the floor and a pile of dirty laundry in a corner.

"Let me guess. You have a stowaway who's a major slob," Mae said.

Book nodded emphatically. "That's it, of course. Definitely not my mess."

Her smile faltered. She leaned casually against the doorframe as if she felt that relaxed with him, but her pallor had grayed and her skin had a feverish sheen.

"Are you sure you're okay?" Book asked.

Mae cleared her throat again, nodding. "Right as rain."

"If there's something—" he began, but clanging steps interrupted.

Ruby emerged from the steps, back the way they had come. She carried Aiden against her chest, patting his back as she paused to peek into the room with the dirty laundry.

"Wow," Ruby said. "This is not the bachelor pad I imagined."

Book opened his mouth to protest, then saw the mocking expression on her face. It was the first time he thought that maybe they could put the past aside long enough to become friends again.

"Continuing the tour," he said, pointing to the end of the corridor. Beyond that last room, another hatchway stood open, revealing dimly lit metal stairs. "There's a storage room just before the stairs. If you go through that hatch and down a few steps, you'll find the head."

"The *head* is what sailors call the toilet," Ruby explained.

"I'm aware," Mae said. "I always thought it was bizarre."

"Oh, it is," Book replied. "Just a toilet and a sink, by the way. There's no shower. Nobody wanted to invest money into making the *Christabel* habitable for guests, but you could survive out here a long time. There's also our little galley and mess hall down there. It isn't much, but it's all we've needed so far."

"And what's beyond that?" Ruby asked.

"I was just telling Mae," Book replied. "There are more crew quarters down there, but they haven't been fixed up at all. We didn't have the budget. Beyond those are cargo holds and more cargo holds, but the lower parts of the ship are completely flooded. There are places where the mangroves have grown up inside the ship, twisted around, nature laying claim to this thing built by human hands, instead of the other way around."

A look passed between Ruby and Mae, a kind of grim acceptance.

"I really am grateful," Ruby said to Book. "Maybe it's not the Four Seasons, but it's what we needed. Us and Aiden, too. It's a relief."

"It's not the kind of place where you expect guests," Book replied. "You won't be comfortable, and you'll probably be pretty chilly tonight, and you'll get bored out of your minds . . . but you're more than welcome. All three of you. As long as you need shelter."

"Thank you," she said. "Really."

Mae echoed her thanks, but Book noticed her glancing down the corridor toward the mess hall and remembered his promise.

"Coffee." He pointed at Mae. "Almost forgot."

Aiden had been nuzzling against Ruby, but now he started to fuss. He looked on the verge of another crying jag. Mae reached out for him, and the baby twisted in Ruby's arms to lunge for the other woman. Whatever time they had spent together, and even though Ruby was Aiden's biological aunt, the baby clearly preferred Mae.

"I've got him," she said. "You guys see to the coffee, and I'll get this little guy to sleep."

"Fair enough," Ruby said, handing the baby over. She lingered before releasing Aiden, a moment of hesitation—or perhaps regret—that Mae did not seem to notice.

Book led the way down the short corridor. The ship's real galley was partly underwater, but their little mess hall did the trick. A small refrigerator ran off the same generator that powered the other electronics on board. There were groceries and snacks and two different coffee makers, one for the snobs and one for the people—like Book—who didn't mind making single cups from those little plastic pods.

"All I've got is dark roast, unless you want decaf," he said, keeping his back to Ruby.

"Decaf might drive Mae to throw herself overboard. I think we'll both go for the dark roast. I don't know if we'll get much sleep tonight, so we might as well get fully caffeinated."

Book popped the first pod into the machine and slid a mug into place to catch the coffee that would dribble out once it started shrieking. He'd always thought of the sound it made that way—shrieking.

"Charlie," Ruby said softly.

Book stiffened. He knew that tone. Remembered it well.

"We don't need to talk about it," he said.

"I think we do."

He sighed and turned to look at her, even as the coffee maker started to hiss. There were dark circles under her eyes, even in what dim light they had. She looked exhausted, her hair tied back into a ponytail. Wet strands, still damp from the rain, were pressed against her forehead. And yet she remained beautiful. It wasn't just the echo of the way he'd seen her when they were in love. No matter how he felt about her, no matter how tired she was, Ruby would have been beautiful to him.

"Go on, then," he said.

Ruby had been leaning against the doorjamb as she watched him put the first coffee pod into the machine. Now she straightened up, her eyes searching his face.

"Can I hug you?" she said, starting toward him.

"I'd prefer you didn't," Book replied.

The first coffee finished. He opened the machine, dropped in another pod, and swapped the full mug out for a fresh one. "How does Mae take it?"

Raspy-voiced, Ruby said, "Cream and sugar."

"You still drink it black?"

"Still. Yes."

Book went to the refrigerator and took out a small container of cream. "You can take that first one. The next one's for Mae."

Ruby went to the small table that served as a coffee station and picked up the mug. "I don't think it's fair for you to make me the villain here, Charlie."

"I wish you wouldn't call me that."

"Fine. *Book.* Doesn't change who you are or who I am."

Book exhaled. "There's no villain, Ruby. Just two people with a lot of regrets."

She took a deep breath. He wondered if she was waiting for him to change his mind about that hug. After another moment, she sipped her coffee and stepped out of his way. Book had never understood how anyone could drink anything so hot, but Ruby never waited for her coffee to cool down. If she didn't want it hot, she would have asked for iced coffee—that was what she always said. Book would have scalded the inside of his mouth.

The second pod had finished brewing. He took the mug and added some cream, then reached for the sugar.

"I appreciate that," Ruby said.

"What's that?"

"That you recognize we both have regrets."

Book blew out a small breath as he added sugar to Mae's coffee and stirred it in. He paused, spoon still in the cup, and then he turned to look at Ruby—really look at her in a way he had thoroughly avoided thus far.

"That's all in the past," he lied.

There'd been sex with three other women since Ruby had left him. Laughter. Good conversation. Sweaty enthusiasm. But he had felt adrift on the current, carried along with no way to navigate. Of course, he had told himself that wouldn't last forever, that he would shake off his memories of Ruby, but when things had ended between them, he had truly lost a part of himself. There was no point in pretending otherwise.

"Let's not rehash things," he went on. "Tell me about now. You and Mae weren't exactly overflowing with information."

Ruby lowered her gaze. He could see her thinking, parsing her words, deciding how much she wanted to share.

"Or we could just keep dancing around like this," he said, lightening his tone. "I mean, if you enjoy this awkwardness. It's a weird fetish to have, but—"

"You're so bizarre," she said, laughing softly. "I forgot that about you."

Book frowned. "I'm that forgettable?"

Ruby looked stricken. "I didn't mean—"

"I'm just giving you a hard time."

They smiled at each other. The ache of the past remained, but with it had come pleasant feelings as well. This was all so confusing. Emotions, in general, could be a bitch.

"Tell me about you," Ruby said. "You're living like a hermit out here—"

"Sort of true, but five days a week, I do have my team with me. They're good people. Brilliant, all three of them with a bit of an edge—though it comes through in different ways. I do like them, though. And I trust them."

"Trust is everything."

"Yeah," Book replied, warmth and humor draining from him. "Faith in other people. Sometimes it's hard to come by. But it's not too late to start trusting. You could begin by telling me the rest of the story."

Ruby gave a small shrug. "There's not much more to tell."

Book shook his head. "Come on, Ruby. You track me down with your sister's girlfriend and baby in tow, and you want me to hide you out. You said Bella's been murdered, for Christ's sake. I think I deserve to know how much shit is going to unfold if whoever you're running from tracks you here."

"They won't, or we wouldn't be here," Ruby fumed.

"You agreed to answer my questions, or you wouldn't be here," he echoed. "At least explain where the baby's father is and whether he and his giant redneck brothers are going to come hunting for Aiden. If I'm going to get into the middle of a custody battle and hide a stolen child—"

"You seriously think I'd do that to you?"

Book pondered that question. He wanted to come back with a line about being surprised in the past by things he didn't think she would do, but he knew it wasn't fair. Not only had he already poked that wound a couple of times, but if he had wanted to turn Ruby away, he should have done it back on land. Out here, now that she was basically stuck with him, it would just be mean.

"No," he admitted. "But you said you would explain."

Ruby sighed. "Look, it comes to this. There are people who are looking for Aiden—and consequently looking for me and Mae. These people have no legal right to Aiden. In fact, they mean him harm."

"Then why not go to the police?"

"They'd never believe us!" Ruby snapped. She exhaled loudly, pressing both palms to her head. "Fuck, *I* barely believe us."

Book studied her. How pale she seemed to him. Exhausted, confused, even rudderless, as if her goal had been to reach this moment and after expending all her energy getting here, she couldn't even begin to consider her next step. He missed her, and he resented her, and somewhere in between those two, he just wanted to put his arms around her. Ruby looked at him as if she'd welcome that simple comfort.

"Rubes," he said, starting across the room toward her, coffee mug in one hand and the other hand reaching out to her. "I'm not trying to wind you up. I just want to know what I've gotten myself into. You're talking trouble. Danger. Mae keeps acting like she robbed a bank and is waiting for the cops to catch up to her."

"I'm not trying to be elusive, but can we do this in the morning?" she asked. "It's a lot to try to put into words."

"Fair enough," he said. Curious as he was, he didn't need those answers tonight, and he could see how badly she needed rest.

A scuff of footsteps interrupted them, and they glanced over to see that Mae had stepped into the room with the baby in her arms.

"Somebody's decided he isn't tired after all. Just fussy."

Aiden squirmed as Ruby reached for the baby, and Mae surrendered him gratefully. Ruby began to sing softly, cradling Aiden and kissing the top of his head.

"I'll give you three some space," Book said, heading for the door. "You probably want to get ready for bed. And I should take a look outside, see how the ship's faring in the storm."

"You're going outside?" Mae asked.

"I have a raincoat."

He could have concocted something about the research boat, checking the moorings, or needing to observe the effects of the weather on the floating forest as part of his work. But he didn't have the brain cells for that kind of bullshit tonight. He was going out on deck because he needed to clear his head. Simple as that.

The part about having a raincoat was true, though. It was red, made in Norway, and kept him both warm and dry.

Book went up the steps, through the former wheelhouse, and grabbed his raincoat as he pushed out the door and onto the deck. The rain buffeted him, but he embraced its sting. He was so happy to see Ruby again, but at the same time, he would be grateful when she had gone and taken Mae and the baby with her.

The wind pummeled him. It tried to strip the raincoat from his grip, but he struggled his arms into the sleeves and managed the zipper quickly. When he raised the hood, the wind blew it back, but finally, he cinched the string around its edges, and it stayed put. The rain pelting the outside of the coat seemed impossibly loud.

He watched the tangled black silhouettes of the floating mangrove forest. The broken masts and the one remaining smokestack looked like the ruins of a lost city in the jungle. The wind bent branches so that it looked as if things were moving up there. Moving, slipping from one tree to the next, watching him.

A bird shifted on a branch. He saw its eyes glisten. When it cried out, its voice sounded almost like a warning.

8

Ruby cradled her nephew and thought about coffee. Despite the awkwardness of being together for the first time in so long, she and Book were apparently still observing the weird little protocols of social contact. She had gratefully accepted the normalcy of coffee, drank half the cup, and then abandoned the mug to focus on quieting Aiden.

Her nephew. Her blood. Her sister's son.

Oh, Bella, she thought. Despite the long silence and the resentment she knew had gone both ways between herself and Bella, she had always assumed that someday they would come together again. In a sane world, falling in love and having a child might have opened the door for the sisters to rebuild their childhood bond. Ruby tried to force herself not to imagine what that life might have been, a world where Bella and Mae had escaped the circle of women who had cast such malign influence over them both, where the Cahill sisters had realized how unimportant their past sins truly were, thanks to the laughter of a baby. Aiden could have done that for them.

But Bella had been murdered. The hope that Ruby had taken for granted had been destroyed. She should have tried sooner, reached out to her sister, insisted they keep in touch. But Bella had kept putting more and more emotional distance between them, and Ruby had let it happen.

She'd never forgive herself, but she would turn her regret into love for Aiden. She would give the baby all the devotion that pettiness had kept her from giving to his mother. Aiden would have all that she could provide, as if he were her own son. At least, that was her intention. She and Mae had not yet discussed what might happen when all of this was over.

Ruby hadn't even known Bella was in a relationship and certainly hadn't known she was pregnant. Had her sister really been so in love with Mae that the two had planned to raise the baby together? Aiden was family, and a yearning to watch over him clawed at her insides, but if Bella had meant for Mae to be Aiden's other mother, then who was Ruby to stand in the way? Ruby had wanted a baby, but she had never imagined being in a situation like this. And she had not even begun to consider what might happen if Aiden's father became involved. Who was he? Would he come after them, after his son? Did he even know Aiden existed?

All questions for another time.

"Did you talk to him?" Mae asked.

Ruby turned, thinking Mae had somehow been privy to her thoughts. "Talk to who?"

"Book. Did you talk to him?"

"Did I explicitly lay out what kind of danger we might've put him in by coming here? I did not. How would I even begin to explain?"

The baby had fallen asleep against her chest. There were no nightmares waiting for Aiden in his dreams.

"Don't you think you should give him a heads-up? Just to be fair?"

"That this is about *witchcraft*? He'd never believe it," Ruby said. "Honestly, I barely believe it myself, no matter how sick you got once we came on board."

A ripple of anger passed over Mae's face. "After everything you've seen? After what happened when you insisted we try to get help?"

"People died," Ruby said quietly.

"Yes, people died."

Ruby stared at her. "You say that so matter-of-factly, like it's nothing. And you talk about witchcraft the same way. Like it just exists, like electricity or running water, some everyday thing we take for granted."

Mae met her gaze. "It *does* just exist. Maybe it's not *Hocus Pocus* or 'Surrender, Dorothy.' But it exists. And, yes, people die. What can I do about that?"

"You can care."

"I *do* care. But I can't erase death. I can't dispense immortality. People die, and the living have to move on," Mae said quietly so as not to wake the baby. It would have seemed sweet if not for the words being spoken.

Aiden fussed in his sleep. Ruby rocked him, but her eyes never left Mae. "For someone who claims to have been in love with my sister, that's a pretty cavalier attitude toward death."

Mae flinched, and her upper lip curled in disgust or anger. It was hard to tell which one. "That's a cruel thing to say."

"She's been *murdered*, by the women in this circle of yours." Ruby felt sick, as if the horror she'd been keeping dammed up inside her had begun to poison her at last. "But you stand there and tell me we have to move on."

Mae walked over to where Ruby sat with the baby and went down on one knee as if she might propose marriage. Regret crinkled her features as she reached out to stroke the thin hair on Aiden's head. She swayed a little, sick in a way that no pill or injection could fix.

"Do you really think my love isn't real?" she asked, staring at the baby. "You think this isn't breaking my heart?"

Ruby sagged in her chair. "I'm sorry. I'm just struggling. I'm trying to wrap my brain around all of this. It's insane."

Mae lifted her eyes. "But it's real, Ruby. I promise you, it's real."

Ruby had never been attracted to women, but in that moment, Mae looked so beautiful and vulnerable that she could understand what Bella had seen in her.

"I know," she said. "I felt the way my skin crawled."

They shared a quiet moment, admiring Aiden, letting the peace of the sleeping infant touch and comfort them. Then Mae broke the silence.

"Can I ask you a personal question?"

Ruby nodded. "I've got nothing to hide."

"You and Book. What happened there?"

"I told you."

"Not really," Mae said. "All you said was that he turned out not to be the man you thought he was. But you show up like this, with a stranger and a baby, and he's gone to a lot of trouble for you. Seems like a pretty decent guy to me."

Ruby regretted letting the question get this far, but she could hear the echo of her own reply. *I've got nothing to hide.* "He's probably the best guy I know. But nobody is really who we think they are, not all the way down. Everyone wears masks, and when they slip and you see what's under them, it can be painful."

Mae bent to kiss the sleeping baby's forehead. "What do you think, Aiden?" she whispered. "It sure sounds like Auntie Ruby is dodging the question."

Ruby laughed. "Maybe a little."

"Fair enough," Mae said. "I won't dig any deeper."

"Thank you," Ruby replied. "Maybe now we can get back to the bigger question."

"Which is?"

"We can't hide out here forever," Ruby said. "What the fuck are we going to do?"

The room was silent except for the groaning of the old ship and Aiden's quiet breathing. *She dragged you into this*, Ruby thought. It was an uncharitable thought. She knew she shouldn't be harboring resentment, but it was difficult not to put some of the blame on Mae. The woman had been a willing participant in acts of malice and bloodshed. She was far from innocent.

Ruby's sister had followed that same path, but Bella had already paid the price for her sins. She'd died for them.

Mae was right about Book, though. They had put him in danger by coming here. When they left, the danger would remain. Anyone following their trail might find him instead. Which meant Ruby had to tell him what she knew, even if he didn't believe a word of it. She just wasn't sure how to start.

9

The nighthawks worried him.

Book sat on a plastic folding deck chair in his raincoat. The forecast had called for the wind and precipitation to start diminishing, but it didn't seem to have abated at all. If anything, it had gotten worse. The wild roar of the storm and the water thrilled him. Cold, damp air blasted across the deck, and he inhaled it all, breathed it, swallowed it. With all the bitterness in the world, he sometimes fantasized about being the last man on Earth. Out on the *Christabel*, it seemed possible to imagine, and tonight, that felt truer than ever. No more cruelty, no more pack mentality, no more people trying to diminish their own pain by hurting someone else in their place.

Peace. Or the closest to peace that he could hope for.

He cocked his head, watching the mangroves sway. Over the wind, he could hear the songs of the night birds. They should have been nested quietly, nervously, huddled together waiting for the storm to pass, but a lot of them were making noise tonight. The floating forest was home to many species. Some were ordinary, others surprising, but the nighthawks should have been gone weeks ago. They had one of the longest migratory patterns of any bird on Earth. It was early October. By now, they ought to have been in South America.

Not this flock.

A dozen or so common nighthawks had stopped here mid-migration, lingered for a day and a night, and then flown south over the Gulf. Now they had come back, and that puzzled the hell out of Book. If they stayed much longer, he'd call Jennie Kim at UT and ask if this was as out of the ordinary as it seemed to him. He had been working for Texas Parks and Wildlife for three years, and people often called him smart, but he was the kind of person who knew a little about a lot of things. With a question like this, you needed an expert.

The rain picked up.

Book had brushed off the concerns of his team when they tried to persuade him not to stay on the ship tonight, and he had been confident about that decision until he was about halfway out from Pelican Island with Ruby and Mae and the baby on board. By the time he had seriously considered turning back, they were closer to the *Christabel* than the shore, so he had pressed onward.

Now here they were. Ruby with her infant nephew, her dead sister's girlfriend, and Book. It was already one of the strangest nights of his life. The knowledge that even now Ruby was just inside, closer to him than he had ever thought she would be again, confused the hell out of him.

But there was no romance in this reunion. Ruby needed him. She had promised to be gone as soon as the storm passed, and he was glad. Having her close made it hard to focus on anything else.

The rain slashed down at an angle, pattering his coat. He thought about the rest of his team—Luisa, Gerald, and Alan—back in Galveston in warm rooms with thick walls, hiding away from the storm. They'd be huddled under their covers, reading books or watching television, living their normal lives, and here he was at the edge of the floating forest. It felt as if the stretch of water separating him from land had become the barrier between normalcy and wild possibility.

Book sipped his coffee. A mischievous smile touched his lips. In that moment, nobody else on the planet was doing the same thing he was doing. In a world of sameness, of ordinariness and repetition, even without the addition of his guests, this experience was unique. He cherished that knowledge. Ruby would be gone tomorrow, but the work would remain, and that had to be his focus.

The lower portions of the mangroves teemed with thousands of tree crabs. The tiny creatures blended well with the bark of the trees, but the moment they moved, their scuttling gave them away. The Christabel Project was to study the wildlife and the unique growth on board and to report on the condition of the freighter itself, mostly because Book had a vision. He had spent the past three years first persuading his bosses, and now attempting to persuade the state, that the freighter could be transformed into the smallest state park in Texas—not to mention a prime tourist attraction. A full network of secure catwalks and observation decks would have to be installed—instead of just one main walkway—and that required funding. Book felt confident that once he and his team made their report, complete with plenty of photos and video, the state would agree.

This was the sort of thing people were always striving for, whether they realized it or not. Peace. Nature. An experience no one else could claim. If you could get a taste of it, even for a minute, it made all the sharp edges of human life worth enduring.

If his team could have been out there with him tonight, listening to the birds and the wind, and the waves crashing against the hull, he knew they would feel the same sense of wonder that he felt. And if they couldn't come to him, he would do his best to make them understand.

But not tonight.

Tonight, rain slashed across the deck. The nighthawks sang again, but they weren't the only nocturnal birds still active despite the storm. During a lull in the wind, he heard the five-syllable cry of chuck-will's-widow. The nighthawks, though—they had begun their migration and come back. It was a mystery, and Book did like to unravel a little mystery now and then. He wouldn't have been on board the *Christabel* otherwise.

A crash of metal sounded behind him. Book turned to see the heavy door wide open, pinned to the wall by the wind. Mae stood on the threshold. The wind had yanked the handle from her grip, and now she blinked, staring down at her empty grasp in surprise. She had tied her hair back. She wore an oversize black Phoebe Bridgers T-shirt and a pair of maroon sweatpants spattered with old paint stains. If this had been their first encounter, he would have thought she looked adorable in her ready-for-bed getup. Instead, the sight of her put him back on edge.

"You feeling better?" he asked, raising his voice over the wind.

Mae crossed one arm over her chest and took a step backward to escape the driving rain. "Just wanted to let you know the coast is clear. You won't catch anyone half naked if you come back inside."

Book tossed the last dregs of his coffee onto the deck and set the mug down. The rain pelted him as he folded up his chair and picked it up. Mae stood back as he approached the door. The wind snatched it, tried to slam it shut, but he caught it before it could slam in Mae's face.

I might regret that later, he thought.

The bitter snark didn't sit well in his gut, but it had risen there by instinct. He had no reason to dislike Mae. She seemed intelligent enough, caring and hopeful. But he knew that somehow she had dragged Ruby into whatever danger they were in, and he couldn't help resenting her for that.

"Your color's improved," Book said. "I thought you were going to pass out earlier."

"I'm okay. Thanks."

Clearly, Mae did not want to talk about her allergies.

He set the dripping, folded chair just inside the door. When he glanced up, he found her watching him expectantly, eyes gleaming in the dark.

"Something you need?" he asked.

"I guess I just wanted to thank you."

Book hesitated, but then thought, *Fuck it*. Life was too short to dance around the weird shit.

"I appreciate that, but honestly, I don't want your thanks. This whole thing is awkward as hell, for a lot of reasons—"

"You and Ruby."

"That's not the only reason."

"She didn't tell me what split you up."

"Maybe because she doesn't think it's any of your business."

"Fair enough," Mae replied. "I'm not asking. You were the one talking about how awkward this is. I appreciate you putting us up."

"Hiding you out."

"That, too."

They stood staring at each other. The wind whipped past Book. The back of his coat was soaked through with rain.

"Okay, listen," Mae said. "The important part is that Bella is . . ."

She broke a little then, and Book felt awful for having brought her to it.

"Bella is dead," she went on, cold and sharp-edged now.

"It's awful. I'm so sorry," Book replied. "But I still don't know any of the details of how she died, except that somebody killed her. Don't you think—"

"You love Ruby," Mae interrupted. "Or you loved her, past tense. Enough to let us stay here without pressing too hard. I'm grateful for the shelter, but whatever your expectations are of what you're owed in return, you'll have to work that out with her. For my part, I couldn't give a shit what broke you up or how you're feeling about seeing each other again."

"Anyone ever tell you that you're a ray of sunshine?"

Mae gave him a blank look.

"No?" Book said. "That shocks me."

"Look, we'll be gone as soon as the storm passes. We've got to keep moving, anyway, or they'll find us."

Book frowned, wondering who *they* might be. "Nobody can find you out here."

Her expression said she didn't believe him.

"You're welcome here as long as you need to stay," he added. "Whatever Ruby needs from me, it's hers. She knows that, or she wouldn't have come here."

"Right now, we just need sleep."

He nodded. "Go ahead. I left something out on deck. I'll be right in, but I won't bother you."

Mae went. Book stayed out in the rain long enough to retrieve his coffee mug but hesitated with his hand on the door before going back inside. It might be warm and dry, but unsettling questions and old regrets waited there.

"Fuck," he said quietly.

Over the wind, he heard a sound like a flag unfurling and looked up to see several nighthawks alighting on the deck a dozen feet away. They watched him, cocking their heads in that twitchy way of birds. One hopped a bit nearer, and the others did the same. Book stared. One of the birds fluttered its wings and seemed about to fly away but only moved a few feet to the left, its eyes on him. All three hopped closer, spreading out, always watching like wolves or lions, hunting in a pack.

A ridiculous thought, but he didn't like the way they stared. He felt the urge to toss the mug at one of them, just to get them to scatter, but caring for wildlife wasn't only part of his job, it was part of his life. He smiled at how stupid he felt, letting birds make him nervous, but when he started for the door, he kept an eye on the nighthawks until he had crossed the threshold and shut the door behind him.

"So weird," he whispered.

Soaked through, he hated to drip all over the floor, but had no other choice. If he had been out here alone, he would have stripped off right there in the wheelhouse. Instead, he trudged down the steps, past the common room. As he approached the mess, he heard voices and slowed his steps. Ruby and Mae were talking quietly, but he couldn't make out the words. When he entered the room, Mae clammed up.

"Sorry to interrupt," he said, walking over to the coffee machine on the counter.

"It's your ship," Ruby replied.

"Not exactly." He dug around in the box of coffee pods until he found a decaf, then popped it into the machine. "Everything okay? You two look worried."

Ruby leaned against the table. "I've barely got any service on my phone, but I was looking at social media posts about the storm. People in the area, in Freeport and Bayou Vista, are posting about how much worse it is than the news stations forecast. There are videos of streets flooding, trees and power lines down already. The meteorologist from Channel Thirteen just did a piece about it. All the tracking models showed the storm weakening and moving east. She said she's never seen anything like it, that the weather here has to be an anomaly. The main storm is moving away from us."

Book pinched his eyes shut and shook his head. "Hang on. The storm's either moving away or it isn't."

Mae uttered a dry, sharp laugh, which turned into a grating cough. "You'd think." She cocked her head, listening as if she could pick out unwelcome sounds from the noise of the ship and the storm and the Gulf. On guard, as she always seemed to be.

The coffee machine started pouring decaf into his mug.

"A tropical storm has tails," he said. "Bands of rain and wind that stretch out, whip around."

He took cream out of the small fridge and poured a little into his coffee.

"Don't you think the meteorologist would know that?" Ruby

asked. "She's baffled. If I can get a couple of bars on my phone again, I can show you."

Book sipped his coffee, leaned against the counter. "What difference does it make? We'll get some sleep, wait it out, and see how things look in the morning."

Ruby and Mae exchanged a look. Ruby seemed nervous, even a bit afraid.

"It'll be fine," he said. "You can't sink a sunken ship."

"I know," Ruby replied. "It's just scary."

Book knew her well enough to realize she was far from okay. Whatever they had really been discussing when he came in, they weren't ready to share it with him.

Mae grabbed Ruby by the arm as if to reassure her. "We'll be okay."

She slipped from the room, leaving Book and Ruby on their own.

"Ruby," he began.

"Good night, Charlie," she said. "And thank you."

Stung, he watched her go. She followed Mae back to the quarters they would be sharing with the sleeping baby. *And what about that?* With Bella dead, that probably made Ruby the infant's guardian, but certainly the state of Texas would have something to say about it. Book supposed as long as they didn't take Aiden out of state, they could come up with some kind of explanation if the police became involved.

In the morning, he told himself, she would tell him the story of Bella's murder and how they had come to need a place to hide. After that, he hoped they could repair some of the resentment between them.

She didn't tell me what split you up, Mae had said.

Book was not surprised. How to explain, when it seemed like such a small thing? Even in the moment, it had seemed a very small thing to him, but to Ruby, it had been evidence of a much deeper problem between them.

He remembered the night so well, how happily it had begun, and how sick he had felt at the end of it.

The moment Ruby stepped out onstage at the Blue Ribbon Lounge, Book had known something was wrong. It had confused the hell out of him because he had been with her for sound check, and then he'd run down the block to get enchiladas for both of them from a place Ruby had fallen in love with the last time she had performed in Austin. During that prior trip, she had created a buzz. That night, she was opening for Broken Glass, one of the hottest local acts in a city overflowing with potential stars. When Book had left her backstage, barely twenty minutes earlier, Ruby had been nervous but so amped she had practically been giving off sparks.

The crowd had cheered in anticipation. They were a trio, really, but performed under her name—Ruby Cahill. The drummer and the bass player were competent, but Ruby wrote her own songs, sang, and played the guitar. It was she the audience would remember.

Her shoulders were slumped. Her smile, when she came to the microphone and thanked the crowd for coming out, had looked brittle. Book sat at the bar throughout her set, brow furrowed. The crowd loved her. He heard people talking about having seen her last time, and how amazing she was, what a future she had. Thinking about Ruby's future—their future together—made him anxious but hopeful.

He racked his brain, trying to figure out what could have happened backstage to upset her so much that it impacted her performance.

The crowd adored her, so he supposed they didn't notice. But Book noticed. The minute she took her last bow, he had made a beeline to the stage door. The lounge stank of stale beer and blackened fish tacos, but backstage had an old, dusty smell that he remembered even now. Book thought it must be the scent of cigarettes smoked by blues guitarists half a century before. The

Blue Ribbon had seen it all, and it meant the world to Ruby to be asked back.

When he found her backstage, he saw that none of that mattered now.

The opening act didn't get a dressing room, just a small, dimly lit area hidden behind a curtain that partitioned it off from stacks of beer kegs and cases of cheap wine. The drummer and the bass player were nowhere to be seen when he drew the curtain back and slipped behind it.

"Hey," he said. "Amazing set, Rubes. The crowd loved you. I heard people talking. Broken Glass may be the headliner, but you had the buzz."

Ruby had been crouched in the corner, putting her guitar back in its case. When she closed it, her hand rested on the latch, and she lowered her head, trembling.

"Shit, I knew it," Book had said, almost to himself. He went to kneel beside her, put one hand on her back, and felt the way she shook. "I saw you onstage and I knew something was wrong."

Ruby stood and turned to him. One hand on her belly. Tears in her eyes. The sadness came off her in waves.

"I lost it," she said softly. In her own world of pain but also sorry, apologizing to him. "Right before we hit the stage, I went to use the bathroom. I was bleeding."

The baby. Their baby. Her pregnancy had changed their lives, fast-tracked everything. Book had never felt about anyone the way he did about Ruby. This had to be love, feeling like this. Wanting everything in the world for her, wishing her every dream would come true. He'd been willing to change his life, build a future with her. They had not talked too much about marriage, but with a baby on the way, he had been thinking about it every day and was sure Ruby must be doing the same.

He loved her.

But it had been too much, too soon. Too fast.

Relief had flooded through him. A tightness in his neck and

shoulders relaxed for the first time in weeks. This would buy them time, he had thought, let them chart their own course, at their own pace. Ruby's heart was broken, but a baby would have derailed her career, at least for a while. They would heal from this and build a life together.

Those feelings—the relief that swept over him—lasted only a moment.

But Ruby saw the look on his face. She saw the way the news relaxed him. He had told her he couldn't wait to have a baby with her. They had begun to plan for their future together.

Now she only saw betrayal. She saw that he was glad.

That had been the beginning of the end for them. In the midst of her grief over the baby, she felt she could no longer trust his feelings for her. Ruby had decided that Book didn't know what he wanted, and after such a heartbreakingly painful loss, she didn't want to be with someone who would disguise his feelings. He had tried to argue that he would have come around, that the reason he had remained silent about his worries was that he had been certain they were only temporary.

But that relief in his eyes—she couldn't erase that image from her mind, and it wouldn't allow her to forget or to forgive. She'd told him that, in her mind, she would always believe he had been happy their baby had died in her womb.

There'd been no getting past that.

Now, here they were, eighteen months later, trying to gracefully sidestep the things they had said and felt back then, with Aiden as a constant reminder, just in case either one of them could forget for a few seconds.

Book didn't believe in fate, but life did tend to throw curveballs.

Alone in the mess, with the ship groaning and creaking all around him, he drained his coffee mug and tried to put thoughts of Ruby aside for the night. He went to his room and stripped off his wet clothes. After toweling dry, he pulled on sweats and a T-shirt.

In the small room he had transformed into his own space, he clicked on the reading lamp and grabbed the paperback off his nightstand, a science fiction novel about a planet overrun by a civilization of intelligent spider-aliens. He loved the science in it, the speculation, but more than anything, he loved the spider society. It made him think of the mangrove crabs, all of them busily going about their lives in some symphony of industry that no human mind could understand.

The birds, at least, were thoughtful. Intentional. So much smarter than most people realized.

Thinking about the night birds, hoping they did not visit him in his dreams, Book fell asleep. The novel slipped from his hands. Outside, the storm grew angrier. The waves made the *Christabel* sway. In the floating forest, the nighthawks huddled together and waited for the night, and the storm, to pass.

But both of them, night and storm, had only just begun.

10

Sleep took Alan Lebowitz on a journey somewhere far away. He often found it difficult to drift off and had endured many bouts of insomnia through the years, but once he managed to fall asleep, it was difficult to wake him. His late husband, Steven, had been the total opposite, falling easily into slumber but waking every hour or two. Steven had solved his problem with melatonin and herbal remedies and progressed to narcotic sleeping pills. When he had begun to stockpile the pills, Alan barely noticed.

He'd used them to take his own life. Alan didn't think Steven's suicide had anything to do with insomnia. It seemed more likely that whatever had been gnawing ratlike at his soul had been the thing disrupting his sleep. Some people might have been filled with self-recrimination, perhaps angry that they hadn't seen the signs, hadn't been able to do anything. Others would be furious at the spouse who'd turned to suicide as a solution. But Alan had neither been angry nor racked with guilt. In the wake of Steven's death, his grief had left no room for other emotions.

Nine years had passed. Grief had been tempered by time and now mostly turned up like a song on the radio that you loved once, but which now mostly reminded you of a better time. A more carefree time. Thinking of Steven brought a flood of memories, more sweet than bitter. He'd been on occasional dates since then, but the last one had been so long ago that he'd forgotten what year it had taken place.

Now he lived a contented life full of work and books and the company of interesting colleagues. He liked cozy beds and thick comforters. He loved a good breakfast that involved bacon, and he liked to be looked after. He also spent far too much time doomscrolling, a term he loved. It was an addiction, and though he had few, he never let himself regret them. Life had proven itself too short.

The Bluebonnet Bed & Breakfast was owned and run by Mrs. Jane Mackenzie, a seventy-five-year-old widow who insisted her guests call her *Mrs. Mack*. This sort of adorable affectation tended to get under Alan's skin, but anyone as gifted at cooking the elaborate breakfasts that Mrs. Mack devised had earned the right to be called whatever they wished. She was a sweet woman, more than willing to be his backup alarm clock if he needed someone to come banging on the door if he were more than five minutes late for breakfast.

So it was only natural that when Alan woke in the dark to the sound of banging, his first thought was that Mrs. Mack had come to wake him. In the bleary fog of half sleep, he had the pleasant thought that breakfast must be waiting and wondered if today would be his favorite, Mrs. Mack's stuffed waffles, hot and packed with bacon, egg, cheese, and peppers.

The banging stopped.

The pleasant thoughts warmed him, and he burrowed farther under the thick comforter, shifted his head on his plush pillow. The scent of lavender came up from the pillow because he sprayed it with mist every other night to help him fall asleep. Simply shifting his head was enough to turn his thoughts a bit clearer, and then he heard the bang again and this time realized it hadn't come from the door to his room.

Mrs. Mack had not come to wake him.

Squinting, resentful of whatever had disturbed him, he forced himself up on an elbow to glance around the room. He often played white noise to help him sleep, so it was only when he saw the french doors hanging open that he realized he had been hearing the rain all along. Not against the glass but pattering the carpet inside the room.

The wind sang. The rain was so loud that he realized he could hear it hitting the house and the cars in the parking lot. The french doors opened onto a small balcony, where the little plastic chairs had blown over. A gust of wind tugged at the doors, drew them shut as if they'd been inhaled, and then blasted them open again. The right door hit the curtain and made no noise, but the one on the left struck the wall so hard, he was shocked it did not shatter.

To think he'd slept through most of this.

Alan slid from the bed and hurried over to close the french doors. He took the thin, braided rope that tied the curtains back and used it to bind the door latches so they would not blow open again. The rain had soaked the carpet there, and his feet were too wet for him to climb back into bed right away, so he walked to the bathroom.

He flipped the light switch, but nothing happened.

No electricity.

Damn it.

Alan felt around inside the bathroom for a towel, then went and sat on the bed to dry his feet. When he slid back under the covers, he picked up his phone from the nightstand. It had nearly a full charge, so the power had not been off for very long. He spent a few minutes searching for posts about Galveston Island and the surrounding area, and his fears were confirmed. Some street flooding had occurred. A shore restaurant had its picture windows blown in. Power was out all over the place, and the locals were furious at the news channels, the mayor, the governor, and anyone else they could blame for fumbling the forecast so badly.

It could've been much worse, but compared to what had been predicted . . . Alan thought people had a right to be angry. With bad information, people tended to make bad decisions.

His breath caught in his chest.

"Shit."

Bad decisions. Like going out to sleep on the *Christabel* tonight.

Book.

Alan tapped his phone screen, called Charlie Book.

He heard half a ring, then a grinding noise, and then nothing. Not even a voicemail message. The call dropped, so he tried it again, and this time, it went straight to an electronic buzz and back to nothing.

"Perfect," he rasped.

What was he supposed to do? Thinking about Book, out there on the *Christabel*, there was no way he would be able to fall back to sleep. Alan wondered if he should call Luisa and Gerald, and if he did, whether he should continue to pretend he didn't know they were sleeping together.

Even if he called Luisa and Gerald, what would they do about his concern for Book? Should they call the authorities? Was there anything they could really do for him now, while the storm still churned outside?

Alan didn't know, and he hated not knowing.

11

Book inhaled sharply. *Did I dream of drowning?*

He rubbed his eyes, wondering what the hell had woken him. A buzzing in his ears drew his attention, followed by a sliver of memory—the sound of his ringtone.

In the dark, he rolled over and reached for his phone. His fingers found the smooth surface of the nightstand, and his pulse quickened. Had someone been in his room, taken his phone? Why would Ruby or Mae have done this? He felt a flicker of anger and confusion as he reached for the lamp and clicked it on.

There sat his phone. Plugged in. How his fingers had missed it, he had no idea.

Out of habit, he picked it up. The screen illuminated, and he saw that it hadn't been his imagination. He'd missed a call moments ago from Alan Lebowitz. It was coming on toward midnight, so he hadn't been sleeping very long. Why would Alan call so late?

He tapped the screen to return the call. The line stayed silent and he held the phone away from his face to make sure it had gone through. *Calling Alan Lebowitz*, the screen assured him, yet the line remained quiet.

A clanging sound echoed elsewhere aboard the *Christabel.* Book cocked his head to listen as it resonated dully throughout the ship. Something had come loose. Maybe the storm surge had risen high enough to lift the wreck off the floor of the Gulf, but he doubted it. As he pondered, the dull, resonant bang echoed again.

He looked at his phone. His call to Alan had dropped, and though he was sure he'd had at least a partial signal before, now the connection flatlined. "Son of a bitch."

That bang came again.

Book set his phone down and dragged on a pair of moderately clean sweatpants, slid his phone into the pocket, then went out into the corridor in search of the source of that banging. Something had broken loose up on deck, or a mangrove had snapped off and the wind was driving it into the hull from outside.

He headed for the steps. In the darkness ahead, something shifted. He jumped, heart drumming, and then the silhouette resolved itself into Ruby.

"Jesus," he said, one palm splayed on his chest. "You scared the hell out of me."

"Shush," Ruby whispered. She gestured toward the bedroom she'd been sharing with Mae and the baby.

"Sorry."

"What is that noise?" she whispered.

"I'm going out to look."

Ruby had pulled on a thick burgundy sweater. She wore plaid flannel pajama pants that he recognized as a gift he'd given her during their time together.

She motioned for him to lead the way, and they went up into the wheelhouse. They heard the bang again, like the ring of a massive, cracked bell. This time, the thrum seemed to originate from the starboard side.

"That's got to be the dock," he said.

"I thought the same," Ruby replied, "but you had those bumpers out there. They're huge. Nothing should be colliding."

Book agreed, but they were both hearing thuds against the hull. Bumpers or no bumpers.

He grabbed his jacket, still wet from the rain.

"I'll join you," she said.

"No need. Stay dry."

Ruby ignored him, walking to grab her coat where she had draped it over the back of a chair. She slid into it and began to zip up.

"Seriously," he said. "There's no point."

Ruby shot him a hard look. "I'm curious. Is that a problem?"

Book shrugged. "Suit yourself."

She puffed out a breath, then reached up to run both hands over her face. "I'm sorry. I'm just on edge. It's not about you."

"For once."

Ruby laughed. "Okay. Take whatever shots you want. I won't fight back."

"I don't want to take shots at you, Ruby. Never did."

"I'm just saying I owe you one. So if you feel like antagonizing me, I'll let you get away with it."

Book nodded in appreciation. "Excellent. I've been the bad guy long enough."

She went to the heavy door and hauled it open. The wind burst in like it had been waiting for them. It howled into the wheelhouse, blowing rain across the threshold. Over the sound of the storm, they heard something collide with the hull again.

Ruby stepped outside, squinting against the rain. She hunched over a bit to stop the wind from knocking her backward. Book left the door open and followed her outside. She reached for his hand, gave it a squeeze, and he looked at her in surprise.

"You were never the bad guy, Charlie. You just weren't the man I thought you were."

Then she walked away, in the storm, headed for the railing.

I tried to be, Book thought, but did not say.

Shoulders hunched, he followed her. His boots skidded on the deck with just enough tread to keep him from slipping onto his ass. Off to his left, the mangrove forest's branches swayed violently. Suddenly, he remembered the birds. Waking so abruptly, missing the call from Alan, hearing the banging against the hull, he hadn't thought about them, but now the image of those three nighthawks on the deck came back, and he turned to search the branches, wondering if they would menace him again. He spotted a couple of dark figures huddled inside the tangled branches but couldn't be sure what kind of birds they might be. Neither of them showed any interest in him.

Just more birds, jackass. Trying not to get blown away.

He fought the wind as he went to join Ruby at the railing, struggling to keep his hood up, then giving up that fight. They heard the sound again. Outside, the sound was more a muffled thud than the clang they could hear from inside the ship. Book looked down. At first, the darkness made it difficult to see exactly what had gone wrong, but then a swell lifted the dock and the problem revealed itself.

The engineer who designed this dock had been very pleased with himself. The *Christabel* sat on the bottom of the Gulf, but that didn't mean the derelict freighter was completely immobile. The water was shallow enough that the upper half of the ship was out of the water at high tide, and at least two-thirds showed during low tide. The platform bolted to the side of the *Christabel* had been designed for that high-tide mark—it was permanently affixed, along with the iron steps that led to the deck. Attached to that platform were thick pilings that had been sunk all the way into the floor of the Gulf. The pilings separated the permanent platform from the floating dock, along with rubber bumpers. Metal hoops on the pilings allowed the dock to rise and fall. The research boat was tied up to the dock, cushioned by bumpers.

All of it had been thoroughly vetted. It would work, the engineer had promised.

But it hadn't been designed for this weather. The swells were so high they were lifting the dock up above the height of the platform. The ocean surge forced all these parts to clash and pull in ways they were never intended to withstand. So far, somehow, all of it held together. None of those movable pieces had broken. The problem turned out to be the part of the whole design that hadn't been meant to move.

As Book and Ruby looked down at the platform, another swell rolled beneath them. The right side of the platform tugged away from the side of the ship, then banged against the hull as the water level dropped.

"Fuck," Book said, as automatic as blinking.

"Do you think it'll hold?" Ruby asked over the wind.

He didn't know. Now that part of the platform bolted to the side of the *Christabel* had broken away, every time the Gulf rose and fell beneath them, the stress on the remaining bolts would be greater.

"Depends on how long the storm lasts," he said, wiping rain from his eyes.

The research boat rose and fell. He had tied it off tightly and the cleats on both boat and dock were holding. It slammed against the bumpers with more force than was safe, yanking on the ropes that lashed it down.

She grabbed his arm. When he looked at her, he thought he saw the unshielded Ruby for the first time since she and Mae had approached him.

"Are you sure we're safe out here?"

"No choice now," Book said, using his back to shield her from the wind. "At this point, it's more dangerous to leave than to stay."

"What if that thing sinks?"

That thing was the research boat. She was right to be concerned.

"No point in worrying about what we can't control," he said. "We're here at least till the storm passes. After that, my team would get someone out here. This ship has been here for a century. It's not going anywhere."

Ruby leaned slightly over the railing, looking down at the platform as it slammed the hull again.

Book took her arm. "You're safe, Rubes."

They locked eyes a moment, and then she looked away. "Let's go back inside."

As they turned, they saw they were not alone. Mae stood just inside the wheelhouse door, backlit, her face in shadow. She held Aiden in her arms. With the halo from the light behind her, Book could not decipher the expression on her face. Was she irritated to have been left alone, suspicious to find the two of them engaged in private conversation, or was this some sort of jealousy? Whatever her thoughts, he didn't think they were pleasant, and whatever was triggering her allergies on this ship hadn't made them any more so. Mae coughed twice, a dry, wheezing sound. Book wondered what kind of shape she would have been in without her EpiPen.

Ruby hurried across the rain-slicked deck, away from him, and he couldn't blame her. Being around each other again was so confusing. Running from these feelings seemed an entirely valid response.

He bent against the strengthening wind. Rain dripped down the back of his neck, under his collar. The mangrove forest swayed. From the corner of his eye, he saw something flutter into motion. A broken branch, he thought.

But then he saw fear contort Mae's face. As Ruby approached her unaware, Mae stared up into the trees. She held the baby more firmly, moved her left arm as if to shield him.

The first of the nighthawks darted down toward them, wings slicing through the rain. It passed so close to Ruby's face that she cried out and spun away, grabbing at her cheek. But the bird cared nothing for Ruby. It went straight at Mae.

Not Mae, Book realized. *Aiden.*

Book ran toward them. The night bird shrieked as it stretched its talons toward the baby. Mae twisted, protecting Aiden by offering her own back. Talons tore at her shirt. Book slid on the deck, in the rain. Hands outstretched to keep his balance, he grabbed a fistful of Ruby's coat to steady himself.

"What the fuck?" Ruby shouted, staring at the night bird as it batted its wings, clawed into Mae's shirt, and tried to dart its beak around her.

Book reached for the bird, snagged one wing, and yanked it away. The bird flapped furiously, and he let go, watching it tumble to the deck and scramble back up. He had no idea what would drive it to behave that way, assuming it sought shelter from the storm. But as he turned to explain that to Ruby and Mae, another nighthawk sailed down through the wind and darted toward the open door. Toward Mae and the baby.

Ruby crowded through the doorway, nudging Mae backward, and hauled the steel door closed behind her. The bird tried to follow, and Ruby caught its head in the door. She slammed it hard. Book heard the clang of metal, and the nighthawk's wings spread wide as its skull crunched between door and frame.

In shock, Ruby swung the door open again. The bird flopped to the deck, a puddle of feathers in the rain. Ruby glanced up at Book, and they locked eyes in wordless astonishment. But the nighthawk began to stir. Its wings twitched, fluttered, and then it dragged itself up and took flight, straight back into the branches of the mangrove forest.

Book looked for the one he had tossed onto the deck, but it, too, was gone.

Just inside the door, Mae held the baby close, whispering to him. Ruby stared at the infant—her nephew—and then looked up at Book.

"Come inside," she said calmly. "I think that's more than enough nature for tonight."

Book agreed. He went in and shut the door.

They were the only people on the ship, but even so, he turned the lock and tested it to make sure it felt secure.

He wanted to say they were safe now, but the words wouldn't come. It felt like that would be a lie.

12

For Otis Halstead, the best thing about streaming television was the instant availability of so many of the television series he had grown up watching. People focused on the new stuff, the movies and series of the twenty-first century, or on classic films. Hardly anyone talked about how costly it had once been to collect boxed sets of those series from the seventies and eighties, or even earlier. But on nights like tonight, when he felt sleepy from whiskey and dinner and found it hard to focus on a book, he could spend time in Korea with Hawkeye Pierce or in the Big Apple with Felix Unger and Oscar Madison, and he could relax. These shows and their characters were old friends, and he never tired of their company.

Tonight, he had fallen asleep in his recliner watching Danny DeVito torment Judd Hirsch and Tony Danza in *Taxi.* Classic sitcom—the kind of thing that the TV industry had forgotten how to make. A simple situation, a workplace comedy, great writing, and a cast full of future superstars. He remembered reading somewhere that Tony Danza hadn't even been an actor—he'd been a boxer, just like the character he played on the show—but he'd turned out to be the biggest star to come out of *Taxi*, right after DeVito. Of course, Otis had a soft spot for Marilu Henner. As a kid, it would've been more accurate to say he had a hard spot for her, but age meant it took a lot more to get him stirred up. Now his reaction to seeing her on-screen was sweet nostalgia.

He'd nodded off while watching the episode where Rev. Jim buys a racehorse as a pet and keeps it in his apartment.

Now he snorted awake to a popping sound and found himself blinking in darkness. No lights. No television. No *Taxi*. No Rev. Jim. The power was out.

"Son of a bitch," he muttered.

His options were limited. He had a generator, but it was late, and he didn't feel like bothering with the whole business when he was likely to just fall asleep in front of the television again. That left going to bed and reading a book by candlelight or flashlight, or just going to sleep. On the other hand, if he wanted to sleep, why bother moving to the bed? The recliner was plush and comfortable, and he was warm under a blanket.

Otis burrowed a bit farther down into the recliner and exhaled, getting comfortable. He closed his eyes.

Someone knocked at the door. Solid, three raps in steady rhythm.

Otis rolled his head to the left to stare at the door. "Who the hell?"

Three raps, again.

Reluctantly, he pushed his blanket aside and sat up, forcing the recliner's footrest down with a click. Only as he rose to his feet did his sleep-fuzzed thoughts clear enough for him to consider the gate. Whoever had come to his door, it had to be someone who owned one of the boats that regularly docked here. Some folks had taken their vessels out of the water in the days leading up to this storm, but Charlie Book hadn't been the only one to leave his boat afloat.

Charlie Book. Otis wondered if Book might be his visitor, changing his mind about spending the night out on the *Christabel.* If so, the man had taken one hell of a chance coming back to port with the Gulf so riled up.

"Dumb son of a bitch," Otis muttered as he crossed to the door.

Three knocks, yet again.

Otis unlocked the door and drew it open, ready to bark at his impatient visitor about the lateness of the hour and the incessant knocking. The wind and rain rushed in, knocking him back a step. The door blew out of his grasp and swung wide, leaving Otis to stare at the darkness outside his cottage.

Whoever had been knocking, they were gone.

Otis thought about the gate again. Who the hell would go to all the trouble of coming down here, wake him in the middle of the night, and not wait around long enough for him to answer the door? Cursing under his breath, he shuffled to the threshold and bent to look outside, not wanting to step out and get his socks soaked through with rain.

A sound rose above the wind, an eerie hoot. He flinched and craned his neck around the doorframe, looking into the dark, out toward the Gulf. Something shifted, and he saw a pair of golden eyes staring back.

"Now, what the hell?"

A great horned owl.

Just standing there, watching him. It had to be injured or had something else wrong with it; otherwise, it would never have been out in that storm, but he wasn't equipped to take care of it. If Book were there, he'd know what to do. Wildlife was part of his job. Otis knew he could call someone, but this time of night, nobody would be answering the phone.

"Sorry, gorgeous," he said to the owl. "You're a tomorrow problem. I hope you make it through the night."

The owl hooted again.

Otis went to close the door. From above, there came an awful shriek. He looked up to see a pair of large black birds descending. Wings outstretched, they knifed toward the open door. Otis jerked backward, grabbed hold of the knob, and slammed the door shut with an echoing bang.

Knock, knock.

Only two this time. The birds had to have collided with his door, but if so, the only noise of the impacts were those two heavy, thumping knocks. Like before.

Otis stared at the door.

"Fuck me," he whispered, waiting.

But the only sounds now were the cries of the storm.

13

Gerald loved to watch Luisa sleep. He thought that if she could have seen herself in those moments, she might have finally understood why he called her beautiful. Many attractive people adopted an air of dismissiveness, denying the very idea they might be good-looking, in order to avoid being seen as arrogant. As a young girl, Luisa had been a shy, tiny little nerd, and she still viewed herself that way.

After they had been involved in this secret affair long enough for her to trust him, she had talked about the way other girls had disliked and distrusted her. She had no interest in making herself more interesting to the boys, and that irritated them. It hadn't been that she didn't like boys, she had explained. It was that she had never liked the kind of boy who wanted a girl to make herself seem lighter, more fun—*less than*—just to get attention.

If those assholes had bothered to take the time to know me, she'd told him once, *they'd have discovered the horniest girl on Earth. They didn't know what they were missing.*

Gerald had loved her then. He had not told her, because he feared it would frighten her away. He hadn't fallen in love with her because of the sex but for every word that came out of her mouth, every thought in her head. From the outside, others might have considered them a strange match. Gerald cherished all the comforts the world had to offer, and he liked to dress well, to eat well. Food and fashion, good conversation, thoughtful people. But he didn't spend the money on style because he wanted to be noticed; he liked to look good because it made him feel good. His mother had taught him that one could carve dignity out of every day, in the way one treated others and how one presented oneself to the world.

Gerald declared his own dignity every morning when he dressed. The clothes, the shoes, the hats—his wardrobe cost a pretty penny, but it was worth it to him. Luisa, on the other hand, wore what she liked and never fussed over whether it was fashionable or old or threadbare. She found her dignity in not caring. Anyone who judged Gerald on what he wore would never have understood how much he admired Luisa for that, thinking they had nothing in common. But it was the shared dignity, the mutual respect, that brought them together.

He lay facing her, buried beneath the covers. With his free hand, he reached out to brush her hair away from her face. He ran his thumb along the soft skin behind her ear, and she shivered in her sleep. A tremor of pleasure, he hoped, while she dreamed.

His hand slid under the covers, tracing her arm and then the curve of her hip. A mischievous smile touched his lips. It wouldn't be the first time he had woken her up for another round. Luisa often had trouble falling asleep, but she never minded if Gerald woke her with his hands or his mouth. Sometimes he would kiss her neck and run his fingers over and into her, and her eyes would finally open wide, and she would smile sleepily and happily. People didn't often use the phrase *making love* anymore, but in those times, in the middle of the night, when it felt a bit dreamlike, that never felt like just fucking. That felt like making love.

He edged closer to her, pressed against her. Kissed her gently.

And her phone rang.

The ringtone always made him chuckle. It sounded like the sort of happy, jingling melody white people played on beachfront boardwalks in the 1920s. It was just so absurdly cheerful.

Tonight, he wasn't chuckling.

Luisa stirred. She squeezed her eyelids tightly shut before she opened them. "That my phone?" she mumbled. "What time is it?"

"After midnight. And yeah." He smiled at her. "It's not my ringtone."

Her expression became troubled. She untangled herself from his arms and turned to reach for her phone on the nightstand. Gerald had been half-asleep, despite the hungry thoughts he'd been entertaining, but her troubled features reminded him that a phone call this late at night would never be good news.

"Hello?" Luisa said.

She sat on the edge of the bed. Turned to glance back at Gerald.

"Alan?" she said. "I can barely hear you. What's wrong?"

Gerald propped himself up in bed. "Put it on speaker," he whispered.

Luisa nodded and tapped her phone screen.

Alan Lebowitz's voice filled the room. "—the line cut off. I've tried about a dozen times, but now it doesn't even ring. No voice-mail, nothing."

"I'm not sure what we can do about that, Alan," Luisa said. She mimed a shrug to Gerald. "Obviously, it's not the cell towers or we wouldn't have a signal for this call—"

"This call isn't great, either," he said as static proved his point.

"No, I know, but it went through. Maybe Book's phone is dead. With the solar battery on the *Christabel*, the power should still be on out there. That would mean he hadn't plugged it in to charge, but that's on him."

"Do you think that's likely? He's more responsible than that."

"Everyone forgets to charge their phone once in a while. He was tired. He fell asleep," Luisa went on. "I'm sure he made it out to the *Christabel*. The storm's picked up since then, but we would have heard from Otis or the Coast Guard. As long as he's on the ship, he'll be fine."

"I don't know." Alan sounded truly worried. "Are you watching the news?"

"I was sleeping, Alan."

"I'm sorry. But this storm is bizarre. It's as if we've got our own little hurricane right here, like it broke off the main storm and it's getting worse just around the Galveston area."

Gerald and Luisa exchanged a concerned look, but he kept silent. He might have admitted to himself that he had fallen in love with her, but their relationship remained a secret. He slid out of the bed to sit beside her, then picked up the bedspread and draped it over both of them. It was too chilly to stay naked.

"The *Christabel* already rests on the bottom," Luisa began. "It's not going anywhere."

"Enough storm surge could shift it," Alan said. "What does Gerald think?"

They both stiffened. Luisa turned to look at Gerald.

"I don't know. Have you asked him?" she said.

Alan's sigh was audible over the phone. "I'm not in the mood to play this game, Luisa. I know the two of you are sleeping together. I'm happy for you. You put me on speaker, so I figured Gerald's listening in. Could we focus on the issue at hand?"

Gerald laughed softly, covering his mouth to keep silent. Luisa smacked him on the thigh. He raised one hand, giving her a what-do-you-want-to-do look. Luisa's shoulders drooped in surrender.

"I don't know," she said. "Gerald, what do you think?"

Gerald kissed her temple. "Hello, Alan."

Static on the line. "—lo, Gerald. Thoughts?"

"The Gulf's not gonna surge high enough to completely swamp the deck," Gerald said. "Unless there's a tidal wave like we've never had in this country, and that's not gonna happen in the Gulf. And with the mangroves as thick as they are, there's no way it'll tip on its side."

Luisa took Gerald's hand, squeezed it tightly. "But if he's down below, sleeping, it could flood. If the surge is really that high, what if it reaches him while he's sleeping?"

"Exactly my thought," Alan said.

Gerald shook his head. "Book's my friend, but what are we supposed to do? If it's as rough out there as you're saying, Alan, we're sure as hell not taking a boat out tonight."

Luisa stood up, gathering the bedspread around her, leaving Gerald naked on the bed. Her phone lay on the mattress beside him.

"Now you've got me worried, Alan." Sarcasm soaked her next words. "I'm so glad you called."

"Sorry. I just didn't want to be the only one who couldn't sleep."

"Yeah, thanks for that," Gerald said. "Look, let us try calling him from here. Maybe we'll have better luck connecting."

"Fine. Let me know if you reach him," Alan said.

"Okay," Luisa replied. "Sit tight."

They signed off, and Gerald picked up her phone. He went to her recent calls, found the last time she'd spoken to Book, and tapped the screen. Seconds ticked past. *Calling Charlie Book* showed on the dark background. Alan had said he couldn't even get the call to go through, so Gerald was heartened when it started to ring.

"Here we go," he said confidently.

But it rang and kept ringing. The call didn't cut off, and it didn't go to voicemail. It rang until, at last, Gerald ended the call himself.

Luisa wore the bedspread like a cloak. Gerald got up and went to the chair where he'd left the white undershirt he'd worn that day.

"Are you actually thinking about trying to go out there?" Luisa asked.

He smiled as he pulled on the T-shirt. "Hell no. I'm just cold."

Naked from the waist down, he felt slightly silly until he realized she wasn't even looking at him. Luisa walked to the hotel room's windows and stared out at the rain. The wind buffeted the windows powerfully enough to make it seem as if the glass moved.

"Try him again," she said.

Gerald called Book a second time. Now, as with Alan, it didn't even ring. The seconds ticked by on the phone screen until the call died with a trio of alarming beeps.

Luisa turned toward him. She looked beautiful, with the rain pelting the glass behind her. Her skin glistened, dark hair framing her face. Her worried eyes gleamed.

"I'll bet that little sightseeing boat is still in its slip," she said. "The owner's careful about security, but he's the kind of blowhard who acts like he knows better than everyone else."

"Luisa," Gerald said. "We are not taking that boat or any boat out on the water tonight. If you're worried, we can call the Coast Guard. But we're not taking that kind of risk. We tried to get Book to stay on dry land tonight. He made this choice."

"At least call Otis. See what he says. He might not be able to see the *Christabel* in the storm, but if he can, I'd feel better about it."

"So we wake Otis, like Alan woke us?"

Luisa walked back to him, opened the bedspread, and wrapped it around both of them. There was nothing sensual about the gesture, just her wanting to get closer, to keep them both warm. Even so, Gerald felt his defenses falling.

"What if he went to sleep and has no idea how bad it's getting out there? I've got this image in my head of Book sleeping while the cabins flood. And Alan isn't the type to worry for no reason. If he's concerned, we can at least call Otis. See what we can learn."

Now that she'd painted the picture in his head, Gerald could imagine Book waking up with the water rising around him. They were friends and colleagues, but he found himself as irritated as he was concerned.

"All right," he said. "Let's call Otis. But you talk. He'll be less pissed off that we woke him if you're the one on the line when he answers."

Luisa smiled. "Because I'm a woman?"

Gerald raised an eyebrow. "Because I've seen the way he melts every time you talk to him. Man's got a little crush."

"You're ridiculous."

"Nah. You may not see the effect you have, but I do, 'cause I've fallen prey to it myself."

Luisa laughed. "Oh, so you're my prey now?"

"Since day one, darling. Since day one."

She bumped against him. "Call Otis."

Gerald went back to the bed and picked up Luisa's phone. If Otis saw the call was coming from her, he'd be more likely to answer it.

What concerned him was what they were going to do if Otis didn't pick up the phone.

14

When his cell phone buzzed, Otis jerked awake in his chair. He ought to have gone to bed, but he'd been unnerved by the birds. Getting undressed, lying down on his pillow—that would have felt too vulnerable, so he had opted to stay in his chair, certain he was too keyed up to fall asleep. Soon enough, however, he'd begun to doze.

Now, the phone.

He groaned as he reached to pick it up from the little table beside his chair. Already, he could tweak his neck or back just by turning the wrong direction and end up in pain for days. How did people who lived to be one hundred even brush their teeth without ending up in traction?

The caller ID showed a number that seemed familiar, but it wasn't someone he had in his contacts.

"Hello?" he rasped. He coughed to clear his throat.

"Otis?" the caller said. A male voice. "Sorry to . . ."

The line fuzzed.

"I lost you there," Otis said. "Who's this?"

". . . wake you up . . . wondering . . ."

That was it. More fuzz on the line and then nothing. Dead air. He looked at the phone and saw the seconds still ticking away, so as far as his device was concerned, the call was still under way.

"Hello?" he said. "Can you hear me?"

Maybe they could, and maybe they couldn't. Either way, as far as Otis was concerned, his caller might have fallen off a cliff. He tried a few more times and then surrendered.

"If you're there, listen up. I can't hear a damn thing you're saying. You'll have to try me back." He frowned. "Better yet, wait until morning like a normal person."

With a scowl, he ended the call. Who the hell rings someone in the middle of the night, never mind someone they don't know well enough to show up in his contacts list? If it were an emergency, whoever it was, he didn't know what they expected him to do about it. Probably one of the owners who'd opted to leave their boat in the water and was now regretting it. Was he supposed to lift it out of the water with his bare hands? Sometimes he thought maybe he was too hard on people, and then he had to deal with them again and remembered why he preferred to be on his own.

Otis grumbled and sat back in his chair.

What a weird fuckin' night.

He put his phone on the side table and picked up the TV remote, then remembered the power had gone out. The last few times it had happened, electricity had kicked back on within an hour and he hadn't needed to bother going out to start his generator. But he had drifted off in the chair more than an hour ago, and if anything, the storm had grown stronger, which meant if he wanted electricity tonight, he would need to go out and get the old genny growling. Grumbling, he rose from his chair, wishing he had gone to bed earlier. He probably wouldn't even have heard his phone buzz and wouldn't have worried about the power.

Otis slid his feet into his unlaced boots, slipped on his raincoat, and went to the door. He paused with his hand on the knob, thinking of that horned owl and the birds who'd dive-bombed his door. Animals often behaved strangely in unusual weather. He'd read that somewhere, hadn't he?

He opened the door with caution and peered outside. Rain spattered his face, but he saw no sign of anything alive. No owls, no freaky birds. Just the dark and the rain and the sound of the wind and the gulf waters crashing against the pilings on the dock. A steady *thump thump* rhythm came from down there, where one of the boats surged against its bumpers with every rolling wave. The storm had worsened, but Otis figured as long as it remained like this, these few boats would be safe enough.

Slightly bent, blinking against the rain, he started around the side of the cottage. The wind brought another sound, and he froze. High and sweet, someone was singing. Just when he'd thought the night could not turn any stranger.

He muttered to himself as he turned, squinting. The voice came from the direction of the parking lot. Otis started along the walk toward the gate, and though the voice did not seem to grow louder, the words were clearer, the melody familiar. Though slow and mournful, with nothing like the happiness of the original, it was "Singin' in the Rain." The woman's voice was beautiful. Earlier in the night, it would have amused him, but he was tired and grumpier than usual, and more than a little unsettled.

Otis called out as he started toward the gate. Who would show up in this weather and at this time of night? Hours had passed since Book went out to the *Christabel*, and the storm had intensified since then. Anyone with sense was home in bed, waiting for it to pass by. And singing? The woman sounded as if she were high on something.

He stomped through a puddle, grateful his boots were waterproof.

At the gate, he peered through the chain link. The singing continued, and he caught sight of the woman. Pale white, tall and slim, she had either silver hair or had bleached it platinum blond. She sang sadly, eerily, with her arms raised above her head as if caught in a lonely pirouette.

"Can I help you?" he called.

She danced slowly, languorously, as the rain plastered her long, dark cotton dress to her body.

"Lady, what are you doing out here?"

The dance halted. She interrupted her song. Her head swiveled and her eyes locked on him, and so slowly he almost didn't notice, she smiled at him. She lifted her chin and sniffed the air. Her smile widened and then widened farther, and she dipped her head in a manner that might have been meant to be coquettish but instead sent a shudder through him.

For the first time, he realized there were no additional cars in the lot.

"How the hell did you even get here?" he said as much to himself as to her.

The dance resumed, but this time without the song. She swayed, twirled, and glided through the rain toward the gate. Otis should have called out again, demanded she explain herself, but something made him take a step back. Then another. He'd had enough of tonight.

"Nah. Nope." He backed away, then turned and hurried for his cottage, glancing over his shoulder.

She pressed her body against the gate, still smiling, watching him go.

Without a sound, a nighthawk beat its wings and alighted on top of the gate, watching him go just as the woman did. They stared after him with the same black, glistening eyes.

15

When it seemed impossible, the rain began to fall harder, drumming against the roof of the wheelhouse and pelting the windows with such force that the noise nearly drowned out the howl of the wind. Book sat in his usual office chair, slumped back, gaze shifting from window to window. There'd been something wrong with the birds out on the deck. He told himself animals often behaved strangely in a storm—something about atmospheric pressure changes—but the explanation wouldn't stick in his mind. Instead, what lingered was a mental playback of those birds attacking.

Had it really been an attack?

Logic tried to change his mind. Birds almost never attacked people, and certainly not like this. He had worked with wildlife for years, and to his knowledge, nighthawks would only come at human beings if they felt their territory being threatened. Perhaps he could have persuaded himself that had been what he'd seen out on the deck, if he hadn't been certain the birds were specifically attacking Aiden.

Shaken, exhausted, he glanced up at Ruby. She stood on the other side of the wheelhouse, leaning against a wall with the baby in her arms. After Aiden had calmed down, Ruby could have taken a seat or gone down to the room where she and Mae were supposed to be sleeping. But Ruby stood, watching the inside of the wheelhouse door.

Watching Mae in action.

"You really think this is going to work?" Ruby asked.

Mae ignored her. After they had come back inside, the two women had whispered to each other, urgent and afraid. He felt like a ghost or like he had become invisible to them. Mae had dug around in Gerald's desk and found a black Sharpie, and then she had gotten to work scrawling symbols on the frame around the metal door that led out onto the deck. The tip of the Sharpie squeaked against the metal, a sound that always felt to Book like the scrape of a fork against a dinner plate.

"Did you hear me?" Ruby demanded.

Mae did not lift the tip of the Sharpie from the metal, but she paused to look over her shoulder at Ruby and the baby. "Yes, I heard you. I'm trying to concentrate, okay? If I fuck this up . . ."

Her words trailed off. She glanced at Book as if to remind Ruby he was there. Book flinched as if he'd been in the front row of a theater and the actors had all suddenly broken the fourth wall to include him in their reality.

Ruby held Aiden as if her touch alone might shatter him. Exhaling, she stared at Mae. She looked like she wanted to run but had nowhere to go. Fear radiated from her, and for the first time, Book noticed just how frightened Mae also seemed. Her coldness and urgency were not disdain or cruelty; they were born of fear. Whatever she was doing, she clearly felt she had to hurry.

"Answer her," he said.

Mae kept scrawling, Sharpie squeaking.

"Let her finish," Ruby warned.

Book saw her fear, but he also saw the understanding between the two women. They knew something—believed something—that inspired that fear, and they didn't want to share that knowledge with him.

He stood up from the desk, walked past Ruby, and went to stand behind Mae, watching her work. The symbols she scrawled were foreign to him. Some looked like letters from a warped alphabet, while others swirled and slashed, strange sigils that might have made sense to Mae but looked like doodling to Book.

"Answer her," he said again. "Whatever you're doing, Ruby asked if you think it's going to work. I'd like to know."

"You don't even know what you're asking," Mae muttered. The Sharpie squealed as she scribbled.

Book scoffed quietly. "You think I'm stupid? This shit you're doing is some kind of witchcraft."

The Sharpie squeaked to a halt. Mae didn't turn. A second later, she began drawing again.

"We're not witches," Mae said.

Angrily, Book tapped his finger against the fresh symbols on the doorframe. "Then what the fuck is this? I don't believe in any of it, but obviously, this is some ritual crap. What do they call it when you do something like this to protect your house or room?"

Ruby slid down the wall, cradling Aiden. "It's called a *ward*."

She dropped her gaze, and her breath hitched. "We never should've come here. I'm so sorry, Charlie."

Something thumped against the foredeck window, but when Book looked, he saw only rain and the floating forest out in the dark.

"What was—" he began.

It happened again, but this time, he saw the hawk. The bird hit the glass, seemed to grip the lip of the window frame on the outside, and beat its wings. It pecked the window hard, then again, and Book had to remind himself the glass was two inches thick.

Then a second one landed beside it. *Clack* went its beak against the glass.

Clack clack. Such a horrid sound. Not a crack, yet. But a third bird landed, and then he heard them strike the portside window. His breathing turned deeper, heart pumping, as if his body knew they ought to run. But they had nowhere to go. This was the safest place for them, and suddenly, that seemed the worst thing in the world.

"Ruby," Book said softly. "What the fuck is going on?"

"We never should've—" Ruby started to say again.

Mae turned and snapped at her, "We didn't have a choice!"

Her voice echoed inside the wheelhouse. Aiden stirred but did not wake. With the staccato clack of birds pecking the windows, Mae started scribbling again, but she wheezed with every inhalation now, and in the wan light inside the wheelhouse, her skin looked grayer than before. Mae coughed lightly, cleared her throat, and Book noticed a coppery-red rash on the back of her neck. Whatever had made her sick, it hadn't gone away.

Wings beat at the windows. Night birds edged one another to make room for themselves to attack the glass. Thumps came against the outside walls, as if some were giving up on the glass and smashing themselves against the wheelhouse.

Book went and sat beside Ruby on the floor, leaning against the wall. Shoulder to shoulder, it was quietly intimate, closer than they'd been since the day she had left him.

"I think it's time you told me exactly what's going on," he said, still hushed, as if he thought the birds were listening.

Mae glanced over her shoulder. "You were going to wait until morning."

"I hope you're kidding."

Mae laughed, the sound laced with fear. "Definitely kidding." She glanced back at Ruby and Aiden. "You want to do the honors? I'm a little busy right now."

The squeaking of the Sharpie against the doorframe continued.

Book turned expectantly to Ruby.

"You won't believe it," she said.

"An hour ago, you'd have been one hundred percent right. But this is not normal." The clacking against the windows continued.

He kept twitching, glancing over to see if the glass would break. "Animals go nuts in a storm, but not like this. And the way you two are acting, it's obvious you think that Sharpie's somehow gonna save you from whoever's after you. I'm freaking the fuck out."

Ruby shuddered. She stroked the little wisps of hair on Aiden's head. Book thought she wouldn't look up at him, but then she did. He'd forgotten how green her eyes looked in dim lighting.

"You were the one who said *witchcraft*," Ruby said.

"We're not witches," Mae rasped again, louder now, over the racket of the night birds. The way she leaned against the door, she seemed to be running out of strength, but she kept writing. "We're the reason stories of witches were invented."

Book blinked. He glanced back and forth between Ruby and Mae. It wasn't that he thought either of them was spinning tales—their fear was too real for that. But it all seemed so absurd.

"Doodling with a Sharpie is witchcraft?"

"Book," Ruby said. Then corrected herself. "*Charlie.* Listen to me. I've only known Mae for about forty-eight hours. Two nights ago, I didn't know my sister was . . . that Bella had been killed. I didn't know I had a nephew. And for sure, I didn't believe in black fucking magic."

"But now you do," Book said, staring at Aiden in her arms, amazed the baby could sleep through the cacophony of rain and thuds and ticks and clacks against the glass.

"Now I do," she agreed. "So I guess the best way to make you understand is to tell you about the other night. But please just let me get through the whole thing, no matter how crazy it sounds. After that, it's up to you what you believe."

Mae stopped scrawling with the Sharpie for a moment. "Except not believing will probably guarantee you don't live till morning."

Book pressed himself back against the wall a bit harder as if he could merge with it, retreat behind it. "Mae, if you think what you're doing is going to stop this, can you focus on that? Maybe faster?"

She started scribbling again.

Book nodded. "Go on, Ruby. Tell me."

And Ruby did.

16

Two nights ago . . .

The living room had been Ruby's sanctuary, a place to lose herself in a book or pick up one of her acoustic guitars and try to bring to life the tunes fighting to be born from her head. After time spent on the road, playing gigs to replenish her bank account, she always retreated into temporary isolation. Those times could be lonely, but also wonderful. Loneliness was safe and predictable. Ruby enjoyed people, lived for the music that flowed through her, the feedback loop between musician and audience. But it drained her, and isolation restored her.

The last thing she'd wanted tonight was company, but Mae hadn't given her any choice.

Ruby wanted to be angry, but every time she started to lose her temper, she glanced at the baby sleeping in a nest of pillows on her living room sofa, and the wonder of the infant's presence short-circuited her anger.

Now she sat on the edge of the coffee table and looked up at Mae. "You expect me to believe any of this shit?"

Mae looked exhausted. There were circles under her eyes and bruises on her arms and throat. Wild strands of hair had escaped her ponytail, which she'd apparently tied back just to get it out of the way. Whatever she had been doing before arriving here, it had not left her time to make herself presentable. Ruby had read a hundred stories in which women went on the run from abusive men or to escape crimes they'd committed, and Mae's appearance lent her an air of desperate authenticity.

The witchcraft, though . . . Ruby didn't buy a second of that crap.

Mae sat on the edge of the sofa. She patted Aiden's back. The baby didn't stir.

"Can I just ask you something?" Mae said. "I encouraged you to call the cops. If you tell them the things I've said, they're going to think I've lost my mind or that I'm some scam artist."

"Gee, I wonder why."

Mae kept one hand on the baby's back, head down until she lifted her gaze again. "I encouraged you to call them, anyway, knowing they wouldn't take me seriously. Why would I do that? Can you think of any reason why I'd want you to call the police other than all of us being in danger?"

Ruby stared at her. It was a good question. "Maybe you're just that weird. Or maybe you believe all this bizarre shit."

Mae smiled thinly. "I believe it because I lived it. And I understand that you don't *want* to believe it. If our positions were reversed, I wouldn't want to believe, either."

Ruby stood from the coffee table and walked to the sliding door that looked out on her backyard, into the darkness where Mae and the baby had appeared out of nowhere. She shuddered, a feeling of dread slithering along her spine. Could Bella really be dead? All this time estranged, and yet Ruby had always assumed that one day they would be reunited, that she and her sister would put the past behind them and try to be family again. If Mae's story were true, there would be no reunion. No forgiveness. No more family.

Except maybe this child. Could he really belong to Bella?

Bella and Mae, she thought.

"I don't know what to do," Ruby said, turning to look back at the sofa, where Mae still perched, watching over the baby as if he were her own son.

"We don't need to do anything right now." Mae pushed her fingers through her hair, straightening wild locks, perhaps trying to make herself look more civilized. More like a sane person. "Let's just wait for the police."

Ruby nodded. She put one hand on the cold glass of the slider and looked out into the darkness. This place, this view, were so peaceful, but inside her was only turmoil. Should she be grieving for the sister she had loved when they were children together or the one who'd abandoned their family? They were both the same person, and yet Ruby felt the greatest loss when she thought not of the young Bella but of the Bella she would now never meet. The Bella that her sister would never have a chance to become.

How could any of this be real?

As if in answer, something moved in the backyard.

Ruby's breath hitched in her throat.

"What is it?" Mae asked from the sofa.

Ruby stared outside. The thing moved again. A silhouette with long hair, in a shapeless coat that came to its knees. *Her* knees, because the hair and height and slightness of her pale body suggested a woman. Eight or ten feet to her right, another figure stepped from the dark. The wan light that shone from inside the living room reflected off this second woman's brown skin. She was short but looked powerful, her curves clad in tight, black, clinging fabric.

The short one tipped her head back and sang out, arms opening as if welcoming her child home. "Mae, it isn't too late for you to come back to us."

Ruby backpedaled from the sliding door, whipping around to stare at Mae. "Who are they?"

Mae had already risen to her feet. She stood, slightly bent, head twitching as she glanced around the living room as if in search of a fast exit. But then she glanced down at Aiden, sleeping on the sofa, surrounded by pillows, and her expression hardened.

Outside, the two women called her name from the shadows.

Mae locked eyes with Ruby. "You know who they are. I've told you."

"You want me to believe the women out there are witches."

"You don't need to believe something for it to be true." Mae came to stand beside her, looking out through the glass at the backyard.

Ruby's heart hammered in her chest. Any other night, she'd have opened the slider and told these women to get the hell out of her yard, but tonight, the solidity of her world had already been called into question. Instinct should have driven her, but Mae already had her so off-balance that she could not trust her instincts at all.

Then the witches began to call her name.

"Ruuuuuuuby," they sang, the two of them in some kind of eerie harmony. "Ruuuuuuby Cay-hilllllllllll."

The bony woman began to walk across the lawn toward the slider. The glow from inside the house turned her gray. "Bring out that little baby and carry on with your life, Ruby. We can make it so you won't even remember tonight."

Ruby felt cold, a knot of nausea twisting in her gut. She turned to Mae. "Do something."

"The police are coming," Mae said. Cold. Expressionless.

"But they're not *here*," Ruby replied, anger breaking up the ice inside her that had made it impossible for her to act. "You brought this into my life. Whatever this is, you—"

Mae turned to her, eyes wide. Desperate. "All I did was fall in love with your sister. And Bella's *dead* now, Ruby! She's gone from the world and left her baby behind. I thought you'd want to protect your flesh and blood."

Ruby felt as if her skull would burst from the turmoil in her head. She did want to protect Aiden, but she had been inundated with strangeness tonight, overwhelmed by things that felt like a nightmare, circumstances that she would have called absurd just an hour ago.

"Witches," Ruby whispered. A laugh bubbled up in her chest, and a cleansing breath followed.

Mae went to peer through the slider, craning her neck for any sign of the police. Ruby stared past her at the two women in the yard. The bony one stopped a dozen feet from the slider, while the other hung back as if reluctant to leave the deeper darkness.

They had no weapons. Not a gun or a knife or even a baseball bat. Two of them outside, and two—Ruby and Mae—inside. Mae had talked to her about the "circle." Thirteen women, including Bella and Mae, who had practiced witchcraft together, inspired by some kind of ancient tradition out of Iceland. It sounded like the kind of group that formed around the latest exercise trend or mindfulness practice. She'd known pagans who joined together at the solstices and equinoxes to show their gratitude to nature, or something like that.

Witchcraft. Weavers.

Bullshit, no matter what they called it.

She'd been stunned by the news of Bella's death, by the arrival of this woman who claimed to have fled from her coven in terror. For a few minutes, anything had seemed possible.

But now she looked at these two women in her backyard and all she could think was, *How dare these bitches!*

Ruby walked to the slider, nudged Mae out of the way, flipped on the backyard light, and unlocked the sliding door. Illumination bathed the tall, bony witch. She narrowed her eyes, irritated by the bright light.

"No . . . Ruby," Mae began.

Ruby opened the sliding door and stepped out. "Who the fuck do you think you are? Get off my property. Now."

The bony woman tilted her head, brow furrowed, as if trying to decipher what sort of creature Ruby might be. The stout, muscular one gave Ruby an almost pitying look. Then they ignored her, looking through Ruby as if she weren't there, staring at Mae—who remained inside the house.

"Cruel of you, Mae. To let this poor thing put herself between you and your punishment," said the bony woman. "We can smell that little baby. We've got his scent. Bring him out now. Our patience wanes."

Ruby shuddered, unsure. That only made her angrier. "If you want to hang out back here in the dark until the police arrive, be my guest."

She stepped back inside and began to draw the slider closed. The bony woman took what seemed only one long step and caught the slider before it could close all the way. Her fingers were too long, like a spider's legs, and she grinned at Ruby.

The doorbell rang, followed by a firm hand knocking at the front door.

Mae reached past Ruby and stopped the bony woman from opening the slider any farther. "That's the police, Johanna."

The bony woman—Johanna—only smiled wider. "I love police."

Ruby'd had enough. She backed away, left Mae to deal with these so-called witches, and rushed for the front door. As she ran through the living room, she caught a glimpse of the pillows piled on the sofa and remembered Aiden was asleep, right there. She wished she had thought to grab the baby, but it was too late now. Getting to the door, letting the police in, was the most urgent priority.

Her socks slid on the tiles in the front foyer, and she nearly went down but managed to grab the doorknob. Behind her, Mae started to shout. Ruby glanced back, but at this angle, she could see only the sofa and the pillows keeping Aiden safe.

She yanked open the door. Two uniformed police stood on her stoop, one farther away than the other, her hand ready to draw a weapon if necessary. In the instant after she opened the door, they transitioned from looking bored to seeming very alert. It was her expression, she knew, and she stood out of the way immediately.

"We have intruders breaking in through the back!" Ruby said. "Please, do something!"

The cop who'd hung back—a tall, brown-skinned woman—drew her weapon without hesitation. She scanned the front of the house, then darted off to her right, racing for the backyard. Her partner, young and male and white and nervous, darted past Ruby and into the living room without drawing his gun.

Ruby raced after him.

"Hey, hey, hey!" the white cop said, running for the slider.

He muscled right past Mae, grabbed bony Johanna by the wrists, and shoved her out through the open slider. The witch stumbled, went down onto one knee on the grass, and turned to hiss at the cop as she began to rise.

"Powell!" shouted to the other cop, rushing around into the backyard.

"Right here, Delgado!"

Maybe it was the hissing, or maybe it was the fact that these two women—these two witches—didn't look intimidated by their uniforms at all, but either way, Powell finally drew his gun. He and Delgado spread out, keeping their weapons trained on the witches.

Powell glanced in at Ruby. "The other one's with you?"

Ruby took a moment to realize he meant Mae. "Yes! She's my guest. I don't know these two. They're threatening us. Trying to break in."

The stout witch, the one who seemed wary of emerging from shadows, laughed softly. "Foolish Ruby. We were being so polite."

Powell aimed his weapon at the bony woman. "Turn around and put your hands behind your back. Now!"

The bony woman, Johanna, smiled shyly. "Well, well. A man who knows just how I like it." She turned her back to him, put her wrists together behind her, and waggled those obscenely long fingers. "Come get me, big boy."

"Cover them both, Delgado," Powell said, holstering his gun.

"I've got 'em," Delgado replied.

Powell produced his handcuffs with a magician's flourish. He approached Johanna from behind, but just as he took her hand, she turned to face him. Reached out those spidery fingers and caressed his face. Powell slapped her hand away and just had time to say, "What the fuck?" before he retched, fell to his knees, and vomited a torrent into the grass.

"Jesus, Powell!" Delgado shouted.

She swung the barrel of her gun back and forth between the two intruders. Johanna only smiled wider so that the corners of her mouth looked as though they might rip. But the other witch started toward Delgado, grim with purpose.

"Not another fucking step!" Delgado shouted.

Just inside the house, the wind blowing through the open slider, Ruby watched in rapt fascination. The things Mae had told her had lingered in her brain, but she told herself what she was thinking was impossible. Powell vomited again, so hard that he began to whine in misery.

Ruby could barely breathe as she watched Delgado approach the other witch.

Woman, not witch. They're not goddamn witches.

But what if they were?

Mae took Ruby by the wrist and squeezed hard enough to break her from her horrified reverie. "Get Aiden. Right now. Get him into your car and—"

Ruby stared at her. "I don't have a car seat."

"Get it together, Ruby, or we're all dead," Mae said in an urgent whisper. She shoved Ruby backward, toward the sofa. "Go. I'll be right behind you."

Ruby lingered a moment. Through the open slider, she heard Officer Powell begin to cry just before he threw up yet again.

"You're doing this," Powell said. "What . . . what the fuck did you do?"

On the grass, the cop drew his gun again and aimed at Johanna. "Make it stop, or I swear to God—"

The other witch began to laugh.

"Iris, stop," Mae said. "I'll come with you. I swear."

The witch smirked. "Of course you will. But what do you expect us to do with these storm troopers? You called them, they came."

The house turned suddenly cold. Cold enough that Ruby could see her breath. A stink filled the air, like the rot of dead mice decaying behind the walls.

Iris turned her back and put her hands together, just as Johanna had done, offering herself up for arrest. As Powell cried and pleaded on the grass, aiming his gun at Johanna with a wavering hand, Officer Delgado rushed up to Iris with her gun in one hand and her handcuffs in the other. Practiced, she managed to cuff one of Iris's wrists one-handed, but then she had to holster her gun.

It was the moment Iris wanted.

She turned. Delgado reacted too slowly. She tried to draw her gun again, but Iris ripped it easily from her hand and hurled it toward the woods. When the gun landed on the lawn, Ruby noticed things squirming across the grass. Things that had come from the woods. Snakes. So many of them that just the sight made Ruby turn and snatch the sleeping baby off the sofa. Aiden sighed but did not wake as she pressed him to her chest.

Officer Delgado shouted for help. Ruby couldn't tear her gaze away from the backyard, from the snakes. Delgado didn't see the snakes coming until the first one bit her. The second wrapped itself around her right leg and began slithering upward.

Something darted across the air in the dark. Several somethings. The first one landed on Delgado's face, tangled in her hair, and that was when Ruby knew it was a bat. They got them all the time, especially feasting on mosquitoes at dusk.

Officer Powell still moaned in sorrow. He crawled on his hands and knees, trying to reach bony Johanna, either pleading with her or wanting to stop her with his hands. With his fists. He slid in his own vomit, and the sound of despair that rose from him made Ruby want to weep.

Then Powell aimed his gun and shot Johanna three times in the chest.

The gunshots echoed around the backyard and through the house. There was a moment when even the squeaking of the bats went silent.

Iris whipped around and glared through the slider at Mae. "Fucking traitor. This is on *you*."

Officer Delgado tried to claw bats from her hair and face. She stomped on the grass, either to crush snakes or shake them loose, and she staggered blindly toward the trees.

In Ruby's arms, the baby began to stir, and finally, the truth crystallized for her—they were going to kill Aiden. Her sister's baby. Her blood. They were going to cut him open in some kind of sick ritual.

They were monsters.

Bony Johanna was dead, but Iris shrieked in fury and started toward the slider—toward Mae. Officer Powell had killed Johanna, and now he tried to stagger to his feet, to get in Iris's way, gun leveled at her.

Ruby ran. Snatched her keys from the table by her front door. Left it open as she fled into the front yard. The police car blocked her Honda in the driveway, but it didn't matter. She'd drive over the lawn.

She ripped open the passenger door, laid Aiden on the seat, and slammed it before running around to the driver's side. She slid behind the wheel, jammed the key into the ignition, and fired up the engine. Her door still hung open as she watched the house. The lights on either side of the entrance were on. She craned her neck, listening harder than she ever had before.

Aiden whimpered. In moments, he would begin to cry. Swaddled in a blanket, he began struggling against the fabric. The baby wasn't safe where he was—of course not. Mae could hold him while Ruby drove, until they could figure out something safer.

If Mae didn't die.

A scream filled the darkness. It echoed from the backyard. A woman's scream, but Ruby didn't know if it was Officer Delgado's or Iris's or Mae's.

"I can't," she whispered to herself. Aiden's safety had to be her priority. If Mae had been coming, she'd have appeared already.

Ruby yanked the car door shut, put the Honda in reverse, and backed into the police car. Slamming it into gear, she cranked the wheel to the left and drove onto the lawn, put it in reverse again and backed up.

Just as she put the Honda back into drive, Mae came bolting out of the door. Ruby hit the brakes, unlocked the doors. Mae opened her door, scooped Aiden off the seat, and practically fell into the car with the baby in her arms. She didn't shout for Ruby to drive. She didn't have to.

Ruby hit the gas, and the Honda tore up the lawn as she sped over the sidewalk and into the street. She'd left her home behind. Left her life behind. But her sister's baby was safe, at least for now.

Bella, she thought, *what have you gotten me into?*

As she blew through a stop sign and skidded onto the main road out of town, she started to think about what she'd just seen. About the sick stink in her house and the way her body had turned cold. About Johanna and Iris and the things they had done.

Ruby wanted desperately to tell herself none of it was real.

She wished she could cry, but adrenaline wouldn't allow it.

Instead, she drove.

And kept driving.

They'd have to stop eventually, but it would need to be somewhere safe. Somewhere to hide. Someplace nobody would ever look.

In the seat beside her, in Mae's arms, the baby began to wail. Ruby couldn't blame him. At least one of them could afford the time to cry.

She checked the rearview mirror dozens of times. There were no headlights following them, which was good news, because she had no idea where to go from here. The car whipped past a speed limit sign, and she found she was twenty miles per hour over the limit. Easing up on the accelerator, she spotted the wrought iron gates at the entrance to Culpepper Park. They should have been closed, but the gates stood open, and she began to slow.

"No." Mae reached out and held the steering wheel so that she could not turn.

Ruby turned on her. "Get your hands off the wheel!"

In Mae's arms, Aiden squirmed. She shushed him and bounced him lightly in her arms as Ruby drove past the park entrance.

"It's too exposed," Mae said in a soothing voice, as if the words were meant for the baby instead of Ruby.

Up ahead on the right was a gas station, shut down for the night. The lights at the pumps were still lit, but the little convenience store had been locked up and remained dark inside. Ruby eased her foot down on the brake, not wanting to disturb Aiden again. She turned in to the gas station and drove around behind the convenience store, pulling in between the dumpster and the rusted metal door at the rear.

"This better?"

Mae glanced over her shoulder. "Lights out," she said. "Kill the engine." She craned her neck to look out her window, but she wasn't looking for other vehicles. Instead, she stared up at the sky.

"What do you think they're going to do? Come after us in a helicopter?" Ruby asked.

"Time for you to put all that shit aside," Mae said, almost a snarl.

"What's that supposed to mean?"

"Your assumptions. Your need to believe the world is only

what you've always been taught it's supposed to be. I think you're old enough to realize we've all been programmed to accept the version of reality that makes people the most comfortable or at least makes the wealthy people who control this world feel comfortable."

Ruby shut off the engine. It ticked as it cooled. She stared at Mae. "You're sounding like some kind of conspiracy nut."

"I'm going to pretend you didn't say that. After what you just saw—"

"Okay, okay." Ruby held up a hand to stop Mae's words. "Just talk. Tell me all of it."

"I already—"

"All of it this time."

Mae leaned forward, careful not to crush Aiden. She peered up through the windshield. "Fine. But it has to be fast."

"Nobody followed us. The skinny one, Johanna . . ." Ruby blew out a breath. "I'm pretty sure she's dead. And there's no way the other one—"

"Iris."

"No way can Iris catch up to us. There were no cars following. We're safe."

Mae shot her a hard look. "We are the furthest thing from safe."

"Because of witchcraft."

"We rarely call ourselves *witches*, but that's the closest word," Mae began. "We use the word *weavers*. In Icelandic, it's *Näturvefjar*. 'Night weavers.' The craft we practice, the things we worship, come down from a time so early in the spread of civilization that the idea of 'witches' barely existed. Thousands of years before the Bible first mentioned the Witch of Endor. What we do, what we're a part of, is the reason why stories of witches first existed. But the followers of an Ur-Witch—"

"Sorry?"

"For me, it started out as something wonderful." Mae glanced out the window again. "Something pure. I thought it was some kind of self-help thing, and at first, that was how it worked for me. The circle—what pop culture calls a coven—was beautiful. And it brought Bella into my life, and then it all changed."

"Changed how?"

Mae looked down at Aiden. His eyes were open, but he wasn't crying or fussing, just watching her with the curiosity and innocence and love of infancy. Before the world could begin the bruising and scarring that ruined us all, in the end. Mae freed one hand from beneath the swaddled baby and reached up to wipe tears from her eyes.

"First with power. You have no idea what it's like the first time you really feel connected to the fabric of the world or the first time you realize it's possible to pull at its threads. I've taken a lot of drugs in my life, but nothing like that."

"Witchcraft is a drug?" Ruby asked, trying to wrap her mind around it.

Mae studied her face. "Oh yes. Like nothing else. It changes you. Otherwise, there's no way Bella would have gone along with what the circle planned. No way either of us would have taken part in those rituals."

"What rituals?" Ruby asked, even though she wasn't sure she wanted to know any more. Her imagination alone unsettled her. This was her sister they were talking about. Her sister, who had been murdered.

Mae cracked the door open a bit. The dome light came on, and she pulled the door shut, but not before taking an unobstructed look at the sky.

"You need to drive," Mae said.

"What are you looking for up there?" Ruby asked. "Please don't say *broomsticks*."

Mae paled, wiping at her tears again, though her eyes were drying. "That's not as funny as you think, but no. There are no broomsticks involved. I'm looking for birds. And I'm looking for Iris."

Ruby shook her head. "People can't fly. You can say *witchcraft* all you want, but that's bullshit. And even if Iris could fly, we had a head start. How would she know which way to go?"

In Mae's arms, Aiden made the most beautiful, adorable baby noise. Despite everything, Ruby could not help but smile at her nephew.

"Scent," Mae replied. "The whole circle—it's Aiden they're hunting. And they can smell him, track him. We can elude them for a while, travel fast and far, but they will find us eventually, Ruby. No matter where we go. All we can do is buy some time to find a way to fight back."

"You're insane."

"That would be better," Mae replied, not seeming offended in the least. "But I'm not. We need somewhere to hide, somewhere they'll never think of looking."

17

The birds kept pecking at the windows. They hadn't let up for a moment. If anything, they seemed angrier, furious that they could not break through. But as Book sat on the floor beside Ruby, trying to imagine the story she'd just told, he felt sure it would only be a matter of time. Any moment, the glass would crack, and that would be the beginning. The night birds would get inside the wheelhouse.

And then what?

Christ, he did not want to know. Ruby's story . . .

How could it be?

Seconds ticked by without any of them saying a word. The old freighter groaned, and the rain and wind smashed against it, but the incessant clacking against the glass seemed like the only sound he could hear. That and the squeaking of Mae's Sharpie as she continued to scrawl on the doorframe.

Ruby looked at Book. "Well?"

He glanced up, watching her eyes. "That really happened? In your backyard?"

"All of it," she said.

He wanted to argue, but with the birds behaving this way, he couldn't think of any explanation that worked better than the one Ruby and Mae had given him. Book did not want to believe them. The world felt safer if he did not.

"I saw it with my own eyes," Ruby added. "What they did to those cops."

Book shook his head. God, he did not want to let these thoughts into his head. He resisted the urge to slap his hands over his ears to drown out the sounds of the birds against the windows, but only because Ruby would have seen him do it and he didn't want her to think him a coward or a child.

He'd never been claustrophobic, but now he felt trapped by the walls around them, by the rusted corpse of the freighter, by the storm and by the sea. His skin prickled with sick anticipation, as if expecting the chill of an unwelcome touch. Heart thumping, he wanted to scream at the birds, and he might have, but he feared it would make him feel even less in control. Only a lunatic would let out such a scream.

"It just seems so ridiculous," he said, helpless to stop the words coming from his lips. But he stared at the foredeck window, at the eight or nine birds there, beating at the glass. They were silent, no cries in the night, only their determination speaking for them.

Mae stood in front of that window, where she had been scrawling occult symbols as she'd done on the frames around the door and the other windows. They were all connected to one another, like black vines. She'd been working much faster, looking up worriedly every few seconds as if racing to the finish. Racing against the determination of the birds to break in.

Now she paused to examine her handiwork, right arm shaking from the effort. The hives on her neck had spread to her arms.

She spoke without turning. "What seems ridiculous? The Sharpie?"

"It's not exactly Shakespeare's witches, is it?" Ruby asked.

Aiden stretched like a cat in her arms, but she rocked him gently, and he settled right away. Book assumed the constant assault from the birds and the rain had become white noise for the baby, but for him, the sounds were an ongoing torture.

Mae turned toward them, Sharpie gripped in her fist.

"It's a modern world with modern tools." She gestured toward the window frame. "Once upon a time, all of that would have been carved into a wooden frame and then scorched with flame, or traced with blood or black char from a fire."

Ruby stared at the markings. "And somehow this is supposed to do the same thing?"

Mae smiled, almost shyly, as if the birds did not terrify her at all. "Like I said . . . modern tools."

She rested a hand on the wall and swayed a bit, unsteady on her feet. Sick to her core. But then she mustered her strength, opened her coat, and unzipped an inside pocket. She drew out a fancy antique cigarette lighter, either tarnished gold or plated in copper. "I've had this a long time. One day, I'll tell you the story of how I got it. Suffice to say, I'm not the first woman to use it in rituals or speak incantations with it burning."

"You lost me," Book said.

Mae flipped open the lighter and flicked the thumbwheel, igniting a flame that had threads of blue within it. Book thought the blue must have been from the type of fuel being burned, but he had never seen a color quite like that before.

"It's witchcraft, Mr. Book," Mae said. "You're not meant to follow."

She muttered something under her breath, not quite humming and not quite speaking. Some kind of chant, Book thought, but not in English. It didn't sound like any language he had ever heard.

Mae popped the cap off the Sharpie. It hit the floor and skittered several feet to come to rest beside Ruby's foot. The blue-threaded flame danced in the draft that slid around the edges of the door. The storm howled outside, and the *Christabel* seemed to breathe with it, the long, ragged breaths of something ancient and dying. Mae held the Sharpie out with one hand, and with the other, she brought the lighter close, until the blue-threaded flame began to burn the ink-sodden tip of the marker. The marker ignited with a pop.

Book stared at her.

"So you're kind of a pyromaniac?" he said. "That's witchcraft now?"

Mae did not smile. Her face had turned grayer. She looked up at Book with eyes that seemed to belong to someone else—someone far older and far less accustomed to sarcasm.

With another, louder pop, the symbols scrawled on the doorframe burst into flame. The whole vine of black marker drawings ignited in blue-threaded flame, and the window frames followed suit. Book cursed loudly, startled, and backed away.

The birds in contact with the outside of the window screeched in unison, their feathers igniting. Some flew away, flapping into the rain, flames doused by the downpour, but others could not detach themselves quickly enough and turned into balls of twitching fire, dead before they could try to flee.

In Ruby's arms, Aiden erupted into tears. But as the flame turned that eerie blue and then diminished, and swirls of black smoke drifted from those symbols, and the fire puffed out, the thing that made the breath rush from Book's lungs was the sudden shift in air pressure in the wheelhouse. The howl of the storm diminished, and the draft he had felt ceased entirely.

The room had been sealed, apparently, in a variety of ways.

"My God," Book muttered, studying Mae with new appreciation. "What did you do?"

Mae nodded to him. "I told you."

"Witchcraft," Book replied. "Or whatever you want to call it."

Ruby stared at the door. "Are we trapped in here now?"

"Not at all," Mae said. "The door works the same. But nothing's coming across that threshold unless it's invited."

"Like vampires," Book said.

Mae shrugged. "Sure."

Ruby tried to quiet Aiden, but whatever Mae had just done had riled him up. He'd slept through all the noise before, but now he wailed. Book told himself it was the stink of the burning marker or the smoke, but in the primitive part of his brain, he knew it was more. Aiden had felt the wave of malignance that had swept through the wheelhouse in the moment Mae had lit that fire. Book knew, because he had felt it, too.

Mae and Book kept talking, but Ruby barely heard them now, focused on the baby. The wheelhouse's transformation into the project's office space had filled it with desks and chairs, computer stations, a glass-fronted cooler containing botanical samples, and more. The work might have interested her another night. She rose from the floor and carried the baby over to the one comfortable-looking piece of furniture—a love seat that looked as if it had been rescued from the waiting area at a dentist's office. Ruby sat on the edge of its cushions and rocked Aiden back and forth.

"Mae," Ruby said, "tell Charlie the rest of what you told me about my sister. And your coven, and Aiden."

Book felt numb and disoriented. His insides were a cold hollow. But he turned to Mae as if coming out of a trance. Fading, she managed to reach the chair at Luisa's desk before dropping into it. Mae caught her breath, wheezing, but after a moment she turned to look at him.

"Might as well sit down," she said.

Book laughed. He felt sick. Whatever she had done might have stopped the birds, but now he wondered what else might be out in the storm. Ruby and Mae had told him they were in danger.

"I can't sit," he said. "Not right now."

"Suit yourself." Mae lowered her head, exhaled. When she continued, her voice revealed her obvious reluctance. But she spoke nevertheless.

"Sometimes I wish I had the kind of story so many older witches have. Abusive husbands. Horrific tragedy. There's one who calls herself Autumn, whose parents ran a day care. They never touched her that she remembers, but the children who didn't belong to them were not so lucky. When the police came for her parents, there were guns. Her father used her as a human shield, gun to her head, to try to escape. She bit his hand to get away, and he shot her. The police put thirteen bullets in him. Autumn survived, but her father had shot her in the leg, shattered her knee, and she never walked right after that. She was nine years old at the time."

"Jesus," Book whispered.

"Yeah, that reminds me. Autumn's parents were all about Jesus." Mae looked up, hardening. "On her eleventh birthday, she learned her mother had been stabbed to death by another prisoner, who had just discovered why she'd been locked up in the first place."

Ruby cleared her throat. "Nothing like that happened to me and Bella."

"Your parents were no prize," Mae said. "At least to hear Bella tell it."

"You really want to have this conversation now?"

Mae sat back in her chair. "I guess it doesn't matter." She scratched both of her arms, and Book saw angry red welts there. More hives. "Bella left home much too young. She ran away. Her parents thought she had been doing drugs before she ran, that it was her reason, but she always swore to me that she hadn't begun until she was already on the street. It started simple. A pretty young girl gets offered all kinds of things, free of charge, sometimes by people who just want that pretty girl to smile at them but all too often by people who want to fuck that pretty girl until they've completely used her up. Some people take pleasure in ruining pretty girls.

"Bella turned into a junkie and a thief. She knew it when it happened, she told me. Woke up one night and realized she had broken something in herself that might be repaired but never healed. The next morning, she tried getting clean for the first time. I suspect you've heard versions of this story—cable TV bullshit, grim documentaries—so I'll cut to the chase. Bella finally kicked it, left all that behind. Like she said, not healed but repaired. But she told me a hundred times that she never would have managed it without the Näturvefjar."

Book lifted a finger. "What language is that?"

"Icelandic," Mae replied. "It means 'night weavers.' You'd think of them as witches, and it's easy to make that mistake. Pop culture has trained us so well. But this is so much older than that. It started before the written word. Maybe before early humans started painting on cave walls. There were creatures in the world then that are the roots of most of humanity's nightmares. Some of them were the Ur-Witches."

"Ur-Witches," Book repeated, trying out the word.

"There were a lot of them, then. Hundreds, I think. One of them was Stratim, who was supposedly the mother of all birds in the world. The stories say one movement of her wings could create a tidal wave, and her screams could raise storms."

Book stared at her. She looked like hell, but her eyes were bright with sincerity. "You believe all this," he said. It wasn't a question.

Ruby sighed. "Just listen."

"I'm listening to a fairy tale," Book said. Even with what he'd seen, he couldn't wrap his head around this.

Mae shot him a hard look. "You asked for the truth, and this is it."

"Go on," Book replied.

"The Näturvefjar were a cult that worshipped Stratim. Their existence is the root of every legend about witchcraft there's ever been. There are threads connecting them to every story about malevolent women with terrifying power. They're like shadows in our ancestral memory, things we're afraid of without even understanding where the fear comes from."

Ruby nodded. "And men have been scapegoating ordinary women for thousands of years because of that fear."

"Because of these weavers?" Book asked.

"And Stratim and the other Ur-Witches," Mae replied. "When men wanted to exterminate women who stood up to them, what did they call us? During the Inquisition and in seventeenth-century Salem? In order to scapegoat women who bristled at the structure of society, all men had to do was start calling them 'witches,' and fear spread like a forest fire."

Book shuddered. He glanced at the foredeck window, then port and starboard. He felt himself trembling and imagined he must look like a heroin addict or something, the way he couldn't stand still.

"Okay. If all this is true, you're talking about prehistoric times. You expect me to believe some ancient Icelandic cult exists in twenty-first-century Texas? That's a lot to swallow."

Mae flicked her lighter. The expression on her face wasn't quite a smile. "They gathered in circles, first in Iceland and then in other places around the world. When I met the women in the circle here, they embraced me. The same thing happened to Bella. I felt safe and loved, and I felt strong for the first time in my life."

"You found people who fed your bitterness and anger and told you it was beautiful," Ruby said, and for the first time, Book saw the disdain she felt for Mae. "You didn't want to be hurt anymore, and they taught you the way to avoid that was to hurt other people first. You loved the taste of whatever they were feeding you."

In her arms, Aiden squirmed and unleashed an angry cry, but he didn't open his eyes. The three of them paused, watching the baby, hoping he would settle back down. It felt like an absurdly ordinary moment in the midst of such a conversation, but when Ruby slipped his pacifier into his mouth, Aiden sucked on it a few times, exhaled, and sank back into sleep.

"I won't argue that," Mae said quietly.

Brow knitted, Book look at Ruby. "What is she not saying?"

Ruby wouldn't look at Mae. "This wasn't a coven of soccer moms who got into Wicca through some yoga instructor. Every one of them—no matter what drove them to it—chose to get involved and stay involved with some kind of blood cult, obsessed with worship and power, and Mae was one of them. So was my sister."

"We didn't know any of that at the beginning," Mae said. "But I'm not going to make excuses. If there's a hell, I'm damned for sure. I've done ugly things; I wanted the power the circle promised. I'd have done anything for Stratim, and then I fell in love with Bella, and the idea that we were going to sacrifice a newborn baby—"

"Jesus Christ!" Book hissed.

Mae coughed. "Where did you think this story was headed, Book? That was literally the reason for Aiden's birth. But then Bella and I were in love, and she couldn't go through with it, and neither could I, and they murdered her, and I took Aiden and ran, and here we are."

"And the birds? What the hell was that about?" Book asked.

Ruby met his gaze. "Mae tells me there's another name for the weavers. In ancient Greece, they were called 'the night birds.'"

"Stratim is the mother of all birds, remember?" Mae said. "The weavers can command them. Or become them."

Book could only stare at her.

"Go ahead," Ruby told him. She glanced at the burning scribbles on the frames around the door and windows. "It's quiet, but I don't think it's going to stay that way. If you have more questions, get them out now."

Book narrowed his eyes, studying Mae. "What was their sales pitch? I understand you had been through a lot, and finding a group that accepted you . . . maybe that meant everything. But they didn't start with ritual murder. So how did they sell this whole thing to you?"

"It wasn't hard for them," Mae said. "Any cult scoops up the people who are broken and whose need to belong, or be strong, or to hurt someone else is so powerful that they're willing to do almost anything to fulfill that need. For me, that was how it started. I didn't know the witchcraft was real until I had become fully immersed. They were my sisters by then. Hell, they were my world. When Bella found her way to us, I believed the greatest gift I could give to her was to lure her down the same path I had followed. In some ways, it was easier for her since she had no contact with her family."

"Do you have contact with yours?" Ruby asked.

"My father is dead. My mother's alive, last I checked. I have an older brother I cut off contact with years ago," Mae said. "When I told my mother why I cut him off, she refused to believe it. When I told her I belonged to the Näturvefjar and that she wouldn't hear from me again, she told me if I wanted to dance naked in the moonlight and paint myself with organic plant dyes, that was my business. I think my vanishing from her life made it easier for her—she didn't have to wonder whether I'd been telling the truth about my brother. She could pretend none of it ever happened."

Her words faltered. Book could see the pain inside her and wanted to reach out, but what could he do to help heal this woman who had been broken so young? She might be put back together, but the cracks would always be there. Broken people found a way, somehow, or they surrendered, and Mae did not seem like the surrendering type.

"After Bella told me she was pregnant, we grew close," Mae said. "We were almost the same age, and we'd come into the circle to find peace and dignity and some kind of harmony with the world. We shared secrets, but it wasn't until she was pregnant that we started spending basically every waking moment together. I took care of her when she felt sick, and I held her when the worry for her baby tore her apart."

"So she knew," Book said. "*You* knew?"

"I knew there was to be some kind of offering," Mae replied. She glanced away, finally finding something of which she felt ashamed. "Either ritual sacrifice or . . ."

"You hinted to me about this before," Ruby said. "You want to fill in the blanks here? They were going to kill Aiden, and then what?"

Mae stopped itching. Stopped coughing. She fixed Ruby with a steady gaze, not trying to escape the truth now. "Stratim would be born inside him."

Book sniffed. "Oh, bullshit."

Mae shot him a dark look. "Which part? Murdering an infant or believing in ancient evil? Because I can tell you, the circle would absolutely do the first, and they utterly believe the second."

"Don't you?" Book said.

Mae sneered. "If you'd seen the things I've seen, if you felt the presence of things that seem to fill the sky and choke the air you breathe, you wouldn't dismiss evil. I've heard Stratim speak from the smoke billowing up from a fire I built with my own hands."

The ship swayed, just a bit, under the onslaught of the wind or the rise of the gulf waters. Book stumbled, but caught himself. He felt sick with revulsion.

"You're talking about a coven of twenty-first-century women who want to sacrifice a baby. To murder him. And you were one of them."

The air in the wheelhouse had turned sour. Whatever tension had existed because of the past Ruby and Book shared, that was nothing in comparison to this new tension over what Mae had been a part of.

"Whatever you think of me, I'm sure you're right," Mae said. "But it doesn't matter now. Here's the end of the story. The closer Bella came to her due date, the harder it became for us to reconcile. We'd both been drawn into the circle because we needed love and acceptance. Once we had a taste of witchcraft, of the power to protect ourselves . . ."

She faltered.

"Whatever I did or didn't do, what matters now is Aiden," Mae said.

She walked toward Ruby and the baby as if she wanted to hold him, but Ruby made no effort to offer the child up to her. Book was glad to see that whatever comfort Mae sought, Ruby was not inclined to give it to her.

As hard as she worked to appear tough, Mae wiped at her eyes. She pursed her lips, fighting back emotion. "These women . . . When Bella tried to stop them, they killed her, and they would've gone ahead and cut open that baby if I hadn't taken him and made a run for it."

"I'm glad you did," Book said, trying to process all he'd learned. "But I have another question. Bella had told you about Ruby, and you tracked her down. But Aiden's father must've been closer. Why didn't you run to him?"

Mae narrowed her eyes. She didn't like that question.

Ruby sat up straighter, watching Mae closely. Suspicion shaded her eyes.

"When I asked you who he was," she said, "you told me you didn't know. A local guy she met at a party. A one-night stand."

"That was true," Mae replied. Her jaw tightened.

"Maybe the one-night stand part was true," Ruby said, "but I think you're too tired tonight to be a good liar, Mae. I think you definitely know who he was, so I have the same question as Charlie. Why didn't you go to him instead of coming to me?"

Mae laughed softly. "Fine. Fuck it. We're in the middle of this thing together, no matter what you think of me. Not that I would have gone to the father instead of coming to you, anyway. His name was Scott. He was a roofing contractor. Bella picked him up at a bar and fucked him in the woods, under the moonlight, nice and romantic if you like dicks and think sex with drunken strangers is romance."

"You keep saying 'was.'" Book watched her.

"Yeah. Scott is past tense now. That was the first part of the ritual. As soon as we confirmed Bella was pregnant, the circle got to work planning. It was my first time participating in ritual murder."

Book hung his head. "Holy fuck."

"If you think I don't have nightmares about it, you're wrong," Mae went on. "But I fulfilled my role in the ritual, so yes, I'm an accomplice to murder."

"Why are you confessing this?" Book threw up his hands. "You're not worried we'll turn you in?"

Ruby wetted her lips with her tongue, staring at Mae. "She's not worried, because she thinks we're all going to die."

Mae smiled thinly, a dreadful sadness in her eyes. "I hope not. But either we'll die, or you'll both have seen enough that you'll be so glad to be alive and happy I saved Aiden that you'll let it slide. You need to know what you're up against."

Out on the deck, a flurry of feathers burst from the branches of the mangrove trees. The wind gusted, carrying them up and away, but they banked and circled and sliced the air until they reached the deck once more. They landed one after the other, perhaps a dozen feet from the door to the wheelhouse. Other nighthawks had been scorched, some died, but these birds hopped nearer to that door.

The horned owl did not appear from the floating forest but from the storm. It flew in silence, beat its wings, and alighted only inches from the nighthawks.

The thing that followed, descending through the rain, looked like a bird on the outside. When it landed on the deck of the *Christabel*, however, its talons were no longer talons. They were the bare, delicate feet of an ordinary woman.

But this, too, was only the creature's outside.

Her name was Eugenia, and she had not been an ordinary woman for many years.

Eugenia turned her face to the storm and smiled, waiting for her sisters to arrive.

Around her, the night birds screamed.

18

The revolving door in the hotel lobby moved slowly on its axis, without anyone needing to give it a push. The plate glass windows on either side strained as the tropical storm winds surged against them, then shifted direction. The pressure changes in the lobby made it feel like the whole building inhaled and exhaled.

Gerald clutched a red umbrella, which now felt like foolish optimism as he stared out through the glass. "This is so stupid."

Luisa headed for the revolving door. "Probably. But we can't just do nothing."

He caught up to her, took her hand, and then stopped so that she had to face him. "You need to know, Lu . . . there's a strong possibility that 'nothing' is exactly what we're going to do."

"Gerald—"

"Please, just listen."

She tilted her head, watching him with a curious expression. "Let's not waste time, okay? I know what you're saying. What we want is the Coast Guard, or even Otis, to do something instead of us trying to reach the *Christabel* in the middle of this. I get it. But Book isn't just the boss, he's our friend. So if you think you can talk me into just going back to bed and worrying about it in the morning, you'd be wrong."

Gerald pushed a lock of hair out of her eyes. "That's not what I'm saying. I just want to make sure we're on the same page. I don't want anything to happen to Book, but if I have to choose between making sure he's okay and making sure you're okay—"

Luisa laughed. "You pick me. Which is perfect, because I pick me, too. Can we just go?"

They spun out through the revolving door. The porte cochere should have kept them dry, but the wind blew the rain nearly horizontal and it swept under the overhang. Gerald wished he had left the useless umbrella in his hotel room.

Squinting against the storm, he spotted headlights crawling toward them. Alan drove slowly even on the sunniest day—and who else would be out in this weather? Gerald's assumption proved true a moment later when his red Hyundai pulled beneath the porte cochere.

Luisa tugged Gerald's sleeve, standing on her toes to speak over the storm. "One of us should've driven. That thing's going to get blown right into the Gulf."

But it was too late for second thoughts. Alan honked his horn and bent over his steering wheel so they could see him gesturing for them to climb into the Hyundai.

Gerald opened the door. Luisa clambered into the back seat, and he slid into the front and hauled the door closed. "You sure you don't want me to drive?" Gerald asked.

Alan pulled out from beneath the overhang and drove out of the parking lot. "You think I'm not capable of getting us there?"

Gerald glanced over his shoulder at Luisa. She smiled at him, in on the joke. As worried as they were about Book, they were sharing this adventure, and there was something exciting about that.

"I know you can get us there, Alan," Gerald began.

"Okay, I'm old." Alan scowled. "But I'm not so old I can't handle driving my own damn car."

Luisa reached up from the back seat to put a hand on the old professor's shoulder. "We know you can. We just want to get there before Christmas."

One hand slipping off the steering wheel, Alan wagged a finger, staring at Luisa in the rearview mirror. "Don't *you* start. If there's ever been a time you want me at the wheel, it's right now. It's dangerous out tonight."

Gerald let the words sink in. *Dangerous out tonight.* As much as he liked to tease Alan, there was no arguing the point.

"Besides," Alan went on, "distract me all you want, but it won't stop me from mocking you two about your half-assed attempt to keep your relationship a secret."

Luisa coughed.

Gerald only smiled and let Alan be as careful as he liked. Now that the secret was out, he didn't mind anyone knowing that he and Luisa were together. They were supposed to be keeping things casual, and he imagined that would continue, but at least this way he no longer had to avoid displays of affection. He had fallen in love with her, and though she seemed not to have noticed the seismic shift in the dynamic between them, Gerald hoped she had felt it. It had begun to torture him, having to pretend he didn't have those feelings, and not being able to be open about their closeness made it worse.

That was over now.

Alan started talking about the latest weather forecast, wind speed and rainfall, and just how high the swells might be. The *Christabel* wasn't far offshore, so if they were lucky, the Gulf would not be too rough for them to reach the ship. Alan didn't talk about his concerns for Book—that fear churned in each of them as they drove along the Gulf, headed for the bridge to Pelican Island.

Gerald looked out at the water. In the dark and the rain, visibility was miserable, but he could see the whitecaps near the shore. The Gulf looked angry.

As they crossed the bridge to Pelican Island, he heard Luisa mutter something to herself in the back seat. She sat directly behind him, so he couldn't see her face.

"What's that, Lu?" he asked.

"Look out the window. Look at the water!"

Gerald peered through the rain-slicked passenger window again. The scenery hadn't changed. The roiling Gulf, the dark, and the storm were all ominous, but they were safely ashore. The bridge was sturdy.

"What am I looking for?" he asked.

Alan glanced into the back seat. "Are you all right, Luisa?"

"There was a woman," Luisa said. "I can't see her now, but I swear she was right there."

"Swimming?" Gerald rolled his window down. The wind and rain buffeted his face, but he scanned the whitecaps. "Anyone in the water right now has to be batshit crazy."

"She wasn't in the water," Luisa said, almost reluctantly. "She was up in the air."

What the hell? Gerald fought his seat belt so he could turn around and look at her. "What do you mean 'up in the air'?"

The back seat strobed with light from the streetlamps they passed. Luisa's face went from brightly lit to a ghostly blue gloom, then into brightness again, but her expression remained the same. Her eyes were too wide, and she looked back at him with an expression that seemed half apology and half fear. "I saw her."

Gerald could see that she believed it. Unsettled, he forced a smile. "It had to be a seagull or something."

The tires rumbled over a seam in the pavement—they had reached the other side of the bridge and were on Pelican Island. Not far to the marina now.

"Yeah," Luisa agreed, staring at him with a smile that looked like the prelude to a scream. "Had to be."

She turned to look back out the window. Gerald did the same, settling into the passenger seat. He made sure his seat belt was secure and then stared out at the churning Gulf and the air above it. There were no women floating through the storm. No seagulls, either. Luisa had never been the kind of person to panic over some trick of the light, but he wondered how well he actually knew her.

Not as well as he'd thought, apparently.

Seagull, he thought, wishing he could read her mind.

Alan tapped the brake. The windshield wipers could not keep up with the rain. He bent over the steering wheel, squinting to try to make out the road ahead.

"I've driven past the road half a dozen times in broad daylight," Alan said. "Make sure I don't miss it."

Gerald pointed ahead. "It's about fifty yards past the old Chevron station."

Alan shot him a mystified glance. "There's a Chevron?"

"Not anymore. It's been sitting empty a long time. Sign's gone, but you can still make out the logo on the garage."

"That place?" He nodded. "Yeah, of course. I barely notice it."

Gerald wasn't surprised. For most people, a spot like that—gray and faded and abandoned—might as well have been erased from reality. Eyes skipped past them because they had no practical use. He had always thought such places more interesting than those still in operation. Abandoned places were haunted with the stories of their failure. Places like the old Chevron station and the *Christabel*. It occurred to Gerald that dead relationships were much the same. No matter how much time passed since a relationship crashed and burned, their failure still echoed.

"Is this it?" Alan said, still bent over the wheel.

Mind wandering, Gerald had been staring at a tree that bent out over the road. A massive limb had fallen partway across the road, and the tree itself looked as if it might rip its roots out of the ground and topple over.

"Gerald?" Alan said, a bit more loudly. "Is this it?"

The old gas station appeared on the right. A gust of wind pushed against the Hyundai, and for the first time, Gerald realized how much Alan was fighting the wind to keep them on course.

"Yeah, sorry. Take a right here."

Alan turned down the road to the marina. If they had gone straight, they would have come to a cluster of run-down shops and bars and the little breakfast place that had become the highlight of many of Gerald's mornings. But they had missed last call at any bars that hadn't closed due to weather, and they were still many hours away from breakfast.

They passed the old salvage yard and then the naval museum. Alan hit a flooded pothole so deep that Gerald was surprised the axle didn't snap. Then they rolled into the parking lot at the marina. *Not much more than a pier*, Gerald thought. But tonight wasn't the night to argue semantics.

"There's Book's car," Luisa said.

Gerald had spotted it at the same time. Without being asked, Alan slow-rolled past Book's vehicle, and they all stared, trying to see if somehow he might still be inside. It was an absurd thought. If Book had been scared off by the storm and decided not to go out to the *Christabel*, he would have come back into Galveston and gotten a hotel room for the night. He wouldn't be sleeping in his car. Yet all three of them peered at the car as they passed, still hoping it would be that simple.

Alan drove them over to the parking spot closest to the marina gate. Gerald found himself happy to have brought that umbrella after all. He climbed out of the car and raised the umbrella—if the wind destroyed it, at least he would buy himself a few seconds of protection.

"Stay here," Gerald called into the car. "I'll open the gate."

They watched him trot over to the gate, tilting the umbrella so that the wind could not get up beneath it and turn it inside out. At the gate, he pulled out his ID badge and swiped it through the reader. Nothing happened, so he dried the card on his trouser leg and swiped it again. Still nothing happened, and then he realized that no red light had gone on. No buzzer had sounded to indicate the card had been rejected.

Shit. Power's out.

He thought about shouting for Otis, but the chances were fairly slim that the old guy would hear him over the storm. The fence went as far as the edge of the pier and jutted out eighteen inches over the water. Gerald had passed through the gate dozens of times without ever realizing how little protection it actually provided to the owners of the boats moored on the other side. He had to be careful, of course, but Otis should have put barbed wire on the outside edge of the fence if he really wanted to keep people out.

Behind him, Alan's car window slid down.

"What's going on?" the professor called.

"Power's out!" Gerald replied. "Just give me a second."

As he went to close his umbrella, the wind shifted direction. A strong gust nearly stripped the umbrella from his grasp. He held on tightly, but it turned inside out, and several of the spokes snapped. Gerald wanted to laugh as he struggled to close the thing. It was garbage now, but he didn't want it flying into the water. The Gulf had enough shit floating in it.

Once he'd managed to close the umbrella, Gerald dropped it on the ground in front of the fence. The rain soaked him as he went to the edge of the pier. He grabbed hold of the chain link with his left hand and swung his right leg out and around the fence. With his right hand, he grabbed hold of the chain link from the other side. It felt a bit like dancing, but in seconds, he found himself on the other side of the gate.

He waved to Alan and Luisa. If he could find a release for the gate, he could let them in. There had to be something, in case of a power outage just like this. But even if they had to go around the fence as he'd done, he had faith in them both. Luisa might be tiny, and Alan getting up there in years, but it shouldn't be too great a challenge.

Luisa was the first one out of the car. As Alan turned off the engine and climbed out, she hurried toward the gate.

"We should try the Coast Guard again!" she called. "If the power's out, Otis might not even be here."

She put both hands on the gate, lacing her fingers through the chain link.

Gerald studied her worried expression. "We're already here, Luisa." She had been so worried about Book, and now she wanted to leave? "If you want to stay in the car, that's okay. You two can wait while I check on Otis, see if he spoke to Book. It won't take five minutes. I'll ask if any of the owners of these boats are stupid enough to run us out to the *Christabel* in this."

"And if it's safe," Luisa said, wiping the rain from her face. Her hair had already been slicked to her head, but she pushed it away from her eyes.

Alan came up beside her. "It's definitely not safe. But we need to do what we can to check on Book. Cell service is out, but Otis can radio him."

Gerald clapped his hands. "Yes. I hadn't thought of that."

Luisa slapped the fence. "Come on, then. Get us in there."

Nodding, Gerald started to look around for a gate release. In among the sounds of the storm, he heard another noise. It sounded for a moment like a flag flapping overhead, but when he glanced up, he found there was no flag. No flagpole. Just the rain.

He thought about the woman Luisa claimed to have seen, out over the water. Gerald realized how rude he had been, shutting her down like that. He had never thought of himself as that kind of man. But as much as he respected Luisa, impossible things were still impossible.

Seagull, he told himself.

But he glanced up into the rain once more, and he hurried to get the gate open.

19

Book stood by the starboard window. Through the rain that pelted the glass, he peered out at the churning darkness of the Gulf of Mexico in search of night birds. There were feathers stuck to the glass, some of them burnt. The wind tugged at them, but somehow they held on. Fortunately, he saw no sign of the birds. Mae's witchcraft had driven them off, at least for now.

Mae's witchcraft. He couldn't believe the thoughts in his own head. If he allowed himself to believe in this, where did he stop? Mae had said her circle, these women who worshipped an ancient witch-creature called Stratim, could transform themselves into birds. So he was supposed to believe he stood in the wheelhouse of the *Christabel* with a woman who could shape-shift into a hawk?

He cursed softly to himself. How could he allow himself to believe this?

And yet, how could he risk not believing?

The night had been a long spiral of ratcheting tension, and now that he could exhale, he found himself exhausted. He longed for his pillow. Across the wheelhouse, Ruby still sat cradling a sleeping Aiden in her arms. Mae stood just inside the hatch—the door that led out onto the deck—playing with the cap on her Sharpie marker.

"Okay," Book said. "If you're gonna tell me what we're 'really up against,' I'd like to wrap my brain around this Ur-Witch thing. You said there were hundreds of them. How do you know the one you worship is the only one left?"

Mae shook her head. "I don't. Autumn told me they all died, but what does death mean to things like that? Stratim may have died, but she still exists. I've heard her voice, seen her possess a living person—though only for a few minutes."

"So she's some kind of evil spirit now?" Ruby asked.

"Not for long. Not if she has her way."

Book felt his thoughts turn slippery—too many questions and too many ideas at once. "But the others might have followers, too. Circles like yours."

"I've never heard of any, but I guess it's possible," Mae replied.

"Which means all the stories of witches—some of them could be about those circles," Book said.

Mae snapped her fingers three times. "Can we fucking focus here?"

"I'm just trying to understand."

"Look," Mae went on, "I'm not saying there were no witches in Europe or in the American colonies. I'm sure there were healers and herbalists or whatever, but most of the women tortured, or burned, or hanged for the crime of witchcraft . . . they were innocent. Nearly all of that was inspired by the Näturvefjar and the Stratim and the Ur-Witches, who came before any of it."

"You've said that," Ruby replied, "but where did *they* come from?"

Mae huffed. "They came from *nowhere.* Whatever Stratim is, or was, she was in this world long before we got here. Think of evil like the deepest roots underground. The Ur-Witches were some of those roots, and only one thing grows from that tree. They're the reason even infants are afraid of the dark corners in a room. Stratim's circle came here in the late nineteenth century. I've read the journal of one of the first weavers to arrive in America—"

Book had glanced out the window again, and now he froze. "Fuck," he said. "Anyone else seeing this?"

"What is it?" Ruby asked, still rocking the baby.

Book barely heard. He backed away from the window, bumping Alan Lebowitz's desk. A coffee mug full of pens and markers spilled across the desk and rolled onto the floor.

"Book," Mae said, crossing the wheelhouse toward him. "You want to tell us what's got you freaked out?"

The breath that left his lungs must have sounded like a laugh.

"What's funny?" Ruby asked.

He couldn't tear his attention away from the glass. "Are you blind? Look at the window. Look at the *rain*."

Mae came and stood beside him. Ruby carried the baby over, approaching him from behind.

"Oh no," Mae whispered.

Ruby said her name as if it were the only question that mattered. And maybe that was true, because Book and Ruby sure as hell had no answers.

The rain had turned black. It spattered the window, beaded up, and ran in greasy rivulets down the glass. Book reached up to touch the window but halted with his fingers an inch away, hand trembling. He had been so tired moments ago, and now his whole body prickled with alarm. A cat would have hissed and arched its back, hackles up, and he felt the primal urge to react the way an animal would.

"Mae," he said. One syllable, but it carried so much. Acceptance. Fear. Because they were out here alone, and though none of this could be true, suddenly it felt like the only truth that mattered. Out here, away from the safety of land and the company of people who would never believe in such things, it all felt possible.

He turned to her.

As he did, he caught a glimpse of something through the foredeck window. Through the veil of black rain that smeared the glass, driven into horizontal streaks by the storm.

Pale. Hunched. Long hair hanging down, soaked through but still moving in the wind. Tracking his gaze, Mae whipped around and stared out the window. She crossed half the distance to the window, then turned to him.

"They're here," she said.

Book blinked. No, no. She was wrong about that. He felt a flutter in his chest that should have come out a laugh. Through the foredeck window now, he could see that the hair had been a nighthawk's wings. The bird flapped against the glass, driven by the wind, a survivor of the previous assault. He told himself it must be injured, that it had tried to flee and the storm had disoriented it.

Book looked again. He saw no bird. Only the black rain against the window. Everything felt wrong. His skin went cold. He thought he must be sick. Some kind of fever.

Then he heard Ruby say his name. Not the name he preferred but the one she had always spoken in quiet whispers, urgent and intimate. Until she spoke that name in hurt tones or shouts of anger.

"Charlie?" she said, sounding small and confused. "Charlie, help me."

Book turned and saw Ruby, unsteady on her feet. She staggered to one side, baby held loosely in her arms, about to drop him. She said his name again, and her arms spilled forward, not quite releasing Aiden but about to. Her cheeks were flushed pink, darkening to red, and her eyes went wide and wandering, as if unable to focus on anything.

His mind snapped into focus. Fear and confusion lost their importance. Book lunged forward, toward the only thing that mattered in that moment. Behind him, Mae cried out for Ruby, shouted at Book to grab the baby, but he was ahead of her voice. Ahead of her instincts. He wanted to protect Ruby, keep her from crashing to the floor, but he knew he could not.

So he let her fall.

But he caught Aiden in his own arms as Ruby stumbled into Luisa's desk, knocked her computer to the floor. Ruby hit the ground at the same moment as the computer. The screen shattered. Book stood holding Aiden, who squirmed in his arms, still miraculously half-asleep.

"Mae, do something!" Book snapped. "What's wrong with her?"

Which meant, *What did I see out that window?* And, *Why is the rain black?* And, *God help me, what is real?*

Mae rushed to Ruby, knelt beside her, but in the same moment, Ruby curled up on the floor and clapped her hands to her skull. She began to scream, jerking her body, pounding her feet on the floor as if having a tantrum.

"Ruby, it's me!" Mae shouted. "What is it? What do you feel?"

A terrible hissing came from Ruby's throat. She arched her back against the floor. "It hurts! Jesus fucking Christ, it hurts!"

"Ruby!" Mae shouted.

She grabbed Ruby's wrists, trying to pull her hands away from her skull. Ruby twisted around and rose up on her knees. Again came that awful hiss from deep in her throat. She turned her eyes toward Book. They had turned a diseased yellow, and he watched in horror as the blood vessels burst in a wave that radiated out from the iris. Ruby looked at him with animal panic, desperate to flee the pain but unable to escape.

Mae pulled Ruby's hands away from her head and froze, gaping at her. "Oh my God. Ruby."

Book would have asked what had stunned her so completely, but he took one step closer with Aiden in his arms, and then he could see past Mae—could see what Ruby's hands had been clawing at.

The baby woke and began to scream.

Book wasn't sure, but he might also have been screaming.

Sharp prongs of bone jutted from Ruby's skull, streaked with her blood. As he watched, the skin of her forehead stretched over a pinpoint that pushed up from inside. The prong burst through, spraying crimson droplets. Ruby's breath turned rapid, frantic, and she tried to reach up for the jutting bone. She cut her palm on its tip.

"Horns," Book said. "They're horns!"

Mae whipped around to face him. "Give me a fucking knife!"

Book shook his head. They were in the wheelhouse. No knives here. "There are some in the mess."

But he could see the panic in Mae's eyes and knew there was no time to run for the mess, to dig into a drawer for a kitchen knife. Aiden wailed in his arms while Ruby shouted in frantic pain. Book felt rooted by the baby, bound by him. Though he wanted to find a knife for Mae, to do whatever could be done to stop Ruby's terror, with the infant in his arms, Aiden had suddenly become his responsibility.

Mae spotted something and rushed to one of the desks to grab the pair of orange-handled scissors. Ruby flailed as Mae darted back to her, but Mae shoved her to the floor and straddled her, holding her wrist down.

"Keep still, Ruby! Do everything I say or you're going to die!"

The word snapped Book into action. He cradled Aiden more tightly to his chest and went to hover above Mae and Ruby. "What the hell is *happening*?"

To his own ears, he sounded over the edge.

"Mae!" he shouted.

"I need a flame," she said. "My lighter's over by the door! Get it!"

Book shouted her name again, but Mae ignored him. She picked up a handful of Ruby's cotton shirt and fed the fabric into the open maw of the scissors, almost savagely, without caution or precision.

"Jesus Christ!" Book shifted Aiden to his left side and reached his right hand out to stop Mae.

She turned and shoved him away. Book stumbled and fell, twisting as he toppled so that he could protect Aiden. As he struck the floor, the baby went silent in surprise. Aiden's breath hitched several times, as if shocked into uncertainty about his next step.

Book rocked up to his knees, staring at Mae, about to shout at her for the risk she'd taken with Aiden's safety. But Mae wasn't having it. She knelt on one of Ruby's arms and had put the scissors aside.

"Help me!" she called to Book as she tugged Ruby's pants down over her hips. "No fucking questions. I told you, I need fire!"

Book hesitated another moment before rushing to retrieve her precious lighter.

"Got it!" he called. "Now what?"

The horns jutting out through Ruby's hair and from the skin of her forehead continued to grow. They branched off like fast-growing antlers. Ruby stopped pulling at them, stopped screaming, but the pain and shock still made her cry.

"Burn something," Mae said. "A candle, some paper—"

Ruby jerked against the floor. She stared at Mae with pleading eyes. "What are you *doing*?"

A hundred questions churned through Book's mind, but Ruby's was chief among them. What the hell was Mae doing? Some kind of ritual, some witchcraft, he supposed. But she hadn't paused to explain any of it.

She scissored off Ruby's panties. There'd been no bra. Now Ruby lay naked on the floor, writhing, eyes wide.

Mae straddled her again, leaned over so they were face-to-face. "Do you give your blood to the sky?"

Ruby stared like a horse about to bolt. She nodded.

Instinct told Book to hold on to Aiden. Nothing was more vulnerable than an infant. But he needed his hands free to help Mae, or to stop her, if it came to that. He slid the baby into an alcove between two bookcases. Even if Aiden could have crawled, he was in a kind of straitjacket. He would be safe, Book thought. He had to be.

An old *Houston Chronicle* lay on Luisa's desk. Book snatched the newspaper, rolled it, and jammed it between his knees while he sparked the lighter. He didn't look back at Ruby and Mae or over at the baby. It felt as if he were hurtling forward at lunatic speed and if he dared to shift his focus, he would crash.

The newspaper ignited. The flame began to spread. He needed to give it a few seconds to really catch. Across the wheelhouse, Aiden launched into a fresh round of wailing.

Behind him, Mae shouted at Ruby, "Focus! You've got to answer, or you're done! Do you give your blood to the sky? Say yes, Ruby!"

Hyperventilating, jerking against the floor, Ruby managed to force out a yes.

Book turned just in time to see Mae slice into Ruby's flesh with one blade of the fully open scissors. Ruby's eyes went wide. She threw her head back and forth. Horns cracked against the floor.

Blood welled up from the wound.

Ruby's blood.

Book sprang to his feet. The lighter dropped from his hand, but he managed to hold on to the burning, rolled-up newspaper.

"Get the fuck away from her!"

He started for Mae, but she spun and glared at him. Her lips were curled back, and her eyes had become black pinpoints, haloed with gold. She pointed the bloody scissors at him. "If you want her alive, you stand there and do what I tell you!"

Uncertainty paralyzed him.

Mae flicked her wrist upward. Droplets of blood flew and sprinkled to the floor. She started to slice again. Book stared at Ruby's face, waiting for her to beg him with her eyes, to tell him what to do. How could this be helping her? Mae cut something that looked like the Roman numeral ten, but as the blood dripped down between Ruby's breasts and trickled toward her navel, he realized it might have been the symbol for infinity.

Again, Mae spattered the blood around them. Focused and purposeful.

A rash broke out on Ruby's face and neck. A moment later, the skin of her arms and abdomen and thighs reddened, and raised patterns appeared. Designs, sigils. Book felt a wave of nausea. Something had joined them in the wheelhouse. The weight of the air changed. The desire to scream, to surrender to despair, became nearly overwhelming.

"Do you give your heart to your—"

Ruby screamed.

Mae slapped her hard across the face. "That's not you, Ruby! Listen. Do you give your heart to your sisters, and to Stratim, our mother?" She bent low, urgent in Ruby's ear. "You have to say it in Icelandic. '*Ég gef hjarta mitt.*' Say it like that!"

Ruby mumbled something that might have been those words.

Book had seen enough. He tossed the burning newspaper to the floor. The baby's wailing filled the wheelhouse as he grabbed hold of Mae with both hands and hauled her away from Ruby. It felt like a sickening dream. Ruby lay there, naked and bleeding, body covered with a rash that ran in lines and swirls, symbols. She had stopped crying, stopped thrashing. Nothing Book had ever known could have done this. Witchcraft seemed real to him now, or weaving, or whatever Mae's circle indulged in.

Mae.

She twisted from his grip, turned on him. "Listen to me. If you love her—"

"Fuck you," he said, pointing at her face. "Whatever you're doing to her, stop it. This is you!"

"You don't understand."

She tried to rush back to Ruby. Book grabbed her collar, twisted, choking her without intent but also without regret. "I don't need to—"

Mae grabbed his hands but didn't try to force him to let her go. "*Veikindi.*"

One word and the touch of her fingers to his. It felt as if the floor had tilted under his feet. His guts churned, his skin flushed, and Book dropped to his knees, retching. A knot formed in his stomach; pain made him topple to his side. He vomited, unable to rise as the stink of it filled his nostrils.

From that spot, he watched as Mae picked up the still-burning newspaper. She turned on Ruby, and he wanted to roar, to stop her. But then he saw the blood-smeared tangle of sharp horns like antlers that protruded from Ruby's skull. One had a slick, waxy coating, and when he looked, the tip of it ignited like a candle. A second horn did the same, as if these were actual candles jutting up from this hideous, bony crown.

"Give your spirit to the dusk and dawn," Mae said, straddling Ruby again.

Ruby's eyes were completely bloodshot. Her tears had turned black as ink.

Mae pressed the burning edge of the newspaper to the fresh wounds on Ruby's chest. Ruby should have screamed, but instead, she hissed in pain, baring yellow, jagged teeth. Book could only lie there, convulsing as he retched again.

"Hurry, Ruby," Mae said. "Right now, or it's too late." She snatched up the scissors, still fully open, and pressed them into Ruby's hand. "Draw the blood of another for the glory of your mother."

Mae tried to force the scissor blade toward her own belly. Ruby resisted. Horror and revulsion twisted her features, but then it was as if she understood the moment had come after which it would be too late for her. Her lip curled up in disgust or disdain, and she slashed the scissor blade across Mae's belly. It snagged the cotton of her shirt but did not cut, and yet the blood flowed, soaking into the fabric.

The candle burning at the tip of one of Ruby's horns snuffed out. Red smoke rose from it. Mae nearly collapsed in relief.

"It worked," she said as if she'd never had such a surprise in her life. Then she scrambled off Ruby and reached for Book.

She took his face in both hands as his stomach lurched again. Mae kissed his forehead and rasped something else in that same, strange tongue, and the twisting in his gut vanished. He felt weak, drained, shivery, but the nausea had left as suddenly as it had seized him.

As Book struggled to rise to his knees, Mae looked around the wheelhouse. On Gerald's desk there sat a light blue canister, one of those ridiculously large metal water bottles. Mae lunged for it, went back to Ruby, clamped one hand on Ruby's forehead, and raised the heavy metal cup.

Book shouted at her to stop.

Mae brought the canister down onto Ruby's horns. The breaking of those new bones made a sickening crack, and Ruby cried out in pain and despair. Mae did it again, twisting Ruby's head to attack each of those bone prongs. Most of them snapped off at the skin, but several broke higher up, leaving stubs that protruded.

Finally, Mae slid to the floor, tossing the metal cup aside.

Ruby lay nude, sheened with blood and sweat. Whether from pain or shock, she had fallen unconscious. Book stared, unable to find the words to demand answers.

Tucked in his corner, Aiden sniffled and whimpered. The old freighter creaked and lumbered as the storm kept pounding. The wind howled through the open guts of the *Christabel.*

Outside the foredeck window, something began to scratch at the glass.

The power went out.

20

Luisa stood on the pier, already soaking wet. There were several boats still in their slips, tied securely to the pilings. Extra bumpers had been put in place, but she could not imagine any of them would escape without damage. The one nearest to her—*Oracle*—had spiderweb cracks all over the fiberglass bow. The meteorologists had blown the forecast, but even so, this boat should have been taken out of the water. The owner had to be either too rich or too stupid to care. It would not surprise her to find, when the storm was over, that the *Oracle* had been sunk.

A small but luxurious fishing charter had already paid the price for its owner's bad decision. The marlin tower poked out of the water, smashing against the pier with every swell. The waves lifted it, crashed it into the pilings, then receded. Whoever owned it would be eager to lay blame, but it wasn't as if you could sue the local news for screwing up a forecast. Nobody controlled the weather. This would be a matter for insurance companies to fight over.

The rain hammered her. The wind gusted and nearly knocked her over. Luisa knew she should have held on to Gerald—she was too small, too light, and it occurred to her now that if the wind shifted the other direction, she might blow right into the Gulf. It would have been funny if the idea did not scare the shit out of her.

She started up the pier toward Otis's cottage. There ought to have been at least one light burning in the window and one outside the door, but the electricity had been out when they arrived. Even in the darkness, she could make out the silhouettes of Gerald and Alan up ahead. Gerald remained at Otis's door and knocked again, while Alan walked around behind the little house.

"Maybe he's not there?" Luisa said as she approached, raising her voice to be heard over the rain. She pushed her fingers through her hair, and rainwater ran down the back of her neck.

Gerald put an arm around her, and they huddled under the eave at the front of the cottage. "Where would Otis go, this time of night?"

"The power went out," Luisa reminded him. "Maybe he went to a friend's place."

Gerald smiled. "He'd go to the Three Sheets if the place was open, but it's closed now."

Luisa did not pursue the unspoken addendum to that sentence, the question as to whether Otis had the sort of friends whose door he could knock on at midnight and find himself welcome. At the Three Sheets, he had many comrades. Every salty dog in the place would gladly clap him on the back and buy him a drink, share a story or two, and talk about their cherished bond. But would they invite him home? Luisa wanted to think they would, but she had her doubts, and it was clear Gerald shared those doubts.

Gerald knocked again, this time pounding with his open palm.

The wind gusted so hard it pushed Luisa up against him. Gerald's free hand snaked down to clasp hers. When they had first climbed out of the car into the rain, it had felt refreshing. The storm made holding on to an umbrella impossible, but she hadn't minded the soaking. It reminded her of childhood days when she would run into the street to dance in the rain, her father shouting at her in frustration. She remembered the way the fresh air had filled her lungs and that she could barely catch her breath because of the wind.

The rain felt different tonight. Thicker. Almost oily. And the air had turned from fresh to rank, like the stink of a dozen low tides. Luisa held her free hand beneath her nose, trying to breathe through her mouth.

"God, what is that?" she said.

Gerald flinched away from the door. He glanced at her. "Did you hear something?"

They both stood listening, waiting for any sound above the howl of the wind.

"Alan?" Gerald called, although it seemed unlikely their colleague could hear over the din. He'd damaged his hearing at dozens of concerts and blamed Black Sabbath for a ringing that never went away.

Luisa would have asked Gerald to describe what he'd heard, but a sound came from inside the cottage. A thump of wood. A shudder passed through her. Something was definitely off. She pounded her fist on the door.

"Otis!" she called. The wind snatched up her voice and carried it away, so even she barely heard. This was pointless. If he was inside, he wasn't answering. She looked at Gerald. "What now?"

On the other side of the cottage door, someone screamed.

Luisa grabbed the doorknob, but of course, it remained locked. She threw her shoulder against it. The rubber of her raincoat squeaked wetly as she tried again. She half expected Gerald to stop her, to suggest calling the police despite the way the storm had disrupted their cell phone signals. But Gerald had heard that scream as clearly as she had.

He paused her with a hand on her shoulder.

Expression grim, he nodded to her. "One, two, three."

On three, they smashed their shoulders against the door. Luisa had no illusions that her butterfly-weight assault had done the trick, but Gerald had size she could not match. Together, they got the job done.

Gerald went over the threshold, into Otis's cottage. Outside, still in the rain, Luisa heard another cry, but this did not belong to any human being. She looked up into the storm and saw a dark figure slicing through the rain. Had she ever seen birds out in weather like this? She didn't think so.

She went into the cottage.

Four steps, until she came to a halt, taking it all in.

The back door hung open, crooked on its hinges. Alan must have come in that way, because he stood in the little living room with Gerald. He might have found the door open back there or forced his way in. It didn't really matter which, because the man they had come to see—the man from whom they had sought help—had died.

Died. So simple a word. So final, and quiet, and unfussy. She might as well have said that Otis's candle had gone out. But although what had happened there had certainly been final, it had been the opposite of quiet and unfussy.

"Jesus Christ," Gerald said, and then he said it again, and again.

Alan wiped his hand across his mouth like an alcoholic who'd just decided he wasn't ready to quit. Pale, unsteady on his feet, he took one more long look at the mess on the floor and then strode from the cottage, leaving through the back door, just as he'd entered.

Otis's corpse lay belly down in the middle of the small kitchen. The skin and muscle along his back had been sliced open, ragged flaps pulled away to reveal his spine. The vertebrae had been separated by force, the spinal cord severed. A variety of knives lay scattered on the floor, sharp islands in the shallow pond of his blood. His murderer seemed to have tried several of them, and it was impossible to know which tool had done the trick.

But the scene had worse to offer.

Luisa tried so hard to look away. Numb with shock, she found she could not.

Otis's neck had been broken, his head corkscrewed around so that his dead eyes stared at the ceiling instead of the floor.

Or they would have, if he still had eyes.

They might have been plucked out, dug out, scooped out, but no matter the method, his eyes were gone. In their place were a pair of thick red candles, still burning, dripping wax into ruined sockets. Black smoke eddied up from those twin flames.

A single black feather lay across the dead man's lips, as if to silence him.

21

Book stood in the center of the wheelhouse, the dense air crawling on him like spiders. Even with the groaning of the storm-battered ship, the darkness enclosed them as if all had gone silent. Ruby lay naked on the floor, shuddering and cursing quietly to herself. Mae knelt beside her, trying to give her some solace.

Ruby shoved her away. Mae sprawled to the floor.

“Don’t touch me.” Ruby wiped at her eyes, but that only brought more tears. She turned on her side, curled into a fetal position, and kept whispering to herself.

Book didn’t like those whispers.

Outside the windows, the storm brightened with distant lightning. Shadows crawled along the walls and floors, and painted their faces. Book spotted the undulating blanket against the wall and remembered the baby. The instant the solar generator had snapped off, Aiden had stopped his caterwauling. Now Book rushed to him, knelt there, and looked down at the swaddled infant as the lightning flare faded. Even in the remaining darkness, Aiden gazed curiously up at him. He had stopped crying, but his eyes still glistened with earlier tears. In shock, or just curious, or too exhausted to know what to do next, the baby seemed almost to be waiting.

Book slumped to the floor. Sitting next to the baby, he stared at Mae as she sat up. He heard the scratching again, the scrape like a fork on a dinner plate. He followed Mae’s gaze to the portside window. Rain pattered the glass, tracing diagonal windblown paths. Another flash of lightning ignited in the heart of the storm, and then he saw what Mae was really looking at.

"Jesus," he rasped. Instinctively, he shifted to put himself between the baby and the thing outside the window. The witch.

The weaver.

How many were there?

Her long, bony fingers scratched at the glass again. The scribbles Mae had drawn on the window frame flared like campfire embers. Outside the window, the weaver's eyes narrowed, brightening with a dark gleam that seemed to come from within. The left side of her scalp had been shaved and tattooed, while the hair on the right hung long and soaked, a silver cloak.

The symbols on the window frame flared again, and the weaver backed into the storm. Something took flight out there, in the dark. Book could make out the dense tangle of the mangrove forest, but not much else.

"Is it gone?" he said softly.

Mae glanced at him as if she'd forgotten he was there. "That's Annika. She's still there. The whole circle is gathering."

"But what you did, the marker—"

"The wards."

Book nodded. "It burned those birds. And it kept *her* out."

"For now. But once they're all here, I don't know."

Shock, he thought. *I'm in shock.* How else to process what he'd just seen, what he had experienced in the preceding minutes? Numb and hollow, confused and terrified, he glanced at the baby again. Aiden made a small noise, the kind of baby coo that he figured parents might be able to interpret. To Book, it felt like a release. *I'm okay*, that noise seemed to say. *What now?*

"What now?" he whispered aloud.

Abruptly, he stood. The storm moaned, shifting the derelict *Christabel* enough to tilt her slightly. His stomach churned. How powerful was this storm? There were enough things to fear without worrying about the freighter breaking apart and drowning them all. Although one glimpse of that woman outside the window made him think drowning might be better than what else awaited them. The birds attacking had frightened him, but this . . .

Move, he thought.

And did.

Keeping low, wary of what might be watching through the windows, Book grabbed a hooded sweatshirt from the back of Alan's office chair and hustled over to kneel beside Ruby. Mae watched as he brushed the hair away from Ruby's face and helped her into the sweatshirt. Her breath hitched as he examined the jagged shards of bone that still jutted through her skin. Ruby looked at him with the eyes of a frightened animal. Book saw shame in that look, but also anger and despair. This had been done to her against her will. Whatever *this* was.

"Talk fast, Mae," he said. "What did you do?"

"Saved her," Mae replied. "No thanks to you."

He wanted to snap at her, but that would serve no one. "You did some kind of ritual."

Mae approached them. She went to her knees by Ruby again.

"No," Ruby said, waving her away.

Mae nodded. She wouldn't argue. Instead, she went and picked up Aiden, holding the baby protectively against her chest.

"The circle has thirteen weavers."

"A coven," Book said. That was what he'd always read. Thirteen witches make a coven.

"There can't be more than thirteen in one circle," Mae went on. "When Johanna and Iris came for me and Aiden at Ruby's house, the police killed Johanna. That left an opening."

"Explain."

"Stratim hasn't existed in her own flesh for centuries, at least. Probably longer. But she can be called by any circle that worships her. That ritual is easier. And once she's called, she can invade the body of any nearby woman, except a member of the circle."

"Why not one of you?" Book asked. Anger and suspicion simmered. "Why not *you*?"

Mae shook her head. "The women in the circle all have a piece of her inside us already. We serve her. If she took one of us over, the summoning would end. Connection severed."

"So she was . . . what, *manifesting* inside Ruby?" Book felt sick.

The storm flickered with diffuse lightning again. Book hadn't noticed Ruby sitting up, and he flinched to find her so close beside him, her blood-streaked face inches from his own.

"What did you do, Mae?" Ruby asked, practically spitting the words.

Mae held the baby close, as if he could shield her from the fear and confusion that filled the wheelhouse. "I told you. The ritual I did . . . you're part of the circle now. You're one of the Näturvefjar. It was the only way . . ."

Ruby behaved as if she'd stopped listening. Her fingers traced the sharp edges of the broken horns on her head. Book thought of the candle, the strange burning wax that had ignited on the tip of one of those horns.

"You said your magic would keep them out," Ruby said quietly. Broken. Just how broken, it was difficult to tell.

"It's not magic. It's witchcraft," Mae replied. "It's weaving."

Frantic, gaze hungry for something that made sense, Ruby laughed softly. "Who gives a fuck what I call it? You said your goddamn Sharpie would keep them out!"

Mae bristled. Eyes slitted. "It will keep them out for a while. But it couldn't stop her. I saved you from her, Ruby. I did that."

Unsteady on her feet, Ruby stood, glaring. "This?" She wiped tears and blood from her face with both hands and showed them, palms out, fingers extended. "This is saving me?"

"Ruby—" Book said.

She slid her fingers into her hair, feeling the torn skin and the jutting, broken horns. "*This?* You knew what they could do. You knew what could happen, and you came to me." Ruby shuddered with emotion. "Why couldn't you just stay away?"

Aiden began to fuss, thrusting out his feet beneath the blanket. A small fist rose up from where Mae cradled the baby. He stretched, and mewled, and *needed*, the way all infants do.

Mae took two steps forward with the baby in her arms. "I came to you because Aiden's your blood. I thought you'd—"

Ruby went toward Mae so fast, Book was sure she meant to hurt her. Instead, Ruby took the baby away. Mae held on a moment, but neither woman would have endangered Aiden with some kind of tug-of-war. Mae let him go, and Aiden began to cry softly, a hitching sound not unlike the quiet sobs that had been issuing from his aunt a few minutes earlier.

Book glanced at the portside window, then to starboard, and finally out at the floating forest. The mangroves swayed. Did he see the flutter of dark wings? He thought so.

He had to accept the impossible things now. Right now. Another minute of denial might kill him.

"How do we get out of this, Mae?" he asked. "Can we wait them out?"

Ruby and Mae glared at each other, a silent war over an infant who did not belong to either of them. The storm churned outside.

"He would have been mine," Mae said at last, and the steel in her gaze faded, revealing her pain. "My son with Bella."

Ruby shook her head. "I have only your word on that. For that matter, I only have your word on anything involving my sister."

Mae's expression curdled. "What is *wrong* with you? Why would you—"

"Whatever you and Bella had, that's over," Ruby said. "She's dead. I've got no family left except Aiden. My sister's dead, and you share in the blame for that."

Mae looked as if she'd been slapped. "Seriously? What about you and your family? You think a person with a healthy homelife goes along with something like this?"

Book couldn't let it go on. He glanced nervously at the windows. They were in the dark, with the storm howling, and no matter how protected Mae claimed they were, these so-called night weavers were gathering out there.

He stepped between them, facing Ruby.

"Stop. Look at you, Rubes. After what just happened to you, maybe we can save the custody battle for later?"

Wrong choice of words. He knew it even as they left his lips.

Ruby looked stung.

"You know what I mean," he said. "We have to figure out how to get out of this!"

She nodded slowly. He could see the pain in her eyes. "That's what you're best at, right, Charlie? Finding a way to get out of a jam?"

All he could do was exhale. "I'm on your side. Whatever this insanity is, we're in it together."

"I'm sorry I got you into this, *Book*." Ruby shot a withering glance at Mae. "I knew it was dangerous. I shouldn't have come. But let's make one thing clear." She shushed Aiden, rocking him gently. "You didn't want to be responsible for anyone but yourself when we were together, and you're not responsible for anyone but yourself now."

Something struck the starboard window.

"Ruby," he ventured.

"No," she said. "You owe me nothing. Let's just survive."

Let's just survive.

Book stared at her, haunted by the past and the fear of what was to come.

22

The door to Otis's cottage blew open, swinging so hard it struck the wall with a bang. Framed seascapes leaped from their hooks and crashed to the floor. Sheets of rain gusted over the threshold, but the three people inside the cottage made no attempt to close the door. They barely flinched.

The three living people, Gerald thought, staring at Otis's desecrated corpse.

He knew he should look away, but it felt as if he could not shift his gaze. Alan had gone to the window at the rear of the shack and slid it open. The old professor pushed his fingers through the thin white strands that were all that remained of his hair. He whispered to God and wiped his eyes, shaking his head.

Luisa stumbled away from the corpse. She went into the cottage's little kitchen and started opening cabinets. Gerald cringed, thinking this was an intrusion, but then he realized Otis had been murdered and was past the point of caring about his privacy. When Luisa found what she'd been searching for, she stretched onto the tips of her toes to reach a shelf inside the cabinet. Her yellow raincoat squeaked and crinkled as she grabbed a bottle of whiskey and pulled it down.

Gerald understood. Otis would have understood, too—and approved. Luisa leaned against the counter, uncapped the whiskey, and took two quick slugs. The power might have been out, but even in the storm, the darkness was not total. In the deep gloom, he could see her trembling. Whatever she truly felt for him, Gerald knew he loved her. If he hadn't already been sure, the ache in his chest confirmed it. The stink of blood had begun to permeate the air, with worse odors beneath it. He had seen death before, but nothing as horrific as this. Yet his own revulsion paled beside his desire to comfort Luisa. All he cared about was protecting her from the horror they had discovered, but of course, it was too late for that. This moment would echo in all three of them for the rest of their lives.

Still, he could try.

"Luisa," he said, walking toward the small, open kitchen area.

Alan went to the window and held up his phone, trying to get a signal. Gerald left him to it, focused on Luisa.

He said her name again. She whispered something in Spanish and poured herself another shot of whiskey. Exhaling, perhaps in an attempt to control her trembling, she lifted the glass.

Her whole body jerked. The glass flew from her fingers and shattered against the wall, showering shards and whiskey to the floor. Gerald swore, reaching for her, and Luisa jerked again. She went down on one knee. Her spine straightened, then she threw herself forward. Her skull struck the edge of the counter with a sickening crack that made Gerald think of a bat nailing a baseball.

"Jesus!" He reached for her. Grasped her hands.

Luisa slid to the floor, jerking and shuddering all the way down. She weighed next to nothing, a wisp of a woman, but still he struggled to keep her upright.

Alan called to him from the darkened living room.

"Alan!" Gerald said, barely aware of speaking. "Help me!"

The professor moved swiftly for his age. As Luisa's seizure worsened, her skull began to smack the floor in a drumroll, and then Alan was there. He groaned as he went to his knees and reached out to grab Luisa's head in both hands. He cupped the back of her skull, keeping it from striking the floor again. Gerald felt like a fool for not thinking clearly, acting quickly. He felt helpless, and he hated that.

"What's happening to her?" he asked.

Alan shifted Luisa, cradling her head on his lap. "Seizure."

"But *why*?"

"I don't know!"

Gerald started to glance around the kitchen, which was darker than the rest of the cottage. He fished his phone out of his pocket and tapped the light on, racking his brain, trying to think of some way to help.

On the floor, Luisa's seizure simply stopped.

He swung the glow of his phone light over and saw that her eyes were open shockingly wide. Their whites were a sickly yellow, and strands of red swam in them as if the blood vessels had burst and were twisting like worms.

"Lu?" he said. "Can you hear me? Can you talk?"

The sound that emanated from her throat did not seem like speech. It reminded him of the whistle of the wind battering the cottage, slipping through every crevice it could find. The noise in her throat turned wet and ragged.

"Alan," Gerald said, "we have to get her to a hospital."

Only seconds had passed since the seizure had ended. Alan still cupped her skull, as if afraid it would begin again. He studied her, hesitating, and then nodded.

"Okay. We get her to the car."

Alan glanced up at Gerald.

Luisa cried out, going rigid with pain. Alan joined her with a scream of his own, jerking backward, eyes wide, but unable to free his hands from around her skull. Gerald stared, not understanding until his phone light found Alan's hands again. The old man screamed and swore and blood blossomed from the backs of his hands, where sharp, blood-streaked spikes had punctured his flesh and pushed up between bones.

"Oh my God!" Gerald slid to his knees and reached out to grab Alan by the wrists.

As he did, the seizure began again. Luisa wailed and thrashed, and Alan let out a deep roar of pain and panic.

"Get her head!" the professor snapped. "Hold her still!"

Gerald did, one palm on Luisa's forehead, pinning her against the floor.

Alan screamed as he tore first his left hand and then his right away from Luisa's skull. Blood matted her hair, but it wasn't only Alan's. The sharp things jutting from her head were not spikes but bones like enormous thorns. They grew as he watched them.

Something stabbed into his palm even as Gerald jerked his hand away. His skin had been punctured and he was bleeding, but he'd been just in time. Other sharp bones emerged.

"Are they fucking horns, Gerald?" Alan asked, on the verge of hysteria. "Are they?"

The bones began to weave themselves together like some rustic crown, and then the sharpened tips bent upward again. The light from his phone wavered. Gerald loved her, he knew he should be doing something, anything, to help her, but nothing in his life had prepared him for this. What was he meant to do?

The tops of those bones, the teeth of that crown, began to grow a glistening, waxy coating, and one by one, the tips of Luisa's horns ignited in flames.

They were candles.

"Mother of God," Gerald whispered.

Alan slid away from her, holding his bleeding hands out before him. Gerald used his free hand to help him up.

"Is this real?" the old professor asked. "Am I seeing this?"

Gerald didn't respond. The light from his phone waved in his trembling hand, strobing across Luisa's face as the terror left her eyes. Her cheeks looked sunken, skin dry, and she began to wither. Her pupils turned oil black, and that gleaming black began to spread, as if each eye were being eclipsed.

He didn't say her name this time. Her eyes narrowed and a smile cracked the edges of her lips, the skin dry as ancient parchment. The yellow raincoat crinkled as her already petite body sank into itself. She looked taller, but perhaps it was only that she had grown even thinner. The sound of cracking bone came from beneath the raincoat. The rubber shifted and popped as if something moved under there of its own accord.

"We have to . . ." Gerald let his words trail off.

Alan's voice had turned brittle. Desperate. "Have to *what*? Look at her! Look at my goddamn hands!"

Horror filled Gerald's thoughts. Whatever was happening to Luisa, in the back of his mind, he knew there was no coming back from this. But he couldn't accept that. She needed help, needed doctors. Someone, somewhere, could explain this. Hadn't he seen images online of some kind of hideous rapid tumor growth?

"Maybe . . . maybe if we're quick enough . . ."

Alan crossed his arms, held his bleeding hands against his chest. He stared at Gerald with a lunatic's eyes. "Those horns are fucking candles!"

Gerald wouldn't listen. He shut out the fear and the knowledge that what they were seeing was impossible. He shook his head to clear it, then stuffed his phone into his pocket, thinking if he just got enough distance from here, he could get a signal strong enough to call 911. He knelt beside Luisa again and slipped his hands beneath her. The yellow raincoat squeaked.

"Stop," Alan said. "Stay away from her."

Instead, Gerald lifted her. She couldn't have weighed more than eighty pounds. Perhaps less. Most days, she tipped the scales at about one hundred and twenty. He ignored the disparity and started for the cottage door. The wind howled all around them, pushing its way through the open door. Rain had soaked the threshold and the floor just inside.

He refused to acknowledge Otis's mutilated corpse.

"Look at it!" Alan snapped at him. "Whoever did that to Otis, they're responsible for this! What they did to him . . . it's like some kind of human sacrifice. Like . . . like . . ."

On the threshold, rain soaking him anew, Gerald spun with Luisa in his arms and shot Alan a withering look. "What? What are you gonna say this is, man?"

Daring him to put a name to the impossible.

Alan extended a bloody hand, thrust out an accusatory finger. "Look at the flames, you crazy son of a bitch! The wind, the fucking rain, and those candles are still burning! How can you explain any of this?"

Gerald threw his head back. Shouted, "I can't!"

He stepped out into the storm. Onto the pier.

Alan came after him, shouting at him to leave her, that they should run. But Gerald wouldn't do either of those things. This woman had changed him so thoroughly, changed everything he'd ever thought he might expect from his life, and if he left her behind, he knew he would lose the man he'd become.

"Goddamn it!" Alan caught up to him, grabbed his arm.

Gerald sprawled forward and spilled Luisa out of his arms. She tumbled onto the pier, and he stared at her in shock, lying there with that crown of horns and candles jutting from her skull. Alan stepped past him, putting himself between Gerald and Luisa.

Bereft, bleeding, Alan pleaded, "We have to get out of here!"

Behind him, yellow raincoat glistening and flapping, Luisa rose from the wooden planks of the pier. She did not stand. She rose, swaying in the wind, boots a full two feet above the wood. Alan must have seen something in Gerald's eyes, because he began to turn. Luisa reached out and tangled her fingers in the thin wisps that were all that remained of his hair. She yanked his head back and with her other hand, she clawed at his face.

Delighted.

Alan screamed.

Gerald rushed at them. He grabbed fistfuls of that slick raincoat and shoved Luisa backward. Her boots touched the pier, and she stared at him, bent and savage, black eyes gleaming. She bared her teeth in a silent snarl, and he saw teeth that were sharp and yellow and too large for her mouth. The flames flickered atop the candles in that tangle of horns, dancing in the whipping wind.

"Luisa."

At the sound of him speaking that name, she frowned. Then she smirked, as though he'd just said the stupidest thing imaginable. And Gerald thought perhaps he had. How else to explain the way his skin crawled, and the sickness in his gut, and the way he wanted to run?

"Are you . . . ?" he asked, but he couldn't finish the question. Whatever words came next, he knew he didn't want the answer.

She turned and walked toward the edge of the pier, near the empty slip where some rich asshole's boat had been. The wind bore down, hammered at them, and she opened her arms to let it take her. Undulating in the storm, she began to rise again.

"No!"

Gerald ran at her. Tried to grab her by the raincoat. Wet and slick, he could not get a grip, but he caught her by the wrist.

Luisa twisted around, smashed him in the temple, hooked two fingers into his open mouth, and yanked hard. Gerald went headfirst into a piling. His nose crunched as it broke. Pain exploded, and he tasted blood as he staggered, trying to turn toward her. He stumbled to his left, over the edge of the pier. As Gerald's arms pinwheeled, he spotted Alan rushing at Luisa, arms open to embrace her, to capture her, and then he plunged into the waters of the Gulf.

He went under. Flailing and kicking. Swallowing water and blood, he fought to the surface. Gasping for breath, he spit and coughed, twisting in the water to find the nearest edge of the boat slip. Gerald swam toward it, grabbed a cleat, and held on as the waves crashed against the dock and the pier and the undertow tried to drag him under.

Over the wind, he heard a scream. He looked up to see Luisa smash Alan against a piling. One of his arms hung at his side, broken and twisted. She gripped his throat and used one long fingernail to carve into his face, then his throat. His screaming cut off, and he fell limply, dead or mercifully unconscious.

Luisa sailed aloft with the next gust of wind.

Gerald could have called after her, but remained silent. Bobbing in the water, he held on to the cleat and the dock and watched the wind blow her out over the Gulf, torn yellow raincoat flapping in the dark, and the candles still burning in the tangle of horns on her head. Impossible, but Gerald knew nothing was impossible now.

The cold water dragged at him.

He said her name, quietly, wondering if it really was her name anymore.

Holding tightly to the cleat, he began to drag himself from the water.

23

Something had changed in Ruby.

No, not something, she thought. *Everything.*

She sat on the coffee-stained love seat, the only piece of furniture in the wheelhouse that had been made for comfort instead of for its usefulness. Her skin prickled with new sensations. The air inside the wheelhouse felt cold and damp, but she wore the temperature and humidity like a layer she might peel off anytime she wished. She had the sense that she could change the air around her, but didn't dare try.

The smell and taste of the salt of the gulf waters, the acrid odor of Aiden's diaper, the rust on the derelict's hull, and the fragrant green life of the mangrove trees were all around her. Sharper than any scent she had encountered before. Along with those smells, the copper stink of her own blood filled her nose.

Mae had taken a turn holding the baby, pacing with him in her arms, but now she sat down beside Ruby. The pressure of her weight on the love seat's cushion made Ruby blink, as if her mind were sobering up from a drunken blindness.

"I know this is a lot," Mae said gently. "But it was the only way."

The rush of sensation had more than distracted Ruby. It had lured her attention away, mesmerized her. Now that her thoughts began to clear, she glanced over at Book. *Charlie*, she thought. Moments ago, she had been angry with him. Deeply frustrated. Those feelings remained, the bitterness that still lingered from the moment she had realized he was not the man she'd thought him to be. But he had never meant to hurt her, and in spite of how much he had, Ruby knew he would never do so on purpose. She trusted him that much.

Mae, though . . . how could she trust this woman? When Mae had come to her with Aiden, Ruby had felt she had no choice but to trust her. They were in danger and had the shared desire to protect Aiden. They shared grief over Bella's death. But Ruby pondered on just how little she knew about Mae, and she reminded herself to be careful now. Whatever had happened to Bella, and whatever Mae had done to her, she had to focus on Aiden. That little baby was the only family she had left.

Her mouth had gone dry. She wetted her lips and tasted more of her blood. A cough shook her.

Reaching up, she ran her fingers carefully over the sharp nubs of the horns that had grown from her head. Ruby had been in a car accident at the age of nine. Her mother had been driving in the left lane and tried to overtake a tractor-trailer rig. She never liked to drive beside one of those enormous trucks and wanted to pass it as quickly as possible. But as her mother had accelerated, the truck had drifted into their lane. Its front left tire had pressed against their old Ford's passenger side—right next to Ruby. The massive tire had brutalized the door, wrecking the metal and shattering the window. Ruby had screamed as the car had gone up on two wheels before slamming down again.

Her mother had managed to keep her hands on the wheel. Face deathly pale, she had pulled over and held young Ruby while she cried. Later that day, when all her tears had dried, Ruby had felt completely wrung out. Numb, empty, and without direction.

She felt that way now. Only Aiden gave her purpose and focused her on just how dangerous her numbness might be. The threat remained, which meant she couldn't indulge her shock for much longer. The trouble was that shock did not respond to rationality or responsibility.

I'm a witch, she thought. But that didn't sit right. Mae kept making the distinction between stories of witchcraft and this ancient tradition, this circle of weavers. Näturvefjar.

Book stood looking out the long window onto the foredeck, where the mangroves bent in the punishing storm winds.

"What do you see?" Ruby asked.

Book nodded slowly, though she wasn't sure what she had said that he might be agreeing with.

"They're out there," he said without turning to look at Ruby and Mae. "The birds are in the trees again, but they're not alone. It's dark as hell, but I've seen at least four of them."

"Birds," Ruby said.

Book glanced back at her, frowning. "Not birds."

Ah, she realized. Of course. He'd suggested as much. "Weavers."

"There was an owl," Book said. "But I think it's really one of them. A witch."

The urge to giggle bubbled up in her chest. Ruby pushed the temptation away. Madness felt alluring, something she could embrace to escape this ugly, painful reality. But that sort of escape wouldn't help anyone, and it wouldn't last very long.

She turned to Mae, who had been waiting patiently, almost penitently, to be noticed. Mae held Aiden and seemed to comfort him in a way that Ruby had not yet been able to manage. Was this witchcraft, too? The weaving of some kind of charm or influence?

Did it matter at this point?

No, it did not.

"I'm having a hard time summoning up any gratitude for what you just did," Ruby said.

Mae looked down at the baby in her arms. "I don't need gratitude."

"That's good."

"If I hadn't made you part of the circle, you'd be . . . not dead, maybe, but gone," Mae said, her tone defensive, as if she did actually want that gratitude after all. "Stratim would be here in your place."

"Would I have known it, or would my mind be gone? Because if my mind and soul were gone and I was basically dead and she had my body, then at least I wouldn't be sitting here like this, terrified and wanting to scream and wondering what it means that you did that ritual on me. I feel so different. My skin, and my . . . What the hell am I now? I feel like I'm connected to the trees out there, and the salt in the water, and thousands of little crabs and who knows what else?"

Mae smiled as if she'd just handed over the most wonderful gift. "It's beautiful."

Ruby shuddered, teetering on the edge of hysteria. "It's terrifying!"

The moment turned silent and cold.

Ruby hugged herself. She wanted to take the baby from Mae but didn't trust herself not to drop him, and she wanted a few more minutes to collect herself. She wanted to ask if the broken horn stubs on her skull would go away or if they could be removed, but she feared the answer. Had anyone ever done this before? Had Stratim ever begun to possess someone, only to be stopped partway through? It seemed unlikely, which meant that Mae wouldn't have any answers for her.

Surgery, Ruby thought. She might need surgery to fix her fucking skull.

What the hell was happening? How was any of this real?

"Tell me more about Stratim," she said.

Mae shifted toward her, exhaling in apparent relief. Aiden cooed in his sleep.

"I honestly don't know much more than I've told you," Mae said. "I learned rituals, tried to understand what it meant to 'weave the night,' as the older ones say. But I never really studied as much as I should have. Bella said I didn't have enough 'intellectual curiosity.'

She was a much better student, more dedicated, really swept up in it all. She dreamed about Stratim all the time."

Still by the front window, Book shifted. "Just dreams, or some kind of connection?"

"I wondered the same thing. Even Bella wasn't sure."

"Will she find someone else?" Ruby asked. "You stopped her from taking me, but that doesn't mean she won't find another body to hijack."

Mae glanced at the starboard window. "I suspect she will. She could only do this in the first place—try to invade your body like that—if the circle summoned her. So we need to prepare for that."

"How long will it take?" Book asked.

"She'll have to find someone she thinks is suitable," Mae said. "But I'm not Stratim. I don't know what that'll mean to her. All I know is—"

Ruby didn't want to hear more about what Mae *didn't* know. "The rest of them are either out there on deck or on the way. They've got to be. So yeah, if she can just hijack anyone she wants, she'll be back soon. Maybe they're waiting for her, or maybe they'll kill us before then and take Aiden to present to her when she gets here."

"They can't get to us," Mae protested.

"For now," Book said.

Ruby felt a bit stronger, so when Aiden began to squirm, she reached out to take him. For the first time, she noticed just how tired Mae looked and wondered if the rituals she had performed had drained her physically as well as mentally.

"I'll give him a bottle," she said.

As she stood up, Book started toward her, one hand out as if he thought he might have to catch her. But Ruby was in no danger of collapsing now. Despite all she'd been through, she felt sturdy. Powerful. The old hoodie Book had given her fell mid-thigh, so she wasn't flashing anyone, but Book had seen all she had many times over. It didn't seem important just now.

Aiden opened his sleepy eyes. She had wondered if the blood on her face and the stubs of horns would bother him, but the baby seemed unperturbed. He blinked, and cooed, and pushed his tongue out between his lips the way babies tended to do when they wanted to be fed.

"You don't have to—" Mae began.

"I want to," Ruby said. "First, though, what about Stratim? However they summoned her, is it temporary or permanent? And is there any way to send her back where she came from?"

Mae sank against the back of the love seat. She glanced at Book. "You saw the candle?"

Book scoffed. "Did I see it? Nothing's ever freaked me out more."

Mae gestured with her fingers, making circles around her own head. "The horns grow thirteen candles, one for each of the circle who summoned her. They burn with the life of the host. Bella said Stratim remains until all the candles go out, and then we'd have to start the whole process again. Another summoning, another host. That's why they want Aiden. That's why his father was murdered in that ritual. There's a rite that the circle believes will allow Stratim to stay in our world forever, and it calls for sacrifice. Aiden was born for that, conceived for it. Consecrated for it. Without him, they would need another father, another pregnancy, another baby with a mother willing to give up her child by choice. To hold the knife."

Ruby frowned. "To hold the knife?"

Mae shook her head. "I'm tired. That's all I remember. I told you, Bella studied all of this. It never mattered much to me until I held Aiden for the first time."

All three of them were quiet. The baby made raspberries with his lips.

"I'm going to feed him and put some clean clothes on," Ruby said after a moment. She coughed lightly, and her throat felt sore. The back of her neck itched, and a sudden certainty stole over her.

She glanced at Mae. "How many EpiPens are in that kit?"

The question did not seem to surprise Mae at all. "At least three more. Hang on."

Mae dug into the baby bag, found the kit, and pulled out one of the EpiPens. She handed it to Ruby, who clutched it while still cradling Aiden.

"You know how to use this?" Mae asked.

Ruby nodded. "Upper thigh."

"What are you doing?" Book asked, glancing back and forth between them. "You're having an allergic reaction, too? Enough to use that thing?"

"Short answer, yes," Ruby said. "Long answer will have to wait. For now, keep watch, and shout if the shit hits the fan."

Book narrowed his eyes, but let it go. "Fine. But if the shit hits the fan, I'll probably be screaming."

24

Soaked to the skin, Gerald knelt on the dock and tried to quiet the hammering of his heart. He whispered to himself, denials of the things he'd just seen, but he could not convince himself it hadn't happened. A wave crashed against the dock, washed over the wood, and nearly toppled him back into the water.

Catching his breath, he forced himself to stand. The wind at his back helped him reach the metal ramp from the dock to the pier. Halfway up, his sodden boots clomping on the aluminum walk, the shock began to abate enough for him to remember he wasn't alone.

"Oh shit. Alan!"

His exhaustion and bruises forgotten, Gerald bolted to the top of the walkway and spotted Alan lying on the pier a dozen feet away. Cursing, he rushed to the old professor and fell to his knees again. One of Alan's arms had been so badly broken that it looked bent the wrong direction in at least three places. Blood soaked the sleeve of his coat, which meant bone had broken through the skin. One side of his face had swollen fat and purple, while the other had ragged furrows where she had raked her fingers down his cheek.

Gerald held his hands over Alan, aching to help but afraid to touch or move him. He glanced out across the water, where Luisa had gone. Was that a light out there, coming from the *Christabel*? He thought it must be.

Luisa. He squeezed his eyes shut as if that might erase the last images of her in his head, but it only made things worse. In the dark inside his head, nothing could distract him from wanting to freak the fuck out.

Eyes open, he turned back to his friend. "Alan? Can you hear me?"

He stared. Fuck. Fuck. Fuck. Was Alan dead? At this angle, in the dark, it was hard to tell if his chest rose and fell, but . . . no. There it was. He was still breathing.

Gerald buried his head in his hands. Alan needed help, but could he risk dragging him to the car? He didn't know how bad Alan's injuries were. If he had internal bleeding, broken ribs, anything like that, Gerald could make it so much worse. But he couldn't just leave him here.

He took out his phone. No signal, just like inside the cottage.

Again, he looked out to the Gulf. To that little light offshore, where Charlie Book was definitely in trouble. Did Book have any idea of the insane, evil shit coming his way? Gerald could not imagine it. How could Book be prepared for this? And what about Luisa? Whatever had happened to her, Gerald could not just let it continue. There had to be a way to cure her, to save her. Fix her.

There had to be.

"Hey, Fancy Dan," Alan mumbled.

Gerald flinched and looked down to see his eyes open. Pain twisted Alan's features, and his eyes were glassy, but his gaze fixed firmly on Gerald.

"Go after her," Alan said.

"How? And even if I did, what am I gonna do for her?"

"Her, and Book, too," Alan reminded him. "You won't know unless you go find out. You won't be able to live with yourself."

Soaked with rain and gulf water, Gerald felt as if he weighed a thousand pounds. The storm wind tried to knock him over, but he refused to topple.

"What about you?" he asked.

Alan had never looked so pale. He closed his eyes. The space between breaths grew longer, but then he spoke. "Otis . . . I know he owned a gun. You ought to bring it with you."

Numb, Gerald took Alan's hand, careful not to touch the one attached to that badly broken arm. He started to shake his head, afraid of the truth, feeling as if he needed to keep arguing. If Alan could stand, Gerald could get him to the car, drive him to the hospital. Then he would come back . . . but he wondered how long that would take and what would become of Book and Luisa in the meantime.

Luisa. The memory of what he'd witnessed made him want to scream.

Alan extricated his good hand from Gerald's without opening his eyes. He reached up, cupped Gerald's face in that leathery hand, patted his cheek, and then exhaled once and was gone.

Gerald saw that stillness and understood immediately. "Jesus Christ," he whispered, choking on the words. He hung his head, said a prayer to a God in whom he'd never had much faith, and then stood.

"I'll be back," he said, and he turned and left his friend's corpse to soak in the rain.

He ran to Otis's cottage. The door still hung open. The wind had knocked over framed photos and blown things off the coffee table. The body of the drunken harbormaster remained, head still facing the wrong direction, snuffed-out candles where his eyes should be.

"Sorry, Otis. Goddamn, I'm sorry."

Gerald moved fast, ignoring the voice in the back of his head asking him just what in hell he thought he was doing. He started in the bedroom, yanking out drawers, tossing clothes onto the floor, digging through the closet. The cottage would look as if burglars had turned it upside down, but what did that matter to Otis now?

He found the gun in a wooden box at the back of a shelf in the closet, along with a pair of US Navy medals, one for good conduct and one for being an expert with a pistol. Gerald froze for a moment, staring at those medals, but he didn't have time for sentimentality. He had never known that Otis had been in the navy and never would have imagined the old drunk receiving either of these medals, but here they were. It made Gerald wonder about his uncle Clarence, who'd loved to talk about being at sea but never about serving in the navy, or the men he'd met during those years, or if anyone had ever shot at him. The gun Uncle Clarence kept in a glass case on a bookshelf in his TV room looked an awful lot like this one. Clarence Coleman's gun had been a Beretta M9. When Gerald had been ten years old, his uncle had let him hold that gun, just for a minute. Unloaded, of course. But unloaded or not, Gerald's mother had raised hell about it and never left him alone at Uncle Clarence's house again.

In the kitchen, he found a long butcher's knife that came with a hard plastic sheath. He snatched a plastic bag off the top of the refrigerator, a shopping bag from Health Mart, and stuck the knife in there along with the Beretta and a half-full pint bottle of Wild Turkey that had been tempting him from the kitchen counter. If he was really doing this, if he'd really seen the things he'd seen, a couple of shots of bourbon would grease the motor to keep him going.

He bolted, bag in hand. The door still hung open, and he didn't bother trying to shut it. Otis wouldn't mind.

The thought made him giddy with horror. If he'd stopped moving right then, he'd have thrown up his guts. Nobody should die the way Otis had died. The image would haunt him the rest of his life, but nowhere near as badly as watching those goddamn candles ignite on the tips of the horns that grew out of Luisa's skull, or the feeling of Alan's gentle hand on his cheek as he breathed his last.

You should run, he thought. *Go, now.*

Instead, Gerald ran to the metal cabinet affixed on the wall just inside the gate. This was the lockbox where they kept the keys to the boats moored there. The owners had access, and so did Otis. Now that he was out here, it occurred to him that he should have searched for the keys, but that would have meant digging through the dead man's pockets, and honestly, fuck that.

Gerald kicked open the door to the utility shed, splintering the lock. Inside, he found a shovel, which he used to pry the lockbox off the wall of the shed. It clattered to the walkway in the rain, and he went at it with the shovel. Smashing it, denting it, did nothing, but when he propped it between his feet and pressed the nose of the shovel into the crevice just below the lock on the lid and put all his weight behind it, the box popped open. Keys scattered onto the walkway.

The first key he recognized went to Steve Orway's Chris-Craft, *Country Girl*, which he'd named after his wife way back when. She'd been dead since before the turn of the century. The cabin cruiser was more than forty years old, but Orway kept it in beautiful condition, running like a dream. Gerald had seen it still in the water, which had saddened him because the old man was in a nursing home and his sons cared even less about his pride and joy than they did about their dad. They hadn't bothered to have it pulled from the water for this storm.

Gerald snatched up the keys, grateful for Orway's ungrateful sons.

He ran down to the *Country Girl*. The wind tipped the boat sideways. His boots splashed in an inch of rain on her deck, falling so fast it couldn't drain quickly enough. Still, it only took him minutes before he had her ready to go. Hoping she had enough fuel to get out to the *Christabel* and back, he cast off, darted to the cabin, and backed her out of her slip.

When he pointed her into the surf, a wave lifted the cruiser and smashed her backward into the dock. Gerald wanted to check the damage, but the next wave rolled in, and he throttled forward. The Gulf churned in front of him, but he aimed for the little point of light in the storm, just offshore, and wondered if he would drown trying to reach it.

He wanted to puke.

Fuck it, he thought and sped up.

Luisa had screamed. Bleeding, she had screamed in pain and fear like Gerald had never imagined. He didn't know if there was any way to bring her back from what had happened to her, but if he didn't try, he'd be hearing those screams in his head for the rest of his life.

25

Book sat at his desk in the wheelhouse and thought he might explode. His right knee bounced incessantly. His body demanded that he move, that he do something—anything—to burn off the nervous energy coursing through him, but the best he could do was to get up and pace the wheelhouse again. Twenty minutes had passed since Ruby had taken the baby down below to feed him, and those twenty minutes had been excruciating. Book moved from port to starboard, staring out the windows, studying the orange-blue flames that flickered, barely visible, along the window frames. It felt like a dream, and perhaps it was for the best that all of this was happening in the dark, in the storm, out at sea, because it would have been so much harder to let himself believe any of it during the hours of sunlight.

He went to the foredeck window. Through the rain, he could see the mangroves sway, but otherwise, nothing moved out there, at least for the moment.

On the love seat, Mae coughed. Her pallor had become more sickly, and when Ruby had gone downstairs, Mae had curled up on the love seat and closed her eyes. Her breathing had grown labored, and she shivered as she napped, leading him to think she must have developed a fever. Whatever was wrong with this woman, it wasn't anything as simple as allergies.

He paced from port to starboard again. The thudding of wings and beaks against the windows still echoed in his mind, and he allowed himself to wonder how long this would continue. When the storm had passed and the sun returned, would the birds continue to behave so bizarrely? If there truly were some malevolent power guiding them, what were the rules governing that power? Would he and Ruby and Mae and Aiden be able to leave this ship once the wind and the surf died down? He wished he had asked these questions before Ruby had gone below, but they had only occurred to him when his heart had stopped its deafening hammering in his ears.

Staring out the windows, he knew he ought to find something to distract him. He could read a book or get some work done. But how was he supposed to concentrate on anything? Book glanced at Mae and felt profound envy. She might be sick, but at least she could retreat into sleep.

Mae took a rattling breath, and her eyes opened. "Book . . . come here."

He hesitated. Mae seemed to like to command people, but he didn't enjoy being told what to do.

"Please," she rasped.

Curious, he did as she asked. "What is it?"

One hand extended, finger pointing to the small, zippered satchel that still lay on Gerald's desk where she had put it down after giving Ruby an EpiPen.

"There are a couple others in there," she said and coughed dryly. "Could you get one for me?"

"Another injection?" Book wondered how often a doctor would recommend a second shot and how bad an allergy had to be in order to require it.

Her fingers clutched at the air, reaching toward the satchel. "Could you just . . ."

Book picked up the kit, unzipped it, and sat on the arm of the love seat while he poked around inside. His fingers grazed a plastic nasal spray bottle as well as a few punch tabs of other allergy medication. He found several other EpiPens inside, and he plucked one out.

Mae reached for it. "Thank you."

Book made no move to hand it over. "I've never seen allergies like yours. The rash you've got, as sick as you are . . . what are you allergic to out here? You and Ruby both?"

She strained, reaching her fingers for the EpiPen in his hand. When she coughed again, her eyes were bloodshot, and she winced with pain in her chest.

"Please," she said again.

"I'll give you the shot myself. Just tell me what you're allergic to."

With an almost feral snarl, she thrust out her hand and snatched the EpiPen from his hand.

"Christ," Book hissed.

She fixed him with a grim look, eyes reddening further. "You're going to trade medication for answers? Maybe I'm starting to see some of the bullshit that drove you and Ruby apart."

Book wanted to argue, to defend himself, but he wouldn't give her the satisfaction. Mae had been an accomplice at a ritual murder, and there was no way for him to know what else she had been involved with. She worshipped this Ur-Witch and performed what amounted to black magic. According to her, the women in their circle could transform into birds. Could he even consider her a human being anymore?

He glared at her. "I'm in the middle of a nightmare you brought to my door. I deserve answers."

Mae flicked the cap off the EpiPen. Her breathing had become more ragged, and she erupted in a burst of coughing so fierce she seemed about to pass out. It subsided and she took a few shallow breaths before she jammed the needle into her upper thigh and injected herself.

Book watched as she leaned back into the love seat, thinking of junkies getting a fix. This didn't seem much different from that.

Allergies.

"Tell me," he said.

Her eyes flickered open. She bared her teeth. "Why not? I don't know why I'm trying to play coy, given what you already know." Mae sat up a bit, took a few experimental breaths, and exhaled. "It's rust."

Book stared at her. "Rust."

"You've read fairy tales. A lot of creatures in those stories can't stand the touch of iron."

"This isn't a fairy tale," Book said. But even as he said it, he realized that it felt like one.

"The whole ship is iron," Mae said, rubbing at her itchy eyes. The rash on her skin had spread to the backs of her hands. "Being around so much of it at once would be difficult enough, but being inside . . . all the rust is in the air. Breathing it in . . . it's poison."

Book glanced at the satchel, then at the EpiPen she had just discarded. Mae had come prepared. His mind went back to the moment she and Ruby had first entered the wheelhouse, when her allergies had come on so quickly that they had to rush to inject her. Neither of them had seemed surprised.

"You knew it would be like this on board, but you came here anyway," he said.

Mae coughed lightly. Her color had begun to improve. "The others are coming for us. They'll be weaker this way. With luck, they won't be as prepared."

A sick feeling churned in his gut. They hadn't sought him out only because the *Christabel* was so remote or because nobody would think to look for Ruby out here with her ex-boyfriend. They had come because if they had to make a stand, being aboard the ancient, rusting freighter would poison their enemies. Sicken them.

He'd let himself believe that one of the reasons they had come to him was that Ruby felt safe with him, that she trusted him, despite the way things had ended between them. Now . . .

"That's why you came here," Book said, staring at her. "To even the odds."

Mae lay down on the love seat again. The injection made it easier for her to breathe, but evidently, it didn't stop her from being exhausted.

"It doesn't even the odds," she said. "But it might buy us enough time to put up a fight."

Her eyes closed. Book slumped into his office chair and waited for Ruby to come back upstairs with Aiden. He tried to put a label on how he felt but found it impossible. Even when he had thought Ruby had run to him for safety, he had known it was more about the isolation of the *Christabel* than the idea he could somehow protect her. But he had been happy to give them shelter and a place to lay their heads. It had felt like they were putting the past behind them, and he could finally let go of the queasy feeling of disappointment—in her and in himself—that he'd held on to for a year and a half. But this was different. Ruby had come to him, but she would have gone to anyone who could shelter them somewhere their enemies might hesitate to attack.

It shouldn't have made a difference, but it did.

Book heard Mae begin to snore lightly. Ruby and Aiden had still not come back upstairs. Even weakened as she was, how could she sleep? Could she be that confident? Did she really feel safe? Because he had never felt less safe in his life.

The *Christabel* tipped slightly to port. When the wind gusted hard enough and a wave struck at the same time, the storm had the power to do that. It hadn't lost any of its strength. If anything, it churned even harder. He wanted to ask Mae what they were going to do now. Did they wait out the storm? Would daybreak do anything to drive the weavers away?

They're not vampires, Book, he thought.

But what did he know about this cult of witches? Were they even fully human? It hurt to wonder such a thing, but they were on the outskirts of his understanding now. He thought of old maps whose unexplored edges would be labeled *Here there be dragons.* If the world wasn't structured the way he'd been taught, if science and logic and human nature weren't strict rules about the way life functioned, what did that mean? How many impossible things waited for them out beyond the limits of the mapped portions of the world?

Book steeled himself, reining in his thoughts. Now wasn't the time to obsess over what other monsters might exist in the dark, forgotten parts of the world. If he wanted to survive, he had to fight the ones out there on the deck of the ship.

All he wanted was the tiniest sliver of reassurance, not just for himself but for Ruby—and for her nephew as well. Aiden wasn't his child, and Ruby had played on his feelings for her, but he couldn't let anything happen to them.

Birds struck the starboard window, three in a row. Book jumped up with a shout, but they flew off, and he stood staring, waiting for the earlier assault to begin again. The warding Mae had scrawled on the window frames continued to flicker with little flames, but he did not feel safe. His heart raced and still he waited, but only the rain pelted the glass now, and when he glanced over, he saw that Mae slept on. Neither the impact of those birds nor his cry had roused her. She looked so peaceful, but for the first time, he wondered if the depth of her slumber might be unnatural. Had they done something to her, her circle?

A thump struck the front window, and a flutter of wings. He turned and saw the bird vanish into the rain. Warily, he crossed the wheelhouse and approached the glass. As he drew nearer, he could make out the floating forest. The mangroves grew together in a tangle, so with every gust of wind, they bent together and tugged at one another.

His eyes adjusted, and he noticed one tree that did not move with the others. As soon as he saw it, he realized there were more like that. At least three of them out there. Dark shapes in the storm, one up in the trees, two of them on the deck right at the rusted edge of the section that had given way, where the forest grew. Bigger than birds.

Something scuttled across the window. Book flinched. His fingers had been an inch from touching the glass. He backed away, confused. How had he moved so close to the window when he'd been trying so hard to keep back? The movement against the glass caught his eye again, and now he saw the thing crawling out there was a tree crab. He frowned, watching it move, and then noticed there were others, not burned by the protection Mae had crafted. Perhaps they were too small, or maybe it was that they weren't attacking, just existing. They crept onto the window, first a dozen and then two, and then he lost count.

They had never done this before. The wind blew hard enough to strip several away from the glass, but others took their place. Fascinated, Book watched the way they marched and gathered. He swayed, lost in the patterns the crabs formed, and he imagined music to accompany their movements. Did they have an innate connection, moving like a murmuration of swallows? Given wings, would they sweep across the sky in elegant waves, as if their flight could create music?

He cocked his head, looking through the foot of glass not yet obscured by the shifting mass of tree crabs. Were those eyes, peering in at him through the skittering mass of crabs? Book swayed a bit, felt a little drunk. It seemed to him that he could hear someone whispering in his ear, right there beside him, but he couldn't make sense of the words.

Something moved outside, flapping in the wind. Was it the hair of a woman? The wings of a bird? Or some part of the *Christabel* that needed to be battened down for safety?

Safety. He would not risk anything happening to Ruby or their child.

No. He blinked. Not their child. *Her* child. But not even that. Her flesh and blood.

Whatever it was, flapping out there on the deck, it wasn't right. Something had come undone. Something important.

It could be dangerous, he thought. *Go out and fix it.*

He knew there was something strange about those thoughts. They didn't seem to come into his head the way his internal voice usually sounded. A frisson of alarm passed through him, a small part of him that reminded him not to go outside. His body seemed reluctant to move, and yet he found himself crossing the wheelhouse and moving toward the door.

As he reached for the lock on the wheelhouse door, a surge of worry swept over him, but this was worry for the *Christabel*, not for himself or his guests. Deep inside him, like a cry from the bottom of a well, he tried to tell himself not to open that door under any circumstances. But those concerns evaporated, forgotten.

Something had gone amiss out on the deck. He needed to fix it. He barely noticed the Sharpie scribbles on the doorframe and the door itself. He turned the lock and then grabbed the door handle.

Ruby stepped into the wheelhouse just in time to see Book twist the door handle. She had not only fed Aiden, she'd managed to put him down in the bed she should have been sleeping in herself. His safety had worried her, but she'd reasoned that as long as she and Book and Mae were between the weavers and the baby, he'd be okay.

He'll live, as long as we live.

For the first time in hours, despite itchy skin and a painful cough, her head felt clear enough to have a rational conversation about how to survive.

Then she spotted Book at the door.

A disconnect in her brain made it impossible for her to accept what she was seeing. Why would Book go outside? He wouldn't.

He drew the door open a few inches, and the wind blew it the rest of the way. Book stumbled backward, caught his footing, and then raised his head to look out into the storm as casually as if he were checking to see if there were packages on his front step. The rain swept in.

Ruby screamed as she ran at him. There might have been words in that scream. His name, certainly, and probably the word *no.* Book didn't seem to hear her. Instead, he appeared mesmerized by the tall, lithe shadow standing just beyond the threshold. She wore a flowing cream top, soaked through, and pants that belonged in a business meeting. Shoulder-length black hair framed her face, and those blue eyes gleamed. Ruby couldn't see the color of her eyes in the gloom beyond the threshold, but she didn't have to see. She remembered her sister's eyes very well.

Impossible. She's dead. She's dead. She's dead.

Elation lifted her heart. Somehow Mae had been wrong, for here was Bella right in front of her, just beyond the open wheelhouse door. Bella stood in the rain, tall and beautiful, her back straight, and a rush of love washed over Ruby. There were so many things she had wanted to say, so many regrets she had believed she would never be able to correct. The past had been filled with so much pain, and Bella's murder had meant none of it could ever be healed.

Now here she was.

Bella had never looked better. Storm or no storm. Ruby was so relieved . . .

Until she saw the other figures standing in the rain behind her sister. Other weavers, members of the circle. Ruby came to a halt just a few feet behind Book and stared at her sister.

"You're alive," she managed to say.

Bella didn't smile in greeting. She met Ruby's gaze, her blue eyes cold. And then she shifted her attention back to her prey.

"Come outside, Mr. Book," Bella said. Her eyes narrowed. "We need to talk, and a little rain won't kill you."

Behind Ruby, Mae cried out. She must have just woken up. Ruby heard her spring from the love seat and rush across the wheelhouse, shouting at Book not to cross the threshold.

Mesmerized, Book started to move. To obey Bella, not Mae.

Ruby grabbed at Book's shirt, got a fistful of fabric, and pulled him backward. He twisted, scowling in irritation, truly mesmerized after all. He struck her arm, broke her grip, and as she released him, he stumbled toward the open door. From the corner of her eye, Ruby saw the malicious pleasure on her sister's face.

Whatever Bella intended to do with Book, it would be cruel.

Ruby lunged for him. She wrapped her arms around him the way they had once embraced, back when they had meant everything to each other, and twisted him away from the open door. Ruby shoved him as hard as she could. Book went sprawling on the floor of the wheelhouse.

Inside.

But the force of pushing him away had propelled her backward, and now Ruby stood in the rain, punished by the wind. On the wrong side of the threshold.

She stared at the open doorway. Safety lay within.

Bella stepped between Ruby and the door. She seemed taller, somehow. Her hair had been cut so stylishly, what did you call that look? Like a bob in the back, with longer locks framing her face. *These are the things that cross your mind when it's blown.*

Mae had said the circle had murdered Bella in punishment, but here she was. What did that mean? Why had Mae lied?

Bella reached out to push aside the damp curtain of hair that partly veiled Ruby's face.

"Hello, big sister," she said.

Ruby might have screamed. What was real? What was a lie? But despite the chaos and fear in her head, her heart stayed focused on the baby boy she had put down on that bed inside.

"Get out of the way, Bella," she said.

Inside, Mae and Book were both shouting at her. Neither seemed ready to come out and help.

Bella shot out her hand and clutched Ruby's throat.

Book shouted and rushed into the rain.

But by then, Bella had dragged Ruby off the deck and up into the storm. The gulf waters roared, so much louder up here. The wind raged, battering the sisters, but Bella turned and slid and seemed to ride the gusts, carrying her sister with her.

Up inside the mangrove trees, aloft in the floating forest, Ruby began to scream.

26

Mae shouted after Book, but she'd barely gotten a word out before he darted into the storm. Even as the rain blew into the wheelhouse, the ward she'd scrawled on the doorframe ignited again. Out on the deck, Ruby screamed, and Mae knew it was too late. Bella had managed to play with Book's mind, to entrance him long enough to get him to open the door. Whatever happened now, Book and Ruby had brought it on themselves by crossing the threshold. As one of the Näturvefjar, Mae had done hideous things, and gladly. But she had nothing against those two, and they had been willing to risk everything to help protect Aiden. So she would have liked to help them. Mae wished she could save them.

She could not.

The temperature in the wheelhouse dropped thirty degrees in seconds. Her breath frosted the air. The symbols she'd scrawled around the windows burned much more brightly now. The wind and rain might come in, the weavers might influence the temperature, but they could not enter. Not yet. The ship's iron hull would sap their strength, sicken them, and the cloud of rust that tainted the air and the rain would choke them. They would not have known exactly what they would find. Tracking Aiden, they had moved quickly. But now that they were here, they would endure the poison if it meant they could get their hands on the baby. Her ward might be strong, but they would do everything they could to shatter it or convince her to remove it—anything to reach Aiden. In time, they would succeed.

That made her decision simpler.

Mae snatched a fresh Sharpie off one of the desks, then bolted through the open hatch that led below. She held on to the railings and scrambled down the stairs in the deepening darkness. The howl of the wind and spatter of rain seemed to follow her. She told herself none of the weavers could enter the wheelhouse, that it was not possible for one of them to be behind her right now, long fingers reaching out to twine in her hair.

She thought of Zoe and Karinna, how kind they had always been to her, and wondered if they would hesitate to hurt her. An image flashed in her mind, of the three of them finger-painting one another's faces with the blood of baby Aiden's father. Part of the ritual, of course, but they had enjoyed themselves. They had taken the horror Mae knew they had all been feeling and forged it into brittle humor, accepted the darkness of their pursuits. The night had been hideous, but also sensual. Taking a life, spilling blood into the soil, praying to a dark power so ancient that it predated the beliefs of every fool on the planet . . . it had made her feel strong and wise, and yes, goddamn it, she'd felt like she was better than other people. Lesser people, who didn't have the intelligence or courage to break every one of humanity's flimsy rules.

Guilty, she thought as she ran the short corridor. But even now, she meant that she was guilty, not that she felt any of that guilt.

To the Näturvefjar, she was the betrayer, but she felt so betrayed by them. Would she have wanted to protect Aiden if he'd been someone else's baby? If she had not constructed in her dreams a vision of raising this child with Bella? Mae knew herself well enough to answer that. She knew what kind of monster she was.

And she knew which monsters were worse.

Like Bella. *She* was worse. Bella had never changed her mind about the fate of her child, no matter how Mae had begged her. So Mae had been forced to act alone.

She didn't know what would happen to Ruby and Book now, but she couldn't allow herself to care. The ship creaked around her. It canted to one side, and she bashed her shoulder against the wall. The cold seemed to follow her into the guts of the *Christabel*, and as Mae ran toward the room Book had given her and Ruby to share, a terrible silence yawned from the doorway. Not a peep from Aiden? The baby might have been sleeping, but he never slept soundly, and there had been shouting and banging up in the wheelhouse. Could Aiden really have slept through it?

She dug out her phone and thumbed on the flashlight function. Running down here in the dark had been stupid, but now she had the phone's false illumination. In her mind, she tried to calculate how long her battery would last. How dark would it become down here?

Mae stepped into the room. The illumination from her phone did not stretch very far. The darkness seemed to swallow the light, so only a pale glow reached the nearest bed. A pillow lay dead center on the mattress with sheets and a blanket bunched up beside it. The mound on the bed had the rough shape of a swaddled infant, but her heart fluttered as she stared at it, a terrible certainty taking root. The weavers had gotten here before she had. Somehow they had taken Aiden.

Coughing, drawing ragged breaths, she darted for the bed, reached down, and plucked the sheets back. Inside, she'd been hoping that her eyes had misconstrued what she saw, but no matter how much trouble someone had gone to in order to make it convincing, the bunched-up sheets held no infant.

The ship creaked loudly. Mae turned, numb and grieving, and the light from her phone fell on the other bed in the room. Two pillows and a blanket had been used to construct a nest for Aiden—something he could not roll out of. He lay on the mattress, sleeping more peacefully than she had ever seen him.

Tears welled in her eyes.

You can do this, Mae told herself. The assurance wasn't entirely successful. Eleven faithful Näturvefjar would be nearly impossible to survive, but they would be nothing compared to Stratim. Mae had stopped the Ur-Witch from hijacking Ruby's body, but there would be someone else, another woman somewhere in Galveston. She didn't know how long it would take Stratim to come, but Mae knew it would happen. Could she hold off the Ur-Witch long enough for the summoning to run its course? She didn't know, but when she looked at Aiden, sleeping peacefully, eyebrows twitching as he dreamed the dreams only babies knew, she had to try.

She closed the door and latched it, but it had no lock.

The ship groaned and shifted like some ancient beast in its dying hour. Mae took the Sharpie and began to scrawl on the doorframe. She wondered how it had come to this, how she had let her love for this child put her in such danger. But she knew the answer. The first time she had held Aiden in her arms, she had felt sickened by the person she had become. Revulsion had woken her. She could never erase the stain of that prior evil on her heart, but she refused to allow a creature as innocent as this baby to pay the price for it.

If she could have saved Book and Ruby along with Aiden, she would have.

But it was much too late for them.

27

The rust around the edges of the vast hole in the deck had eaten away at the iron for a century. When Book staggered back toward the floating forest, his left boot punched through the rotted metal. He pinwheeled his arms and managed to grab a sturdy mangrove branch to keep himself from tumbling down into the hold. A crab scuttled over his hand, but he ignored it. The wind whipped around him, rain soaking his hair and clothing. The storm bent the floating forest and made a sound more like human grief than the sort of whistle or moan he'd heard before.

Squinting against the rain, he peered up through the mangroves and stared in breathless awe at the two figures dangling in the air, up amid the trees. Ruby screamed at her sister, her voice ragged with some combination of fury and terror. None of this should have been real, but he could see them, up in the tangled treetops. The wind relaxed a moment, the trees calmed, and he had a momentarily clear view. Bella hugged Ruby around the waist, face-to-face as Ruby tried to fight free.

"Don't fight her!" Book shouted. "If she drops you . . ."

He trailed off, certain the wind carried his words away. Ruby would never be able to hear him in the midst of the storm. The only way he could help would be to climb up to them. The thought might have been insane, but every muscle strained to start climbing, to reach Ruby. He glanced at the catwalk that his team had installed to span the hole in the deck. Solid, nearly brand new, the catwalk would be sturdy beneath his feet, a much safer point from which to climb. To reach it, he would have to skirt the edges of the hole, race around to the entrance of the catwalk. But there were other weavers on the deck and they might try to stop him, and after all, what was the point of burning precious seconds being careful when he meant to leave the deck altogether?

Book leaped into the trees. He planted his left boot in the crook of a thick branch, grabbed hold of others, and began to climb. Mangrove trees were not made for climbing. The branches were slick with rain, and far too few were thick enough to hold him. Still, he forced himself up through the tangle, small branches stabbing and scraping and drawing blood, almost as if they meant to. Little crabs showered down upon him as he shook the trees. He crushed one under his hand without intending to.

Voices lifted to him, and he glanced back through the branches and saw two of the weavers on the deck. They were unsteady on their feet, and though it might have been the waves crashing against the hull, he suspected it was something more—the iron of the ship, the rust particles in the air. He had resented the calculation Ruby and Mae had made in coming here, but he was grateful these women were struggling.

One pointed at him, and the other—white hair heavy with rain, like a hood to hide her face—hurried to the broken edge of the deck and took hold of one of the trees. She began to shake it. The motion should not have carried, but somehow it traveled from one tree to the next, and Book shouted in alarm as the trees that held him began to vibrate and then to whip back and forth.

"Ruby!" he called, head tilted back as he hung on, trying to get a look at her face. Somehow that felt important, that if he could lock eyes with her, Ruby would know he was there and that she wasn't alone. That whatever happened to them now, he wouldn't turn his back on her.

A cry came on the wind. He turned to his left, away from the Näturvefjar down on the deck, and saw a nighthawk diving toward him. It pinned its wings back and torpedoed through the branches, and he turned his face just in time, so its talons raked the back of his neck.

Book beat at the bird as it tried to claw his head, seemingly desperate to reach his eyes. He lost his grip, his right foot slipped from a branch, and he fell down through the mangroves. Down below the level of the deck, into the dead heart of the *Christabel.*

Dark as the storm had turned the night, it was even darker in the hold. Branches snapped beneath him as he fell. He reached out to try to catch himself, and his left side struck a thick branch, knocking the wind from his lungs. He felt ribs crack and would have roared his pain if he'd had the breath to do it.

Blinking, he realized he'd stopped falling.

The stink of rust filled his nostrils, along with the damp-earth smell of vegetation. He had seen video of what it looked like down here. They'd used drones armed with spotlights to explore the flooded, overgrown parts of the hold. But the ecosystem of the floating forest was delicate and vulnerable, so none of them had ever physically descended into its heart, until now.

All around him were the lower portions of those trees, growing close together, up through the rotted deck above him, down into the seawater and through the hull of the *Christabel* below. The groaning of the metal as the wind and the gulf water hammered it was so much louder down here. The hull amplified every sound, turning the storm into the howls and moans of the loneliest haunted house imaginable.

Panic ripped into him. The water level inside the belly of the *Christabel* rose and fell with the tides, and now with the storm. The lower parts of the mangroves were submerged. There were no waves in the water trapped inside the old freighter, but still it undulated with the push and pull of the sea outside the ship. The water yawned below, beckoning with the suggestion that he could let go of the trees, sink into the dark, and hide until both the storm and the evil had passed. Ruby would probably be dead by then. Even if she somehow lived, baby Aiden would die, turning her survival into a curse. That curse would ruin Book, too. The temptation to hide might have been small, but it was real. Inside him, there remained a small part of the child he'd once been, frightened and vulnerable and anything but brave.

"Ruby," he whispered. Whatever happened, he couldn't let her lose this baby, too.

Book started to climb. His hands slid on wet branches, but his boots found crooks and ridges, and he looked up into the hole in the deck. Up at the underside of the catwalk that cut across the opening overhead. Up through the trees. The rain slashed down into the hold, but he caught sight of Bella and Ruby again. Ruby thrashed in her sister's grasp, laid back her head, and screamed to be set free. From the tangle of branches and trunks up high, he could see night birds poking their heads out to watch the struggle. He spotted a nighthawk taking flight, blown aloft by a gust. The bird dipped its wings, dove toward the sisters, and snagged its talons in Ruby's hair.

He shouted her name.

A crab fell into his open mouth. Book choked, nearly lost his grip, and hugged himself against the trees, injured ribs giving him spikes of pain. Coughing, he spat out the crab, but others scuttled over his arms and into his hair. Tiny legs skittered on his neck and down the back of his collar. They dropped from above, scrambled off branches, and crawled onto his face. Dozens of them, hundreds of scratching legs swarming on him. He tried to shout again, and several darted into his mouth.

Spitting, he shook his head. Book scraped at his eyes, wiping crabs away, but he could only use one hand, and there were so many of them. Far too many. He hooked an arm around a tree and tried to use both hands in a frenzy of fear that thrummed in his bones.

He screamed at the crabs to get off him.

His boot slipped. Without a handhold, he fell, scraping against the trees.

The dark water waited to receive him.

28

Ruby could see the naked malice in Bella's eyes. Worse than malice—*malevolence.* How badly had life twisted her to make her this creature? They had been raised under the same roof by the same imperfect, sometimes thoughtless parents. Ruby resented them, nursed bitterness, but also carried memories that lightened her heart. What kind of corrupt, selfish nature would allow Bella to follow a path that led her to become *this*?

"Please!" Ruby cried over the wind and the rain. "Put me down!"

Floating. She was floating, buffeted by the storm, held aloft by whatever dark gifts Stratim had given her worshippers. Witchcraft. Ruby searched her sister's eyes, numbed by this new reality.

Their feet floated just above the mangroves, the wind sliding around them no matter how brutal the gust. Ruby had fought back at first, but when she'd scratched her sister's face and felt Bella's hold begin to slip, she realized she would fall. Now they hung above the mangroves with nighthawks and a pair of enormous owls battling the storm to stay close, like excited fans desperate to be near the stage in a concert crowd. Down on the deck, other weavers watched eagerly, waiting for something Ruby did not understand. One of them began coughing so hard it drove her to her knees.

"Mae said you were dead!" Ruby shouted. "That you tried to stop them from killing Aiden and they murdered you!"

Bella's eyes narrowed. "Mae would say anything to save the baby! I should have known the moment she disappeared with it that she'd run to you! Who else would have helped her?"

Ruby wiped rain from her eyes, staring at her sister. "The baby's not yours?"

"He took root in me, but he was never mine," Bella said proudly. "He always belonged to the circle."

"God, what are you?"

"I'm your sister," Bella replied.

"This is *your* child! Aiden is your baby!"

Bella scowled. "That's where Mae went wrong! She had a name for it before it even left my womb!"

A wave of disgust flowed through Ruby with such power that her fear ebbed. The cruelty of her sister, the surrender to utter monstrosity, made her sick. Her life was literally in Bella's hands, their embrace still the only thing that kept Ruby from falling, but she grabbed her sister's face, forced their eyes to meet.

"You really meant to do it," she said, throat aching. "You carried that child inside you knowing they would murder him when he was born?"

Bella laughed. "Open your eyes, Ruby! I've been screaming into the darkness since we were little girls! All the lies about how *good* we were, the bullshit about the kindness of regular people, it drove me insane. People are made of lies and selfishness and fear, and they will do anything to protect themselves. Human beings are fucking evil—"

"That's not true! That's just what you want to see, to make excuses for yourself!"

"It *is* true!" Bella shrieked in her face. The wind screamed around them. "I kept looking for a way to be safe. Someone to protect me. I figured safety in numbers, and then I found these bitches, and I knew I'd been going about it all wrong. The only safety is being able to protect yourself. Being able to hurt anyone who might try to hurt you. If you can make people afraid, you can control them."

Ruby felt sick. "What *are* you?" she asked again, but the question felt different now. Quieter, darker. Had she ever known Bella, even when they were girls together?

Ruby held Bella's face in both hands. She tried to look deeper into her sister's eyes, but that intimacy must have been too much. Bella twisted her head away from Ruby's touch, then simply let go. Embrace broken, Ruby began to fall, but Bella grabbed her wrist before she could plummet into the mangroves. Her shoulder wrenched as Bella's grip brought her up short.

The storm grew louder. The wind had seemed barely to touch them when they were together, but now Ruby swung beneath her sister, hair flying, the storm whipping at her. If Bella released her, she would be swept over the side of the old freighter and into the Gulf. A deep trough rolled beneath them and the *Christabel* canted to one side, then the wave that followed crashed into the freighter, so tall that it washed across the deck and around the legs of the witches that gathered down there now. Ruby looked down and realized they had formed a rough circle around the edges of the hole in the deck, that yawning black throat from which the floating forest grew. Two of them were on their knees now, maybe in worship, but at least one looked sick.

Hanging by one wrist, Ruby looked up at her sister. In the indigo gloom of the storm, for just a moment Bella seemed almost like herself. Broken, sad, searching for connection.

When she spoke, the wind tried to snatch the words away, and Ruby strained upward, barely able to make them out.

"I did love Mae," Bella said. "But she broke trust with the circle. The Näturvefjar will never forgive her, Ruby. She has to die, but you . . . you could live."

Did she care? Was there any humanity left in her, that she

might spare the life of her sister? Maybe a scrap of humanity remained. But it wasn't enough.

Had they still been face-to-face, Ruby would have spit on her. "You think I'll walk away while you murder your own baby? I grew up the same as you, Bella, but I don't know you!"

Any family bond they might once have shared had broken completely.

Bella sneered. "This is out of my hands. I'm a part of the circle—"

"So am I!"

For the first time, Bella faltered. Ruby looked up into the rain, barely able to make out her sister's features until Bella reached down with her free hand and pushed the wet hair away from Ruby's face. Bella saw the sharp ridges of broken horns, and her eyes narrowed.

"Mae is clever," she said with what seemed genuine admiration. "But being part of the circle won't save you from Stratim any more than it will save her."

Another enormous wave splashed over the side of the deck. Water poured down into the hold. Ruby wondered if Book was still alive down there and told herself that of course he was. Told herself that Charlie Book had always been a resourceful man. But that was mostly just what she needed to hear, and she had no one else around to lie to her.

Charlie, she thought.

Bella jerked her arm, twisted hard. Ruby cried out, ready for the revelations to stop, waiting for the fear and heartache to finally end. But Bella seemed satisfied with her attention and started to descend, until Ruby felt the branches of the mangrove trees scraping her legs. She stretched, trying to find a foothold, and Bella lowered her until she could sprawl across the branches of two different trees. Her weight added to the wind in bending those trees, but they did not break. Sodden with rain, she felt as if she might snap every branch, but Bella released her wrist. Ruby held that arm against her chest, massaging her shoulder, wanting to ask why, to know what this batshit-crazy homicidal monster had in store for her.

Women kill their children all the time, she thought. *Like husbands kill their wives.* She had never been able to understand it. All she could imagine was that these were people who were so filled with anger and self-loathing that what they really wanted was to tear themselves apart, to mutilate their own flesh, to die out of sheer hatred and disgust at whatever they despised in themselves. She knew this simplified it all—that it had to be more complicated than people so terrified to admit how craven they'd become that they destroyed the thing that made them feel the weakest, the most cowardly, the most disappointing.

But maybe they were just monsters.

Like Bella.

Ruby clung to the branches, holding in a thousand screams. She stared at her sister, who swayed with the storm as if they were under the waves instead of above them.

The birds began to land all around them, alighting on this thick branch or that treetop. Nighthawks and owls, and something she did not recognize. Down on the deck, the weavers chanted in a guttural language she knew she would not have understood even if she could have made out the words.

"What do you want from me?" Ruby screamed at last, throat raw.

The rain slicked her face, mixing with fresh tears.

But it wasn't Bella who replied.

It was the birds.

The voice came from all of them at once, from open beaks, yet it was the same voice. This was not harmony, not some choir. One voice, a snide, rasping insinuation, a bedtime story read by an aunt who wore a false smile and wished you'd never been born.

"*You serve me now, Ruby*," the birds said. "*I am your mistress. Your goddess. Your mother.*"

The Ur-Witch. Ruby had never understood fear. She knew that now. Behind its mask, true fear was utter hopelessness. Hot urine slid down her thighs, but this brand of terror left no room for humiliation. She felt herself immersed in a miasma of fear, awash in desperate terror like nothing she had felt since before she had the words to describe it. She'd been in a crib then, barely more than a baby, and the power had gone out. The darkness consumed her, and thunder shook the house. This memory returned to her sometimes, her earliest memory, rooted and inescapable. Stratim's mere presence drowned her in the same kind of suffocating menace.

Evil, she thought. *This is evil.*

"*What I want from you*," the birds said, full of spite and rage, "*is that you go inside that ship and take the infant from my prodigal daughter.*"

She didn't know where she found the courage to speak. "Mae . . . Mae won't—"

"*Kill Mae. Bring the infant out into the storm. And perhaps you will live.*"

Ruby gaped, twisting around, trying not to fall down through the mangroves. She wanted to protest, to say Mae would not give Aiden up, and that she would never be able to kill her, even if she wanted to. But just as she became certain no more horrors or shocks were to come, another presented itself.

Bella glided closer to her. As another wave crashed onto the deck, her sister embraced her, looking around at the birds just as Ruby had.

"Mother," Bella said, "I knew what I would sacrifice when I became pregnant. I knew my purpose. And when Mae betrayed the circle, I knew she would die for it. But I begged a boon from you, that you would let my sister live."

Confusion blurred Ruby's thoughts. Bella had bargained for her life? Begged for her? This monster who would grow a child inside her for the sole purpose of its murder? Wherever this had come from, this little trace of love or memory of their childhood bond, she did not want it. Any grace Bella might buy her now disgusted her.

"No," she said. "Fuck you, Bella."

If she had feared her sister before, if she'd felt some kind of sympathy amid the horror, now hate grew inside her for the first time.

Bella grabbed her by the throat as if to cut off her voice. Glaring, furious. "Shut up, Ruby. You don't know what you're—"

Ruby slapped her hand away.

Laughter came from the throats of nighthawks and owls. "*I will be with you soon, daughters. The night closes in.*"

The birds took flight, lifted by the wind, lost in the rain.

To the north, toward Pelican Island, one of them seemed to burst into flame, a bright orange flare in the dark. It flickered, and for an instant, Ruby thought it looked like a crown of fire, then a ring of separate flames.

Pain shot through her skull, radiating from the broken horns, and then she knew what those flames must be. Little fires in the dark, still burning despite the wind and rain.

They were candles.

And, like the night, they were closing in.

29

Book climbed more carefully this time. Weighed down, soaked through, bleeding, he moved inexorably through the trees. His plunge into the water had swept the crabs away, but as he moved upward, they began to scuttle onto his arms and face again. He brushed them from his eyes and mouth but ignored the rest. That moment underwater had cleared his head. Fear still churned in his gut, but he would not try to hide while Ruby and Aiden were still alive.

Despite the wind, the mangroves created a kind of conduit that carried sound down from above. As he gripped one branch, tested the next sturdy foothold, he could hear Ruby and Bella shouting at each other. When he had nearly come level with the deck and halted, trying to figure out how to safely jump from the trees to the broken edge or to the catwalk, he heard the third voice overhead—a dozen voices, but all the same—like rusted door hinges all grinding together at once.

So when Stratim arrived, he knew.

The Näturvefjar all raised their arms in supplication. They were pale, sickly, struggling, but their goddess had arrived. A wave came over the railing and gulf water spilled across the deck and into the hold. Something rustled in the branches overhead. Book craned his neck to get a look at this creature. He caught a glimpse of burning candles flickering despite the storm, but the movement in the trees had been Ruby and Bella, and they were his focus. He had to get Ruby away from her sister, away from this. Away from the ship, really, which made him think about the research boat. The stairs bolted to the side of the *Christabel* had been half torn away earlier, and now he realized that their survival might depend on those stairs still being attached—hanging on, even by a single screw. If the stairs were there, the research boat might still be there. How the hell he would get Ruby and Aiden to the boat, that was a separate question.

And Mae, he reminded himself.

But Mae had betrayed the Näturvefjar. No way would she survive this.

Neither will Aiden. What Stratim really wanted was that baby. But Ruby wouldn't leave her nephew behind, and so neither would Book. He told himself that he wouldn't have left without the baby even if Ruby's desires weren't a factor. Maybe that was true. He hoped so.

Up in the tangled treetops, Bella shook her sister. "Goddamn it, listen to me. In a couple of minutes, it's going to be too late for me to save you."

Ruby screamed, "Then *stop* this!"

"I couldn't even if I wanted to. But I don't want you to die! I never wanted that!"

"I don't know if there's a hell—"

"Goddamn it, I'm not waiting till someday for my eternal reward!" Bella shouted. "I'm grabbing it right here and now. Whatever's beyond this world is just as filled with horror, so I'm doing my living now!"

"You're going to murder your own child!"

Book shifted his head and got a clear view of them just in time to see Bella slap her sister's face, so hard that the sound echoed across the deck, even in the storm.

"Listen to me!" Bella snarled.

Book snagged a branch and hauled himself up, cracked ribs protesting. The weavers were around the edges of the hole in the deck. One of them screamed and pointed at him. His back felt exposed. Vulnerable. He wondered what it would feel like to be stabbed there or to have his spine shatter. His heart beat like hummingbird wings, but he climbed, stealing upward glances, seeking Ruby. The past slipped away. It didn't matter now. They had hurt and disappointed each other, but what was any of that in the face of this?

A pair of mangrove trees bent against the wind instead of with it, and branches snapped as they tried to catch at his clothes, moving with malign intent. The weavers were doing this. They had to be.

Overhead, Bella Cahill shrieked. Book whipped around, saw a woman plummet to the deck. Her body hit hard and wet, splashing in a couple of inches of seawater that still washed across the *Christabel*'s prow. Book nearly screamed Ruby's name, but two of the weavers staggered toward her, and he saw it wasn't Ruby at all but Bella.

Then he heard Ruby cry out and looked up to see her sweep down from the tops of the mangrove trees alongside a creature who carried her by the throat with both hands. Book saw the Ur-Witch in full, her face ghostly pale in the flickering light from the unextinguishable candles that burned at the tips of her many horns. Stratim tossed Ruby onto the deck beside Bella. The drop had to hurt, but not so much that she couldn't stand. Ruby scrambled up and tried to run for the wheelhouse door.

Weavers raced to grab at her. One had long silver hair, the one Mae had called Annika. Another was hunched and pale and wheezing, the third dark and no taller than a middle schooler. The sight should have stunned him. Fear for Ruby should have made him act.

But he couldn't tear his eyes from Stratim.

From the obscene crown of horns and their thirteen candles. He saw her too-long fingers, sharp at the ends, burned black at the tips as if scorched. And he saw the slick, torn, tattered yellow raincoat that hung from her frame. That raincoat that had come from the children's section of some department store, though its owner would never have admitted it to him.

"Luisa," he said, and sorrow choked him.

Stratim had tried to possess Ruby, and Mae had managed to stop her. Mae had said the evil would seek the nearest woman and inhabit her instead. Somehow—he could not make sense of how—that had been Luisa. She should have been in Galveston, downtown, with thousands of others, yet she had been the closest.

Book sagged, barely holding on to the mangroves. *It's you*, he thought. *Whatever else, she was there because of you. Checking on you.*

Small and draped in gleaming yellow, Stratim alighted on the deck between the Cahill sisters. With an obscenely smiling mask that had once been Luisa's face, she pointed a long, scorched finger at the door to the wheelhouse and stared at Ruby.

"*Open it*," she said in the hideous rasping voice the birds had used before. The sound of that voice scraped him to the bone.

Ruby shook her head. She backed against the door, refusing.

"You have to obey her," Bella warned. "I'm sorry, Ruby, but you have to. You're part of the circle."

"Fuck your circle," Ruby said, sneering.

Stratim swept toward her, grabbed her by the throat, and smashed Ruby against the door.

Ruby planted her feet, set her hips, and punched the Ur-Witch harder than she'd ever hit anyone or anything. Book wanted to cheer. Instead, as Stratim reeled, he put his pain aside and scrambled through the mangrove trees, getting closer to the part of the deck where they had all gathered. If some of the weavers saw him, they did not raise an alarm. Maybe he didn't matter to them, posed no threat, or maybe they were too entranced with their goddess's malignance.

The circle began to gather. Some stood tall in the rain, swaying with the motion of the deck and the strength of the storm.

Others staggered like drunks or slunk like predators. One of the weavers wore a tailored business suit that clung, sodden, to her muscled form, while another wore only a tapestry of tattoos that turned her nakedness into art. He spotted Annika with her long, silver hair, and it was this one who walked up to the broad window that looked into the wheelhouse and called out for Mae.

"You're behaving like a fool, Mae!" she called, her accent something like French. "Let us in, sister!"

The others echoed the words. "Let us in, sister!" They were like a flock of birds, all cawing at once.

Book stared at the door, silently willing Mae not to obey. He wondered if she was still in the wheelhouse or hiding somewhere in the belly of the ship. Waiting or searching for some hope of escape.

"*Open it*," Stratim said again. She didn't issue threats of what would happen if Ruby did not obey, but the warning radiated from her.

"No way. If you're gonna kill me, then kill me. But I'm not the coward my sister is," Ruby said. "I'm not going to give you an innocent child to save my life."

"*A part of me is inside you now*," Stratim said. "*When Mae brought you into our circle, a sliver of my spirit*—"

"What, infected me?"

"Blessed *you, daughter*."

"Not your daughter," Ruby spat at her.

The Ur-Witch grinned. Book wondered if Ruby wanted to be killed so she couldn't be used to hurt Aiden. That was the only explanation he could think of for the way she pushed the thing inside Luisa. The thing with that crown of horns and candle flames.

Stratim rolled her eyes in an expression purely Luisa. It made Book want to scream. Was part of Luisa still there, down inside, aware of all this? God, he hoped not.

"*Fine*," Stratim said, striding through the rain toward the wheelhouse door. Weavers called out, offering themselves for this task, some of them visibly weak or coughing. Stratim dismissed them. Her hand touched the doorknob.

Something broke inside Charlie Book. Not for Mae's sake but for Aiden's. The thing that had invaded his friend Luisa's body now wanted to murder an infant. His imagination could not conjure anything that might horrify him more. He'd held Aiden in his arms, sleeping, defenseless but ripe with all the days and years ahead of him. The baby's own mother would sacrifice him to the demands of the Ur-Witch, to this monster's hunger for ritual bloodletting. Could there be a darker magic?

Book found himself moving.

Two of the weavers saw him. The one in the business suit ran to intercept. Annika raised her arms as if to conduct an orchestra, and a nighthawk darted from the storm, talons ready to tear his flesh.

Ruby saw him, too. She shouted for him to stop.

It might have been Ruby's shout that drew Stratim's attention. Whatever it was, the monster in Luisa's yellow raincoat glanced toward him with a smile just as she tried to turn the doorknob to enter the wheelhouse.

Book probably would have died then, but as he hurtled across the deck at Stratim, the wheelhouse door ignited with fiery symbols that mirrored the ones Mae had scrawled on the other side of the door. The ward startled Stratim, and where her hand touched the latch, it burned. In pain and shock and anger, she jerked her hand back, losing a precious second or two.

The weavers tried to grab him. Ruby shouted to warn him.

Book tackled the Ur-Witch, shoulder down, and plowed her straight into the door. The sigils that burned with the defenses cast on that metal seared her flesh, melted patches of Luisa's yellow raincoat.

From the corner of his eye, he saw Ruby try to rush to help him, and Bella holding her back.

Then Stratim turned to look at him, pleading, and she spoke in Luisa's voice—gazed at him with Luisa's eyes. "Charlie, you're hurting me."

But Luisa never called him *Charlie.* Knew he didn't like to be called by that name. She knew a thing that he had confided only in her, and no one else—that the baby he and Ruby had conceived and lost *was to be named after him.* He and Ruby had even referred to the tiny, developing thing as *Charlie,* since he preferred to use his surname, anyway. He might have been relieved not to be rushing into fatherhood, but when Ruby lost their baby, he felt that loss deeply. Mourned for the Charlie that would never be. He might not have been mature enough to be a father quite yet, but he'd already started to love the unborn Charlie.

Luisa knew how much he'd lost that day. She would never call him *Charlie.*

So he didn't hesitate.

He took a fistful of her hair and, even as her talons wrapped around his throat, he smashed her head against the door. He meant to press her there, so the burning symbols would continue to hurt her, but she choked him. Her talons dug into his throat, drawing blood, tearing at his skin, so he grabbed hold of that crown of thorns with both hands and slammed her again and again into the door. The candle flames atop those horns flickered but did not go out.

Weavers grabbed him, dragged at his clothing. They were strong, vicious, and he wondered how fast they could have killed them if the presence of so much rust and iron had not already weakened them. A nighthawk darted toward his eyes, and he dipped his head and felt its claws rake his scalp. One of the weavers began to cough and choke, loosening her grip enough that he managed to shake her off, giving himself time for one more shove. With all his strength, he bashed Stratim's skull off the door.

One of her horns snapped, denting the door. As it broke, the candle on its tip snuffed out.

From behind, he heard a cry of shock and pain, and he glanced over his shoulder to see the naked, tattooed woman jerk upright, cough once, and collapse to the deck. Her eyes were rolled up to white, and he could see, even in that flicker of a moment, that she was dead. Not a breath, not a twitch.

Well, one twitch. Her mouth opened, and a thing like a black worm slipped out, turned to smoke, and swept off into the storm.

Done.

Two of the weavers dragged Book backward. Stratim stalked toward him. The broken horn was jagged, sharp, but the other candles still burned brightly. Rain hissed and sizzled as droplets touched those dancing flames. The wind almost seemed to lift her, slide her toward him. The yellow raincoat flapped, branded and melted where the little flames on the wheelhouse door had touched it. Her eyes glinted with pinpoints of light, and a wave of nausea and fear washed through him. Primitive, childlike fear, the sort of terror he'd felt as a boy when he'd wake in the middle of the night and grow slowly certain that the dull gleam of light he spied in the depths of his open closet came from the eyes of something watching. Something waiting. Something hungry. This fear could not be dismissed any more than he could dispel the cold or the rain.

Stratim sneered at him. His skin crawled. Prickled. Itched, and that itching turned into blisters that rose on his skin. This was something altogether different, not primitive instinct but a deep sickness. An oily stink filled the air, a cloud around him that no storm could blow away. Was this witchcraft, or was it merely what it felt like to be this close to true evil? If malignance and rot had a stink, surely this must be it.

She reached for his throat as the weavers held him.

Ruby broke away from Bella. She cried out for mercy, though they all knew this creature had none. Book thought she might try to attack Stratim as he had, but Ruby was smarter. Instead of trying to overcome the monster, Ruby grabbed Book, assaulting the weavers who were holding him. She smashed the flat of her palm into the throat of the white-haired weaver, and the woman staggered backward. Book wrested himself free from the other one.

Stratim slid toward them in the rain.

A wave washed across the deck. While most of it poured down into the hold, Bella stepped into the Ur-Witch's path.

"Mother," Bella said, even her tone a plea. "You swore if we got the baby back, you would let my sister live."

Stratim paused. Book and Ruby held on to each other, more out of numbness than for protection, and they waited.

Luisa had been a tiny woman. Though Stratim had made her monstrous from the inside out, she had not grown any taller, yet in that moment of indecision, she seemed to loom over them.

A smile touched the corner of Stratim's lips. Luisa's lips. Cruelty still burned in her eyes, the yearning to inflict punishment, but her smile widened.

"*There are other ways to get the child*," she said.

Stratim moved so quickly that Book couldn't be certain she had physically crossed the intervening space. If not for the fact that the candles still burning on her head left a kind of blur as she slid to the edge of the floating forest, he would have been sure she had vanished and reappeared. In the storm, blinking against the rain and wind, he told himself it was simply hard to see. Nothing could move that quickly.

The Ur-Witch stepped over the edge of the hole in the deck and dropped into the darkness with the mangrove roots and tree crabs.

"My God," he whispered.

"Book!" Ruby shouted over the wind.

He barely heard her, still staring at the spot where Stratim had disappeared.

Ruby grabbed his face, turned him toward her so they were

eye to eye. "Is there another way to get inside the boat down there? A way she can reach Aiden?"

Book didn't think so. The whole lower section of the ship had been flooded for a century, and though none of the remaining hatchways below had been sealed off, they were rusted nearly shut. Fish swam freely through the gaps.

She saw the hesitation in his face.

"I don't know," he said.

Yet he did know. Luisa could never have held her breath long enough, and she didn't have the strength to force open iron doors whose hinges were rusted solid. But the thing inside Luisa's body was no more Luisa than a hermit crab was the creature whose shell it had stolen for a home.

"Go after her, Charlie!" Ruby pleaded. "Whatever happens, save Aiden!"

Book hesitated. He couldn't just leave her there. "Come with me!"

Ruby glanced around at the weavers, all of them pale and drawn, but ready to kill. She reached for his hand, and Book felt a surge of hope. Somehow, despite the danger, they would connect. They would find a way out of this.

A hideous screech filled the air, loud enough to cut through the roar of the storm. He twisted away from the sound, just as sharp talons sliced the air by his head. Book turned to see an enormous barn owl swoop toward Ruby's face. She dove aside, sprawling, and one of the weavers stalked toward her. Ruby sprang at the other woman, and Book had to remember that they were two of a kind now. Ruby had the darkness of Stratim inside her, a sliver of the Ur-Witch's power.

The barn owl alighted on the deck between Book and the yawning hole where Stratim had slipped below. Keeping him from pursuing her.

"Charlie, goddamn you, go after her!" Ruby shouted as she fought.

He didn't want to leave her behind, but he knew she would never forgive him if he didn't try to save Aiden. And he knew he would never forgive himself.

He'd grown up to be a scientist, but he came from a neighborhood where jokes and swagger often turned to bullying and broken noses, which meant Book had taken more than his share of punches. He'd bled, and he'd made others bleed, and while he'd only had one genuine fight as an adult—in a bar on Bourbon Street in New Orleans, with a prick from Boston who refused to leave Louisiana without getting his ass kicked at least once—Book remembered what it felt like to give in to violence. The lizard brain, the old part of the human mind still connected to an age when survival required savagery . . . the lizard brain never forgot.

He charged at the barn owl. "Get the fuck out of my way!"

His body tensed as he ran, ready to haul back and punt that massive bird into the mangrove trees. The barn owl turned its head all the way around to stare at him with impossibly golden eyes, and as it did, the wind gusted, and it grew.

He hadn't noticed this woman before. This witch. This weaver.

Had she been among them already? Regardless, she was one of them. At least six and a half feet tall, with a thick bush of wild curls, she wore a long gray coat tailored better than anything Book had ever owned. Who were all of these women, really? He thought of the diverse array of people who might share a pew in a church, or cross paths in an airport terminal, or avoid one another's eyes in group therapy.

It didn't matter. Terrified as he was, fear had become like breathing tonight. He pushed through it, kept running toward her. Ten feet away. Seven. Three.

Standing between him and the catwalk, she lifted her hands, sneered at him, and pushed at the air with her palms turned outward. The storm responded, rain and wind slapping his back so hard that he smashed to the deck and rolled right up to her feet.

Book gazed up into her eyes. She'd have been beautiful if he could have seen any trace of a soul. She crouched, reached out to lay a hand on his forehead the way his mother had always checked to see if he had a fever.

"You poor bastard," she said. "Wrong place, wrong time."

Her hands wrapped around his throat. She went down on one knee for leverage and started killing him.

A gun boomed, the crack so loud it made the storm seem to hush.

The bullet blew a hole through his would-be killer's chest and sprayed blood out her back. Her boots slipped out from beneath her. That expensive coat fanned out, and she tumbled backward.

Shouting, ears ringing, Book scrambled to his feet. The weaver began to wither on the deck beside him, but he spun around in search of the shooter. Ruby and Bella and the rest of the circle were doing the same. They were all staring, and when Book saw what had drawn their eyes, he stared as well.

"Holy shit," he whispered. "Gerald."

30

Gerald wondered if they could see his tears in the rain. He wondered why it mattered to him. Thirty-four years old, a grown man with a career and a history, bearing witness to impossible things and committing violence he'd never imagined, and he didn't want anyone to know he was crying.

Society wires us young, he'd told Luisa once. *And the wiring is a fire hazard from day one.*

Book stepped toward him, glancing back and forth between the gun and the dead woman who'd been a big goddamn owl a few seconds ago.

"Gerald? How did you get here?" Everything about him was urgent. His voice, his stance, his gaze.

"*That's* your fucking question?" Gerald laughed a sick sort of laugh, the kind of sound his sister had made when she'd told him the story of her husband having a heart attack in bed with their next-door neighbor.

The women on deck began moving in one fluid motion, like birds taking flight from a power line. Gerald raised the gun, showing them the barrel, making sure they knew they were all in range. He could do smooth motions, too, when he wanted.

"I don't know the details, but I know this is a grim little circus out here," he said.

There were at least seven of them. He thought there were one or two on the other side of the mangroves, but he wasn't about to circle around the massive hole in the deck to go searching. He kept his back to the railing, certain that none of them were behind him. Nobody would be coming up that way unless they were as stupid and as lucky as he'd been, stealing a boat and driving it out here. He'd nearly been swamped a dozen times. Even now, he wasn't sure Orway's Chris-Craft would still be there for a return trip, but it didn't matter.

He'd followed Luisa.

The monster.

He'd followed her yellow raincoat, those horns, and the candle flames that flickered from them. Any farther offshore and he would not have made it out here, or he would have lost track of her in the storm. Of course, he had been fairly certain where she was going from the moment she floated up into the wind.

"Book, you saw her, right? That was Luisa who went down there, into the hold?"

"It's her, but it's not her," Book replied, lifting his voice over the rain. The wind tried to snatch it away, but Gerald heard. "Did you see—"

One of the witches, if that was what they were, scuttled to his left. Gerald didn't know if she meant to attack or just trap him between herself and the others, but he didn't wait to find out. He shot at the deck six feet in front of her. Her eyes went wide. The wind screamed, and a wave washed across the deck from the other side.

"Listen up!" Gerald shouted. "That's the last bullet I'm wasting!"

He looked across at Book. At his friend's feet, the woman Gerald had shot barely existed now. He could see her coat, but what was inside the coat had no substance, like her body had deflated or dried up. Whatever these things were, they weren't entirely human. That made it easier for him to think about shooting more of them.

"What are you waiting for, Book? I heard all that shit about a baby," Gerald called. "If you can stop Luisa, go and do it!"

Book had been waiting like a runner at the block. He didn't even let Gerald finish before he hurled himself into the mangrove trees. His arms wrapped around several. Branches broke as he slid down and vanished belowdecks.

One of the women held her hands out and started toward him.

"Thank you," she said, like he'd saved her life. "Whatever happens now—"

"That's enough, Ruby!" one of the others shouted, rage making her ugly. "He just murdered one of your sisters!"

Rain slid down the back of Gerald's collar, colder than he'd ever thought autumn in Texas could be. He noticed it, but it was just one of a dozen things vying for his focus. His primary concern was the two women facing off about twenty feet away and the question of whether he would have to pull the trigger again. The gun felt heavy, slick, and he wondered if he would dream about killing the tall woman. He wondered if she would haunt him, and he thought he knew the answer.

Then it hit him. *Ruby.*

"You're Ruby?" he asked.

They didn't hear him over the wind and their own conflict.

"That wasn't my sister!" Ruby shouted, and Gerald thought maybe the rain was hiding her tears just as much as it was his own. "I only have one sister on this Earth, Bella. That's you. I'm standing right here, and I'm telling you if you count these monsters as your sisters and choose them over me, then you're every horrible thing Dad ever called you. Fuck that; you're a thousand times worse."

The other one, Bella, flinched. But then she seemed to laugh in the way people sometimes did when all their hope was gone. "You already called me a monster. Now you want to be my sister?"

"I don't want to be!" Ruby screamed at her. "But I am, and that makes me all Aiden's got in this world, since his own mother wants to kill him!"

They kept it up. Gerald just wanted to buy Book some time,

and he had done that. The rest would be up to Book. Standing in the rain, with the *Christabel* swaying beneath him, he felt his adrenaline begin to wane. His heart had been galloping since the moment Luisa had first screamed in pain, but now he'd reached his goal, and he wasn't sure what would come next. All he knew was that these women had something to do with what happened to Luisa and that Book needed his help, and so he would help, and he would get answers.

Answers.

He pointed the gun at Bella. Maybe she really was Ruby's sister, but he didn't give a shit.

"Now that we've calmed down a little, why don't you tell me what the hell's going on here? That woman with the . . ." His breath hitched. "With the fucking horns on her head. We're together. Her name is—"

Bella waved him away like he didn't matter. Like the bullets in his gun and his finger on the trigger didn't matter. "You're not *together* anymore."

The witch who'd tried sneaking up on him took two steps nearer, but her labored breathing gave her away. Gerald turned the gun toward her. Another tough-guy warning touched his lips, something about how he had told her once already. As she moved toward him, however, he shuffled backward toward the floating forest. He knew the dimensions of that hole in the deck, knew which parts were sturdy enough to hold his weight and where the rust would give way and let him fall. He knew the trees.

They didn't typically move against the wind.

As he backed toward them, the branches of the two nearest trees seemed almost to unravel as they reached toward him. One wrapped around his left arm, and he shouted, yanking himself away. He scrambled back from the mangroves, staring wide-eyed. If he hadn't already seen candles burning atop horns that punched out through the skin on his girlfriend's skull, maybe he would have screamed. Maybe he would have wasted precious seconds denying what he'd seen and felt. But he had passed that point a while back.

The scuttling, sickly looking witch took that moment to rush him. Gerald turned and shot her through the forehead. Off-center. The orbit around her left eye shattered, and the eye seemed to sink into her face. She didn't scream, only collapsed to the deck. A long, hissing noise came from her open mouth as if she'd sprung a leak. Spittle and mucus ran from her lips and nostrils, and then something oil black slid from her throat like a fat worm. Gerald thought it was solid, but the wind swept it up and away.

He turned the gun on Ruby and her sister.

"I don't much care what you two are fighting about," he said, and then he glanced around, watching as the others spread out farther. How many were there, really? "What I know is that I can't fight the goddamn trees, so anytime I think you're up to something, that you're trying to come after me, I'm going to put a bullet in somebody's head. If you hadn't figured it out yet, I'm a very, very good shot. I've got my aunt Bev to thank for that. If I live through this, I owe that old woman the best steak on the planet."

Ruby separated herself farther from her sister. She put her hands out in front of her as though they might stop a bullet. If this was really Ruby—the one Book had loved and lost—then he figured he should avoid shooting her if possible.

"Gerald," she said. "That's your name, right?"

He nodded, but his gaze twitched around, watching the witches. He'd warned them. Goddamn it, he had *shown* them. But maybe they realized he didn't have enough bullets to kill them all, or maybe they figured he wasn't fast enough. Whatever it was, they were right, and it seemed like they might be willing to die.

"Don't do this," he warned them. A terrible sadness seized him, and he looked at Ruby and Bella, pleading. "Tell them not to do this."

Bella shook her head as if in sorrow. "You seem like a good man."

"I try to be."

She smiled, showing all her teeth. "That's how it always starts."

As if on some silent signal, the other witches seemed to vanish in the storm. But as Gerald spun to search the rain-slicked deck, he saw they hadn't vanished at all. They were owls and hawks, swept aloft, racing one another in the rain, arcing around the mangroves, hiding in the trees, sailing on the storm.

Only Ruby and Bella remained on deck with him.

The others were circling. It looked to Gerald as if they were watching for an opening to dart down and kill him.

From the moment of Luisa's first scream, this had felt like a nightmare.

Now Gerald woke up.

He wanted to run, but where could he go that they would not catch him? Maybe Ruby was an ally, and maybe she was not. Book might survive, might stop the thing that had taken Luisa, maybe even save this baby they'd been talking about. But Gerald didn't want to be here anymore. That instinct to run felt like a betrayal, like he was letting Luisa down.

None of that mattered.

He watched the hawks and owls and knew he was going to die.

31

Book plunged into the water down in the *Christabel*'s hold. Thrashing, he thrust out his right hand and grabbed the narrow trunk of the first mangrove he found. He'd never been able to keep his eyes open in salt water, but he forced himself. It stung like hell, with no reward. The briny darkness seemed absolute, and no wonder. Deep in the hold, at night, and underwater? Where would the light come from?

And yet . . . there it was.

Breath held, he twisted underwater and spotted a diffuse glow in the murk. He tried to pull himself along, push between trees, but the mangroves grew too densely and he had to surface.

He bobbed atop the dark water, stuck in the small jungle as the surface undulated around him. Pain clenched at his right side, those cracked ribs. The light beneath the water dimmed but had not vanished completely. It could be only one thing—candle flames, still burning.

Cold bit deep, aching his bones. Far overhead, he heard violence up on deck. Another gunshot. He thought of Gerald and Ruby, but they would have to fend for themselves. Ruby had demanded he put Aiden's life first, and he would honor that. As much as he hated to leave her behind, the baby could not fight for his own life, and Book would never forgive himself if he did not try to protect the child. Fear seeped into his bones along with the cold, but it would not stop him. He pictured Aiden in his arms, remembering what the baby looked like when he slept, and any hesitation evaporated.

He hurled himself after Luisa—after Stratim. Branches scraped and cut and stabbed him as he forced his way through the mangroves. His legs were underwater, but his boots found purchase in the crooks between branches. The soles slipped, his ankle twisted, but he had momentum now, and nothing would stop him. A branch dug deep into his neck and burned as it sliced his skin. He hissed through his teeth but did not slow down, even when he felt trickles of blood on his throat.

Down in the dark water, the candle flames winked out, but he knew they hadn't been extinguished. They could burn underwater, and that hadn't changed. Stratim had vanished.

He closed the gap between himself and the spot where the flames had gone out. Twenty feet. Fifteen. Seven. A dark wall waited ahead. Once, it had separated one cargo hold from the next. Mangroves grew on either side of that metal wall, and Book could have climbed up and over it. Instead, he submerged, following the Ur-Witch. He grabbed branches and dragged himself deeper, descending until he spotted those candle flames burning underwater again. Closer this time. Something had slowed her down, which made Book move faster. Hand over hand, he yanked himself through the water, caught his shirt on a branch and twisted away, tearing the fabric and his skin, bleeding into the water.

Gaining on Stratim.

On Luisa.

She'd been caught on branches as well. By that yellow raincoat, which shone with reflected candlelight. She should have just taken it off, but she struggled with the offending branch and then reached out with both hands and snapped it from the tree. Stratim began to swim.

Book caught her ankle.

Startled, she stopped swimming, turned to look at him in the water as if frustrated that she'd snagged herself again. When she saw it was Book and not a tangle of mangroves that had caught her, she sneered. The light of the candles flared brighter, casting hellish shadows. Her horns threw shadows like the twisted trees themselves. All was gray and pale down below, except that raincoat. She bared blackened teeth and hissed underwater as if she didn't have to worry about such a frail thing as breathing.

The water felt thicker, turning oily. A malignance radiated from Stratim, souring Book's stomach. His skin rippled with a revulsion he could never have described. He'd seen all kinds of horrors in his life, but never felt anything like this.

Stratim lunged for him. Grabbed his wrist and dug her nails in, punctured skin. Book ripped his hand away, which gave her what she wanted—the freedom to move. She bunched herself up, put one foot on a tree, and was about to escape when Book snaked out that same hand, trailing tendrils of his blood, and grabbed a fistful of slippery yellow raincoat.

He held on.

She thrashed, but this time when she went to claw him, Book caught her wrist and twisted it backward. His lungs burned. His eyes stung. The breath he'd taken wouldn't last much longer, so he launched himself upward, dragging her with him.

Laughter burbled from her throat when they reached the surface. "*What kind of fool are you?*"

Book didn't have an answer. Only that he was a fool, indeed. Her eyes were bloody red, her teeth sharp and black. The horns on her skull looked as if they had always been there. One of the horns had broken off, and one snuffed out, but another had just extinguished, no longer burning. He caught all of that in an eyeblink and remembered the way the weaver had died up on the deck when he had broken one of those horns or antlers or candles or whatever the fuck they really were.

The outer hull was three feet behind her. Book pushed off

a tree and smashed her head against the metal. He took those horns in his hands and slammed her skull once, twice, a third and fourth time, and another horn snapped off. It dropped into the dark water, and he kept going. Book smashed off the horn that he'd been gripping in his right hand.

All of this had taken only seconds.

She grabbed his throat. The iron around them, the rust in the water, might have weakened her, but not enough to keep her from killing him. He had a sliver of time to wonder what this ancient thing inside Luisa's skin could really do. He knew a little, so it didn't surprise him completely when his entire body turned cold and weak and shuddery, and bile burned in his gut. Black pustules formed on his arms, and he felt them on his neck and chest. This was her witchcraft, poisoning him.

"Too late," he said, and he stabbed her in the chest with her own broken horn.

Weak, fading, full of sorrow, he stabbed her again. And again.

Her blood clouded the water, but those remaining nine candles still burned.

Then, suddenly, another winked out. Leaving eight.

Gerald.

Book would have smiled if he hadn't been on the verge of puking. Gerald must have shot another one of them. How many were left? He tried to tally the figures he'd seen up on deck and realized in all the chaos he had included the two who were on his side. He wouldn't have to fight Mae and Ruby.

He hesitated. Stratim used the moment. She spat in his face, and the spittle clouded his vision, black mucus that crawled over his eyes. Book screamed and dug into the orbits of his eyes, peeling that putrid, stinking spittle away. With one open eye, he saw her straining to look up, worriedly attempting to glimpse the flaming tips of her own horns. She couldn't see them all, of course, but she had felt them going out. These were the anchors to the body she had stolen like a hermit crab invading another creature's shell, and Book and Gerald had begun taking them away, one by one.

If he could put out all those candles, he thought it might be the end of her. But how could he do that, when snuffing out any one of them might also snuff out Ruby's life?

32

Ruby felt a flicker of hope. They had watched one of the weavers drop dead, and Bella had cried out in grief and panic. Now Gerald had shot another of them—Iris, who had come for Aiden in Ruby's backyard that night. Gerald shot her in the chest, maybe through her black heart, and she'd collapsed on the deck like she'd been dumped from a bucket. Her limbs thumped when she fell and she didn't so much as twitch. The rain continued, and the wash of the massive waves slid around her like she'd been there all along.

But then they were on him. A tall, stooped woman with wild black curls stalked toward him, a painfully thin giant. Two nighthawks darted at his face. True to his word, Gerald did not waste a bullet. He tried to smash one of the birds with the gun but would not fire until he was sure of his target. Then a horned owl spread its wings, dove for his throat, and before her talons could touch him, she seemed almost to unfurl like a flag and then stood right in front of him on the deck, dark brown skin, a shock of white hair, and a long red coat. She grabbed Gerald by the throat with one hand and twisted the gun from his grip with the other.

Gerald could only gurgle. Choking, he couldn't find his voice.

Ruby turned on her sister, thoughts fractured. "Bella, stop this!"

The rain and wind stank of rot and burning. The deeds of these creatures, and the horrors they contemplated, seemed to give off their own repulsive stink. Stratim had gone down into the throat of the *Christabel* in search of the blood she needed to step physically into the world. The body she wore now would let her explore but not remain here forever. Stratim needed Aiden to die, and maybe nothing would prevent her from getting to him. But if anyone could, it would be the baby's mother.

Bella hesitated.

Ruby grabbed the front of her shirt in a fist and slapped her hard enough to echo. She expected ferocity in return, but instead, Bella gaped in shock.

"You're my sister, goddamn it," Ruby said, but without anger. Her chest welled with sorrow. "All I ever wanted from you was to be your family. That's your son in there, your child. Your heart can't have rotted so much that it means nothing to you!"

The last words tore out of Ruby, ripped her open with the pain of her own loss and yearning. Had that anguish been the thing to give Bella pause? She did not know. But her sister turned to the other weavers as they dragged Gerald to the deck, one of them clawing at his face as he screamed, and Bella shrieked in reply.

The sound that tore from her throat had no words, and yet it had power. Like the screech of one of these hawks, it split the air. The other weavers on deck had dropped the guise of birds and were only women now, if they were ever only women. They had Gerald down. Bleeding. He'd been wearing glasses before, but they were broken and askew, and he shook his head to try to get free, sending the glasses flying from his head. But those remaining weavers turned to look at Bella, paused by her cry but bitter about the interruption.

"Don't lose heart now," said the red-coated witch.

"Cassandra," Bella called her, "leave him be. He doesn't matter to us."

She stood, this Cassandra, as if unfolding. Six foot, at least. Startingly beautiful. Her skin gleamed, slick with rain. Her white hair like an aura around her head. Ruby thought she looked as though she had once been a queen. Yet as regal as she seemed, she also looked unsteady, as if nausea plagued her. Interrupted in her fury, she stumbled a bit with the next smash of a wave over the railing.

Cassandra pointed a shaking finger at the weaver who lay dead on the ground with Gerald's bullet through her heart. "This is death, Isabella. This man is ripping apart the circle. He's murdered at least three of us—"

"Defending himself," Ruby said. "And you didn't come for him!"

Bella clapped a hand on her arm, dug in her nails. Ruby got the message, clenching her jaw to keep from speaking again.

But then Ruby noticed the dead one on the deck, in the ripple of water. Another of those black wormlike things had crawled from her mouth and died in the rain. Even now, it shriveled. As it did, the dead weaver shriveled, too, almost as if she were melting. There were scars on her throat that hadn't been there a moment ago. Her skin had a yellow tint, teeth were missing, others were long and sharp. On her left hand were only three long, hooked, gnarled fingers. Her right hand retained all five, but they were also hooked, sharp, vicious. As the face of the dead witch changed, Ruby saw she'd had disgusting sores on her cheeks and one on her forehead. A hole had rotted through skin and started on the bone of her skull.

Ruby wanted to recoil. She looked from the dead thing to Bella, and the question came out before she'd even formed the words in her head.

"Is this what you all are?"

The one called Cassandra laughed, then began to cough as if the laughter choked her. On the deck, Gerald struggled until one of the weavers grabbed his testicles and screamed at him to stop moving. He let out a roar of pain as the heels of his boots slammed against the deck, but he stopped struggling, breathing fast through gritted teeth. That same weaver used a long fingernail to scratch her own face, drawing blood. She smeared it with a finger and drew something on the deck—something the rain did not wash away. Then she reached out toward the mangroves.

Thin branches snapped and twisted, growing, long enough to touch the deck. More branches bent and reached, cracked and grew, and soon they were rigid vines scraping the deck as they raced for Gerald. Ruby saw the terror in his eyes, but the witch crushing his balls had him at her mercy, and so he could only stare and hyperventilate as those branches wrapped around his legs. One of them speared the flesh of his thigh.

The two weavers who'd been holding him let go. Gerald stared at the vines that bound his legs. He looked at Ruby as if she might help him make sense of this, but she could offer nothing.

"You want to know what we are?" Cassandra called to Ruby, forcing her spine to straighten, though she still looked unsure and unwell.

Bella lowered her shoulders, hooked her fingers into claws. "Don't do this, Cass."

Cassandra spit into her own hands. She began to shake her shoulders, tapping one foot, a jerky rhythm, almost a dance. When she clapped her hands together, it wasn't for the purpose of music but some kind of punctuation. The instant her palms met, she shifted. Not a bird, not an owl, and not the beautiful Black woman who'd stood there an instant before. Ruby had been in a church once where the centuries-old body of some alleged saint lay inside a glass coffin, skin dry and tautly drawn across cheekbones. A dusty cadaver with strings of hair. Cassandra looked like that now, but her eyes were sickly yellow, opaque eggs, and parts of her exposed skin were covered with dark feathers. Her teeth were broken and black, and a steady line of thick mucus drooled from the corner of her mouth. The sores on her face and chest revealed pink flesh beneath, burnt or rotten and bursting. Still infected somewhere inside.

Ruby turned to Bella. She had no name for the emotions that

overwhelmed her. Tears welled in her eyes. "Oh my God. What do *you* really look like?"

Bella tried to laugh but couldn't pretend anything was funny. "Cassandra's been part of the circle longer than I have."

"Seven years longer," Cassandra said, relishing Ruby's horror.

Ruby blanched, the implications taking root. Was she looking at her sister's actual face, or was this some kind of masquerade? A *glamour*, they called it in books. That was where the word came from. The illusion of beauty. What did Bella look like, under there?

What will I look like? Ruby thought. Because she was part of the circle now, too. She'd accepted a bit of Stratim's evil, the dark rot from the primordial stew, into her body. If she'd known how much the corruption of her heart and soul would show itself on the outside, she would never have been able to agree.

She moved away from Bella. The weavers' true faces revealed their nature.

What am I now?

Ruby didn't know. What she did know was that she was not the kind of person who would allow a child to die so that she might live. She'd been trying to appeal to the girl her sister had once been, but that girl didn't exist, if she ever had.

Over by the railing, Gerald tried to pry bits of root from around his legs. He snapped off a piece, forced himself backward until he bumped the railing. The two weavers who'd been watching him seemed to have written him off. Without a gun, subdued, they assumed he was no threat. They could kill him anytime they wanted to.

Ruby could see in his eyes that he was steeling himself to fight back again. He had no other choice, and neither did she. Ruby wished she knew even a little about witchcraft. What had she seen them do? They could hide their true faces and take the forms of birds. Some could poison you with a touch or twist nature to their desires. The branches. The crabs. Was this witchcraft, or was it less about what they could do and more about the malice in them? They were called *night weavers*, and Ruby thought what they really meant was that they sowed malignance and darkness to advance their own needs. She'd known people who did the same thing in their lives, but without the slightest hint of witchcraft.

Save it for later, she thought.

Ruby had no choice—she would attack her sister. She hoped neither of them died, but what was life now, anyway? She spotted the gun on the deck, in the rain, about fifteen feet from where Gerald lay, bound by those twisted branches.

She tensed, ready to run for that gun.

Which was when one of the weavers guarding Gerald whimpered, grunted, and sprawled face-first onto the deck. She flinched once, and died.

"Annika, no!" Cassandra cried out and ran to her.

Bella shoved past Ruby, and the two weavers knelt by the dead one, sharing in grief and worry.

"Autumn and Eugenia dropped like this!" Cassandra raged. "What the hell is going on? It can't just be the rust—that's not enough to kill!"

Piss pooled around the dead witch before being washed away by the rain.

As a black worm emerged from between Annika's lips, Ruby understood. The crown of horns. The burning candles. The Ur-Witch.

Book had snuffed another one. Which meant he was still alive.

"Oh my God," she said quietly.

She understood fully now. Mae had explained part of this. Initiation into the circle meant taking a part of Stratim's darkness into herself, a malignant sliver of ancient power. But in summoning the spirit of the Ur-Witch into a human body, the entire circle surrendered a spark of their own lives. That was part of the bargain when joining the circle. Stratim belonged to them, and they to her. Her life was irrevocably tied to the ritual used to summon the Ur-Witch.

Which meant the same thing that happened to Annika could happen to her. One of the candles in Stratim's crown burned with Ruby's own flame. If that one went out, she would not survive. Gerald killing them wouldn't hurt her, but if Book snapped off the wrong horn, Ruby would die. And Book didn't know!

Panic seized her, but almost immediately, she shuddered through a breath of surrender. Ruby didn't want to die, but there were so many ways death might find her tonight. All she could do was try to live and try to keep Stratim from killing Aiden.

On the deck, Gerald fought to break free of the vines wrapped around his legs. He twisted and strained, used both hands to snap and break the vines away. One last weaver guarded him, but she barely paid attention—her focus was on the death that had just occurred and on the face-off between Ruby and Cassandra.

Gerald strained against his bonds, trying to reach his gun.

Ruby knew he couldn't reach it while the vines held him down. Which left it to her.

Ruby ran for the gun.

33

Underwater, Book refused to let go.

His guts churned. He felt himself flagging, even as his lungs burned for air, but at least now the pain in his cracked ribs had turned to a dull, numbing ache. Seized by sickness, he tried to focus, but his thoughts blurred. All he knew was that he could not let go of Stratim—could not let her reach the baby. For a moment, he forgot that Aiden wasn't even his child, but it didn't really matter who'd given birth to him. She had to be stopped, which meant that Book could not let go.

His right hand gripped one of her horns. He knew this could be Ruby's life in his grasp, but what would she want him to do? He could barely think, never mind fight back. Pustules burst on his skin. Stratim had dug into his eyes and into the flesh of his arm, but he held on as she swam, dragging him through the water, weaving among the bottoms of the mangrove trees.

Vomit burst from his lips, fouling the water around him. Book gasped, swallowing salt water, which convulsed his stomach, sending another torrent from his throat. Panic turned his mind gray, fading toward black. Unable to get oxygen, he would soon die.

Then Stratim burst to the water's surface. Still holding on, Book bobbed up and managed a breath. Gasping, coughing, he fought the urge to be sick again. Blinking, he saw a rusted doorway, halfway out of the water. Open just a foot or so.

Book held on as the Ur-Witch forced her body partway through the door. She sneered at Book, cursed him in forgotten languages as he continued to hold on to her. Stratim slipped through the opening into the half-submerged corridor beyond the door, but still she could not break his grip. His arm extended through the opening and he tried to squeeze through after her. Luisa had been so physically small, and he was easily twice her size. Stratim glared at him, radiating a kind of loathing he had never imagined.

"*Let go*," she said, her voice a malevolent rasp, coming from what remained of Luisa's mouth. "*You're dead already. You just don't know it yet.*"

The words barely made sense to Book. Disoriented, terrified, all he could do was hold on tight. Stratim struggled harder to free herself, but he could see her strength flagging. The candlelight from her horns cast infernal shadows on the pitted, rust-orange walls, and when Stratim let out a ragged cough, he remembered. Thoughts fogged with fever, *he remembered.*

Iron. Rust. *Poison.*

Book hauled her toward him with what strength he could muster. Stratim's face struck the half-closed door, and he reached through, scraping her cheek against the rust. She couldn't manage a scream, only a moan. Book released her, but only so that he could use his size against that door. He bent into the effort as he smashed his shoulder into the door. The upper portion screeched as it ground open several more inches, and he splashed through the opening.

Stratim flailed weakly in the half foot of water, staggered to her feet, and tried to escape him. No longer in physical contact with her, some of his own sickness ebbed, or perhaps the recovery he felt came from a surge of hope and adrenaline.

"Mae said they picked this spot to hide from you," he said, "but that was a lie."

Book smashed his right fist against the wall. A little cloud of rust particles churned in the air where he'd struck the hull. Satisfied, he did it again, and again. Rust sifted down from the ceiling above them, motes dancing in the glow of candlelight.

Stratim breathed in and choked. She staggered away, wheezing and clutching at her throat. The tattered yellow raincoat sluiced water as she emerged into a portion of corridor less flooded than the rest. He could see a pink rash on her exposed skin, sores starting to form, and he relished the irony that she had used her witchcraft to sicken him but all he had needed was this ship. The *Christabel.* Left here for a century to rust, and now he could weaponize its neglect.

"*What kind of fool are you?*" the Ur-Witch rasped. "*Poison in your flesh and your gut, beaten and bloodied, and yet you persist. The child is not yours. Stay right here, Mr. Book, and perhaps once I have what I want, I will forget how very much you've irritated me tonight.*"

Book studied her, saw the uncertainty in her eyes, and heard her labored breathing. He smiled and smashed his fists against the walls, and little clouds of rust puffed out with each blow. It sprinkled into the already tainted water and clogged the still, stale air in that claustrophobic corridor, down in the belly of that ship. The iron guts of it. The rusted corpse of the *Christabel.*

"You know what I think?" Book said and spit a wad of blood and sickness into the water. "I think you've shown me your bag of tricks. You and your fucking circle—it's blown my mind. But the items on your magic menu are pretty limited."

He could see he'd struck a nerve. The suspicion had been with him for a few minutes, but really, it was the fact he was still alive that convinced him. The iron sapped her strength and caused her pain, and the rust made her sick. Maybe away from the ship he would be dead already, but not here. If she had some witchcraft that would kill him where he stood, she would certainly use it now.

Book waded toward her, dragged himself from the water, and

they were face-to-face. The candles still burned, and he wondered which one belonged to Ruby. He wondered if he could do what had to be done.

And he wondered one other thing . . . what if it wasn't the candles he snuffed out?

"Luisa, if you're still in there, I'm sorry."

Book rushed the Ur-Witch, wrapped his hands around her neck, and smashed her against the wall. She gasped, already choked by the rust, now the last of her air cut off. He spun her around and drove her down into a few inches of water, back the way they'd come.

Beneath the water, illuminated by the light of her own candle flames, she grinned.

Stratim clawed his face, dug talons into his throat, and Book roared in pain. He stumbled backward, and she surged toward him. The sound that came from her throat might have been the screech of an owl, but loud enough to shake the walls. She grabbed his hair, jerked his head back, and sank sharp needle teeth into his shoulder. Book hissed air, in so much pain he could not muster another scream. He punched her in the throat, got a boot up into her chest, and kicked her across the corridor. She slammed into the wall but did not fall, though dust swirled in the air around her. Her breathing sounded like the slow scrape of sandpaper, but the Ur-Witch looked at him with a hatred so self-satisfied that her sneer ripped the corners of Luisa's face. If not for her hair and the tattered yellow raincoat, Book would have been unable to recognize her as his friend.

Her eyes had darkened, but at the center of each was a pinprick of blue light that glittered as if some other illumination lay within. The presence of her evil had crawled over him, into him, had made him want to curl into himself, to hide, or to destroy it before it could curdle the last ounce of his soul. But one glimpse of that blue light, so pure it seemed unearthly, washed all of that away. He thought he'd felt evil before, but this was something else. This was the absence of good or evil. Looking into that glint in her eyes, he felt as if she were about to eat the world and turn his skin inside out. Nothing had ever felt so wrong.

Book fled.

34

Gerald saw Ruby dive for the gun. The towering Cassandra lunged after her. They hit the deck, sliding in the ripple of rain and seawater. Ruby had the gun in both hands while Cassandra tried to strip it away from her. With a savage snarl, Ruby thrust the gun at Cassandra's face, cracking her nose and teeth.

"Didn't see that coming, did you?" Ruby cried in triumph, and Gerald thought maybe she had gone a little crazy.

How could he blame her? Probably they all had. Ruby's sister, Bella, had gone still, watching Cassandra and Ruby struggle. She looked as if she might be sick, like indecision and confusion had taken her completely by surprise. Her hesitation had given Ruby a moment to fight back.

The other witch, or whatever they were, glanced from Gerald to the scuffle on the deck. He saw the conflict in her—should she keep an eye on Gerald or help Cassandra restrain Ruby? She hunched slightly, salt-and-pepper hair and black hoodie all soaked in rain and draped lankly upon her. Of all of these pale, swaying, sickly women, these things that weren't quite women, this one seemed the least invested in being here. Gerald thought she hesitated because she was trying to decide what it would cost her to simply flee.

Instead, she moved to help Cassandra.

They were fighting over the gun, but the gun hadn't been the only weapon Gerald had taken from Otis Halstead's cottage. The long butcher's knife had been zipped into his jacket pocket all this time, in its plastic sheath, but once he had lost the gun, they had been watching over him. He hadn't had the seconds it would take to unzip the pocket, take out the knife, and snap it out of that plastic safety cover. But if he did it now, and if Bella's indecision lingered just a few more seconds . . .

Now or never.

Unzip. Unsheath. The plastic blew away across the deck as he started to saw at the vines that still wrapped his lower legs. The blade was serrated and very sharp, and he had the strength of a man who didn't want to die. Bella didn't even seem to notice him, locked in some kind of internal struggle. He sawed and hacked for almost ten seconds before the hoodied witch looked up from the struggle with Cassandra and Ruby and saw that he was about to break free.

The witch dropped into a crouch and slapped her hands on the deck. Water sprayed up from the impact. She glared at Gerald with searing hatred. The branches he had just hacked through began to twist and crack, reaching for him again. One of those he'd cut through speared the flesh of his thigh, and he unleashed the sincerest profanity of his life as he ripped himself away, putting distance between himself and those branches.

He stumbled toward her on his wounded leg, knife in hand. Gerald considered himself a good man. Imperfect as all were, but never someone who would turn a blade on another human being. Never someone who would kill.

That had been true until tonight. When he had seen what happened to Luisa, something broke inside him, leaving jagged edges. Whatever power had slithered into the world that could do that to Luisa, he wanted to destroy it. And when he had tied off at the broken platform on the side of the *Christabel* and climbed the steps to the deck—when he had seen these women who were not women but monsters, devils in human skin—the revulsion that swept over him made him capable of anything. He saw the thing wearing Luisa's ruined body, and he saw Book in trouble, and he did not hesitate. Grief carved out his insides so he was hollow, full of nothing but unreleased screams of anguish.

So when he fumbled toward that witch with knife in hand, he intended to use it. But now, at last, Bella seemed to realize she had to get involved. Whatever guilt or anguish had caused her hesitation, the sight of another witch in danger snapped her into action. She started toward Gerald.

Two gunshots boomed, echoing across the deck.

Gerald, Bella, and the hoodied witch all turned to see who the gun had killed. They watched Cassandra flop to the deck, long limbs smacking down with a hideous wetness. Ruby held the gun, staring at the creature she had just killed, pale with shock and grim determination. Immediately, Cassandra began to wither.

Bella cried out. The sound tore from her throat, a hopeless scream of loss. She hung her head in despair.

The salt-and-pepper-haired witch whipped her head side to side, a growl in her throat growing into a roar as she launched herself at Gerald. She moved through the wind and rain with inhuman speed. Gerald barely had time to get the knife up to defend himself when she had her hands around his throat, and he had the knife buried in her chest. As she choked him, claws drawing blood, he had the presence of mind to wonder why she'd attacked him instead of Ruby, who had pulled the trigger.

She tried to drive him to the deck. Gerald staggered backward, fighting to stay upright, and his spine collided with the railing. Desperate for air, he turned and bent, thrust his hip into the witch, and tossed her over the side.

Gerald watched her fall, leaning on the railing to hold himself up. The Gulf churned below, slamming the hull. The witch flailed, plummeted toward the water.

Turned into a nighthawk.

Carved the wind, wings outspread, lifting upward, turning back toward him. Talons out, the hawk dove at his face with all the speed the storm could provide.

Gerald reached out with both hands and caught the hawk as its talons slashed his chest, clawing the shirt and the skin below. The nighthawk screeched, and then he broke its neck with his bare hands.

He dropped the bird, and it hit the water, bobbing and floating. Dead.

When he looked back at the others, he found Ruby and Bella standing together over the leathery corpse of Cassandra. Both sisters seemed to be in shock, and that was fine with Gerald. Wounded and bleeding, he found that his mind had begun to seize up with the horrors of the night. He didn't want to kill anyone or anything ever again.

"I don't want you to die," Bella said loudly over the storm.

Ruby looked at her as if they were strangers instead of sisters. "I think it's too late for that."

35

Three steps took him to a juncture. He darted to the left, smashing his fists against the walls as he went, hoping the rust would continue to sicken her. All these months he and his team had been out here on the *Christabel* and he had spent so little time down here in the bowels of the ship. Portions were flooded, but there were areas that were dry, their walls eaten away by salt and time.

He found an open door, darted through, and found himself on a narrow walkway overlooking the engine room. Down below, seawater slid back and forth. A shaft of gloomy light came down from high above, rusted through, and rain slid through the opening. The steam engine loomed in shadow, a dead industrial god in this ancient tomb.

Book tried to close the hatch he'd come through, but its hinges were rusted in place. All he could do was run onward. He heard coughing that echoed through the corridor he'd left behind and knew Stratim hunted him.

"*I don't think I'll forget how much you irritated me after all,*" she called, her voice slithering throughout the freighter's dark innards.

He could barely see, but he ran along the narrow walkway. Halfway around the outer wall of the engine room, he found another door. The hatch screeched as he pushed it open, but it gave enough room for him to pass through, and he found himself in another corridor.

In the dark.

He waited for his eyes to adjust, fearing that he would be blind now, down in the echoing belly of the ship. But the gloom of the engine room gave just enough shared illumination that he could make out the shape of the corridor ahead. There were doors on either side, perhaps storage, but he thought it might be more crew quarters. That little bit of borrowed light only let him see about fifteen feet, but he hurried along, footfalls echoing, until he found himself in the deeper darkness.

His hands searched in front of him. He quested ahead with the toe of his boot, but he knew he would never get anywhere like this. Book moved to one side, put his hand on the wall, and began to move forward into the darkness by touch alone, still terrified he would trip but with no other choice ahead of him.

The ship whispered all around him. It groaned with the force of the waves that crashed against the outer hull. It breathed with the inhale and exhale of water sliding in and out of its rusted holes.

Six steps. Twelve. Fifteen. His hand found two doorways, but he kept going, knowing this corridor could not go on forever. But what if it did? The glittering blue light behind Stratim's eyes suggested an eternity, not of peace but sorrow.

His skin prickled with the thought of her catching up to him.

His foot caught, and he stumbled forward, knees smashing into metal stairs. Book hissed in pain, the sound echoing up and down the corridor.

In reply, he could hear the footsteps of the Ur-Witch.

He looked back the way he'd come and saw that crown of candles illuminating the hatch he'd used to leave the engine room.

"*You are right that I have limits now, in this tiny corpse I wear,*" she said. "*But quite shortly, you will meet me as I truly am, and I will introduce you to the full array of my skills.*"

Book stared. Even from this distance, in this dark, he could see the blue glint in her eyes. *Fuck.*

Almost growling with the effort of combating the poison in her lungs, Stratim staggered toward him. She began to pick up speed. The candlelight showed him the edges of the stairs in front of him, and he climbed quickly, ten metal steps up into a narrow space like an iron coffin, from where he could no longer see death pursuing him. To the left, stairs went farther upward, and he thought he saw a glimpse of light up there, thought he recognized a rusted latch and a poster on the wall.

Yes, the head they used would be there. The bathroom. He'd come through into the part of the ship below their quarters. That was where Mae and Aiden would be.

He nearly went that direction, and then he realized how little help he would be. Maybe he and Mae together could kill the Ur-Witch, but only if they put out all those candle flames. Mae would die. Ruby would die. He wasn't confident that Mae would be willing to make that sacrifice, even for Aiden—not if it meant Stratim would get the baby, anyway.

All Book could think to do was kill the Ur-Witch himself, and failing that, he could buy time for Ruby and Mae and Gerald to find another way.

He'd come up onto this platform. To his left were the stairs that went up into his quarters. But straight ahead, another set of ten steps descended again into darkness. He remembered this area now. There were other quarters here, as well as rooms that would have been stowage for gear and equipment.

The best he could think to do was hide in one of those rooms. Wait for her to find him. And try again to kill her.

Softly as he could, he descended into the dark. He slid his left hand along the wall until he found a door, slipped inside, and waited.

Waited.

Waited.

Breathing.

Stratim coughed. He heard the rasp and a sick, wheezing laughter. "*I've given myself away*," she said. And then he heard the scrape of her shoes on the metal stairs and the squeak of the wet raincoat.

The five remaining candles in her crown illuminated the corridor, but as he watched, another winked out. He held his breath and tensed to attack, watching as she took another step, just into his line of sight. She winced in pain from the wounds where he had stabbed her with her own broken horn. Did she know where he had hidden himself? Book didn't think so, but she stopped and sniffed at the air as if she might track him by scent alone, and God help him, he thought she could.

"*I do smell you*," she said as if she could read his thoughts.

Like a bird, Stratim turned only her head. She looked right at him, smiled through the gap in the doorway, triumphant.

"*But I smell something better now. Something deliciously innocent.*"

She turned back the way she'd come, headed back up into the gullet of the freighter, coughing as she reached the steps that would lead to Aiden. Helpless Aiden. The baby might even smile at her before she killed him.

"Stop," he said, stepping out from behind the door he'd used to hide himself.

Halfway up the steps to the platform, she glanced back at him.

"I'm right here," Book said, knowing that he was inviting death. Pain caught up to him from every wound and sore and bruise. He fought not to let her see. "You want to finish me, come on and do it."

She hesitated. Licked her lips. She relished the idea of murdering him. But he had injured her badly, and between him and Gerald, they had snuffed out three-quarters of the candles on her bone crown. Another went dark, even now. Most of her circle were dead, and he suspected she worried about risking the last few.

Still, she smiled. Full of hatred. "*Have you wondered how I know your name, Mr. Book?*"

He hadn't. Until now. His skin prickled, and suddenly, he felt smaller. Seen.

"*Briefly, before Mae betrayed me with my own witchcraft, I invaded your beloved Ruby. Her spirit, her flesh, and her mind were open to me. Mae drove me out before I could claim her, but I saw so much. I clawed into her thoughts. I saw the memory of the day she bled, the day she told you about the worst pain she had ever felt. The day she lost the son she wanted to name after you,* Charlie."

Book fell to one knee in the water. "Shut up. You don't know a goddamn thing."

Her voice became a whisper, like a snake gliding over desert sand. "*You were happy your son died. It would have made life so much more complicated, and without him, you were free.*"

"That's a fucking lie."

The Ur-Witch laughed. Most of her face remained, but suddenly, he could no longer see Luisa in her. Not at all. Those twin blue lights burned deep inside her eyes, and he couldn't look.

"*Stay here, Mr. Book. Let this baby die, too. Just like the last time, it will make your life so much easier.*"

Book crumpled to the tilted metal floor, the sickness and exhaustion and wounds catching up to him. The light from the Ur-Witch's crown danced along the floor and walls and then dimmed as she reached the platform and turned to ascend the next set of stairs.

He could have stayed like that. Unable to imagine any way he would survive this night, he could have just let that be the end. But he reached into a part of himself that existed beyond shock and fear, beyond grief, and beyond the urge to surrender. Rage lived in that place, a fury that powered determination. His life had been lived in a culture that insisted everything was a gray area, that good and evil existed on the same spectrum, but now he had *met* evil. Felt its touch. Been sickened and terrified just breathing the same air. Evil had its own insidious purpose. And in the face of that, so broken that fear and hopelessness lost their meaning, he found clarity.

Book rose to his hands and knees. He planted one hand on the wall and forced himself to rise. The corridor had been cast into darkness. Stratim had taken her candlelight with her.

In the darkness, Book reached out, shuffled forward, and found the railing.

He started up the steps, in search of the light.

36

Mae stood just outside the mess, with Aiden held in the crook of her left arm and a chef's cleaver knife in her right fist. She'd had to make the most difficult decision she had ever faced. When the Näturvefjar began to gather on board the freighter, she had known Stratim would arrive soon. She had managed to stop the ancient thing from hijacking Ruby's body but had known the Ur-Witch would find another.

Stratim would be coming soon.

Mae had panicked. All she cared about was saving Aiden, but the baby had been back in the room that Book had given to her and Ruby. In that moment, in her fear, it had felt logical to retreat to that room with the Sharpie and scribble wards on the doorframe. It made sense to her.

It hadn't taken long before she realized her logic had been polluted by desperation.

Her wards had held off the other Näturvefjar so far, but it was impossible to know how long that would last or whether the same would be true of an Ur-Witch. Surely, it was the height of hubris for her to think any witchcraft she wielded could defeat the ancient evil who was the source of that witchcraft. Stratim might be weakened by the iron that surrounded them, choked by the rust in the air, and limited by being in this world only in spirit, but Mae had to assume she would still manage to break through. Maybe the wards would work, but not forever.

Which meant Mae had effectively trapped herself and Aiden in a dead-end kill zone. There was no place to run from that room, and she hadn't even thought to try to find a weapon to bring in there with her.

Grappling with the knowledge that there was no real escape, she lost valuable time frozen by indecision. At last, despite the work she'd put into warding the room, she had taken Aiden and left the illusion of safety behind.

Guided by the flashlight on her phone, her first stop had been the mess. In the kitchen, she had found the array of cooking knives Book's team used in preparing their meals. She didn't know which of them fancied themselves a culinary artist, but when she found the wicked-looking cleaver knife, she was grateful. The best cooking tools often made the best murder weapons.

The thought made her giddy.

Now she smiled a lunatic's smile, knife hand shaking. Aiden squirmed. He was wide awake, watching her. Mae squeezed her eyes shut, and fresh tears spilled down her cheeks. Her lips were pressed tightly together, holding back a wave of chaotic emotion.

When Mae had first begun to worship Stratim, the idea that she might one day encounter her in the flesh had been enough to fill her heart with transcendent joy. Worship had made her feel grateful, lightening her whole body, lifting her burdens.

The purest love she had ever known had been during her sophomore year in high school, when her regular English teacher had been on maternity leave and a substitute named Nina Stokes had taken her place. Twenty-three, gentle, and openhearted, Miss Stokes had seen her in a way fifteen-year-old Mae had never felt seen. Miss Stokes—Nina—talked about the rights of women, and taught Toni Morrison and Maya Angelou, and told Mae she had all the magic she needed to make her dreams come true. She'd worshipped Nina. Felt a love that made her weak and shy and flushed anytime Nina looked at her, never mind spoke to her. Lightheaded. Mae had fucked it up by writing Nina a twelve-page letter professing her love and gratitude, praying that if Nina were still single when Mae turned eighteen, she might kiss her, just once.

Drunk with love and worship.

Nina had never shared the letter with the principal, but she had regretfully tendered her resignation, frightened that her teaching career might be derailed before it even began. A victim of love. Mae knew this because she had tracked her down online after graduation and sent her an email. Miss Stokes had been apologetic and flattered and hoped Mae understood. The hell of it was that by then, Mae understood perfectly that she had put Nina in an untenable position, but somehow logic was not sufficient to cure her of the hurt and disillusionment. She'd been jaded as hell after that.

Until the first time she had prayed with the Näturvefjar, when she'd been inducted into the circle and felt the ethereal touch of the Ur-Witch. The dark breath had slid inside her, and she had inhaled sharply, filled her lungs, shuddering with delight. She'd felt the presence of Stratim in her mind, and she had opened her heart, given all her dreams and hopes and bitterness and resentment, knowing Stratim would cradle them all.

Drunk with love and worship, and sisterhood, and the gleeful need to punish everyone who had ever hurt her.

Until Bella.

And then Aiden.

It had begun when Aiden had started to kick inside Bella's abdomen, and when the boy was born and Mae had been the first to hold him, she had known that all those other moments of love she had thought transcendent paled in comparison to this. When it had become clear that Bella intended to allow the ritual to go on, to let the circle murder her baby, Mae had no choice—she had stolen Aiden away in the middle of the night and fled to Ruby. From all Bella had said about her sister, Mae had believed Ruby was the one person who might help her, especially if she believed the circle had murdered Bella and wanted to do the same to Aiden.

So Mae had lied. Of course she had lied. If Ruby hadn't believed Bella was dead, she would never have gone along with any of this. She'd never have believed her sister was willing to sacrifice her own child. By the time Mae herself had believed that this woman she loved would do such a thing, it had nearly been too late.

Mae had not given birth to Aiden, but she felt as if he belonged to her. She would die for him.

Maybe tonight.

Probably tonight.

Mae had *felt* it when Stratim arrived on the *Christabel*. When her goddess had grabbed the door latch and Mae's ward had burned her, kept her from entering, she had felt such pride in the midst of her terror. But she had also felt it when Stratim descended into the belly of the ship, belowdecks, and that could only mean one thing. Stratim thought she could get into the interior of the ship from below.

And she could. She would.

Just outside the mess, Mae stood trembling. She jostled Aiden, gripping that cleaver knife, trying desperately to think of a way to save this baby's life.

Her head whipped up.

From down the corridor, where an open door led to metal stairs . . . were those footsteps? Climbing?

Heart thundering, Mae turned to look toward steps that led up to the common room and then to the wheelhouse. It was a dead end, of course. In the wheelhouse, her only escape would be out to the deck of the freighter, where the rest of the circle waited to stop her, to punish her, to offer Aiden in bloody sacrifice so that Stratim could remain in this world forever. Something Mae had once wished for more fervently than any wish she'd ever made for herself. Now she would do anything to prevent it.

Anything.

Aiden squirmed again. Watching her. Feeling her anguish. His face scrunched up, and he began to cry, quietly at first, but then he took a breath, and she knew a wail would soon burst forth.

"No," she whispered. "You're okay, baby. We're okay."

Less convincing words had never left her lips.

Aiden's cry grew louder, echoing up and down the corridor. She shushed him. Her tears burned hot. "Please, baby, no. Aiden, my love, we're okay. Shhhh. You're okay."

She glanced toward escape again, and then back down the corridor where those footsteps had echoed.

A dim orange light glowed from the stairwell at the end of the corridor.

Candlelight, dancing as Stratim climbed the stairs. Coming for them.

Mae crooked her arm, holding the baby so he could make out the shape of her face in the dark. In whispers, through tears, she begged him to be silent.

Then she threw back her head and joined him, wailing, because she had seen what her sisters had done to traitors before. She had joined in. This was not the first knife she'd ever held with the intention of parting flesh.

But Aiden was innocent.

The candlelight grew brighter at the end of the corridor, and the candles came into view in the darkness. The face of the Ur-Witch floated beneath it, ghostly in that flickering light.

With baby and knife, Mae ran. She bolted up the stairs, past the common room, and then up to the wheelhouse. Aiden froze, shocked into silence as Mae ran, but when she paused in the wheelhouse to look out the windows, the baby began a frantic huffing that erupted into another round of wailing. Mae didn't try to shush him now, only bounced him a little and swayed back and forth by instinct.

Rain battered the windows. Gusts of wind pounded the

freighter, making it seem as if the *Christabel* breathed on its own, alive and mournful and not giving a single fuck about the lives ending tonight.

Mae saw figures out in the storm but couldn't make out who it was. For a moment, she had tricked herself into thinking it mattered what kind of danger waited for her out there, that she had a choice. But if she looked back the way she'd come, she knew any moment she would see the glow of candles coming up the steps into the wheelhouse.

Steeling herself, she held Aiden close and ran for the door. The wards were still in place, still flickering with tiny, unnatural flames. Cradling the baby with her left arm, Mae struggled to turn the latch while clutching the handle of the big blade in her right hand. She extended two fingers, caught the latch, but as she turned it, the knife fell and clattered to the floor.

Heart thumping hard enough to hurt, she crouched, balancing Aiden, to pick up the knife. The door shook in its frame, bashed by the wind. Her fingers closed on the cleaver knife's handle, and from the corner of her eye, she saw the yellow raincoat.

Mae shot to her feet. Only three candles still burned on Stratim's bone crown. Some horns had been broken, others extinguished. The sight shocked her to stillness. Three still burned. Three still lived. *Me*, Mae thought, *but who are the other two?*

Aiden took a breath, then erupted into another shuddering wail. Stratim smiled. Scraps of skin hung down from her face, and most of the teeth that had been there had fallen out, but in the candlelight, Mae could see other teeth behind them, as if the creature's true, ancient face had grown behind the one she'd stolen. Suddenly, the idea of seeing the true face of the Ur-Witch filled her with unspeakable fear.

She fumbled with the door latch again.

Stratim stalked toward her, confident. A wave of hunger rippled out from her.

"*Give me the child, daughter*," she demanded. "*He lives for me.*

His mother made him for this purpose." Her grin—the grin behind her ruined features—twisted to become a sickening parody of sympathy. "*Most of your circle is dead now. We will rebuild it together. Perform the rite, take the child's heart and eyes, and you will have all the love you have ever desired. Peace and glorious abandon.*"

At the sound of the monster's voice, Aiden had stopped crying. He nuzzled against Mae, hungry, but she had no milk for him. Nothing to feed him. All she could offer him was life.

"There's nothing you can give me that could ever feel like love," Mae said, staring at Stratim, seeing now that there were pinpoints of hideous blue light in her eyes—the eyes behind her eyes. "Not anymore."

Stratim scowled in frustration, and for the first time, Mae realized why she hesitated. Only three candles left. If the Ur-Witch killed her, that would leave only two. If they were all snuffed out, her hold on this poor woman's corpse would be severed, and there was no way to know how long it would be before some other circle of weavers would be foolish and desperate and insidious enough to try this ritual.

"You don't want to kill me," Mae said, surprised she had said the words aloud.

Stratim started toward her. Her grin broadened. The host body's right eye slid down the torn gray flesh of her cheek. "*That does not mean I am unwilling.*"

Behind the Ur-Witch, Book emerged from the darkened stairs. Mae drew a sharp breath at the sight of him. She tried to cover her reaction, but the monster had noticed and started to turn.

With a strangled cry, Book hurled himself at Stratim. Unsteady, face covered in sores from the Ur-Witch's power, he did not hesitate as the monster faced him. They collided and fell to the floor, and Book grabbed one of her unbroken horns.

"Ruby said to save the baby, whatever it costs!" he said, and Mae could see the anguish behind those words. He knew what he was doing, what it could mean. That Ruby might be next to die.

Stratim screamed like a wounded animal.

Mae put the blade between her teeth, opened the latch with her now free hand, and ran out into the rain. Her boots slid on the deck. She grabbed the cleaver knife from her teeth and spun around. There were three others out on the deck in that storm. Ruby, Bella, and a man she had never seen, whose presence shocked her. All she knew about this man was that he was not one of the circle. She prayed that meant he was there to help.

She bent over, trying to shield Aiden from the storm as well as she could. "We might live, baby boy," she told him, her mouth inches from his ear. The sweet smell of his head made her want to cry all over again. Innocence and beauty, that's what he was. "We might live."

The wheelhouse door stood open. Mae looked up in time to see Stratim slam Book into the wall. He ripped off part of the monster's outer face, just trying to keep fighting, doing anything he could to stop her from coming after Aiden. But he hit the wall and he fell, and he was too slow getting up.

Stratim screeched. It sounded like a hawk's cry. She ran toward the open door, three candles still burning, flickering. Mae huddled Aiden against her. At the threshold, Stratim collided with a wall none of them could see. The screech cut off as she stumbled backward. Mae watched this monster who had been her goddess, her mother, glare at the doorframe and then turn hateful eyes toward her. The ward still worked.

For a moment, the only sounds were from the storm.

Then the Ur-Witch started screaming again. Primal, feral, she dug long, gnarled fingers into the doorframe, trying to break the ward.

Mae held her breath, knowing it was only a matter of time now.

Minutes.

Or less.

37

Ruby watched the gleaming black worm slither from Cassandra's body and then looked up at her sister, relieved to see a hint of sorrow on Bella's face. A quick glance around showed they were alone except for Gerald. He stood warily, ready to defend himself again. Weary and disoriented, Ruby exhaled. Could it be they were the only ones left?

Bella deflated. "You going to shoot me next?"

Ruby had all but forgotten the gun in her hand. Now she cast it aside in revulsion.

"No!" Gerald shouted, but too late.

The gun clattered on the rainswept deck, sliding off into the darkness.

Ruby reached for her sister again. "Bella . . ."

Bella flinched away from her, upper lip rippling in disgust at the idea of Ruby touching her. "You want to get all 'big sister' on me now? Fuck that."

"What do you mean 'now'? I never stopped."

Bella sneered. "Okay, Rubes. Okay." She looked down at Cassandra's corpse again.

"Once upon a time, I thought you couldn't hurt your family worse than you already had," Ruby said, barely loud enough to be heard over the storm.

"You don't know what you're talking about!"

"Bullshit! You always figured the world owed you something,

and you were gonna get it. Your whole life, you never made an effort with anything. Not with work, and not with people. Anyone who told you to start taking responsibility for yourself was the enemy."

Bella bared her teeth. "Yet here I am. In command of my life."

Ruby laughed hoarsely. "We know that isn't true. You're more trapped now than you ever were back then."

The rain made her anguish so much worse. She knew Gerald was still there, but what could the brave fool do but stand and watch?

"Fuck you! What kind of life do you lead? Writing songs nobody gives a shit about, playing clubs where no one will remember you a week from now! Well, I won't be forgotten, Ruby. When this is done, I'll be a goddamn queen. I'll have whoever I want and whatever I want—"

Ruby stopped listening to her.

Fifty feet beyond Bella, Mae had just stumbled out the wheelhouse door into the rain. Ruby and Gerald stared at her, but it took another moment before Bella heard the wailing of the baby in Mae's arms. Bella's baby.

The one she wanted to offer up in murder.

"Oh shit," Gerald said. "Heads up."

Ruby wished he hadn't said it. She rushed toward Mae but knew she wouldn't be quick enough. Gerald's words had alerted Bella, who caught her by the arm and yanked her to a halt, choking Ruby with her free hand.

"Back off, sis," Bella said. "He's my son, not yours."

The malice in her voice, the cruelty in her eyes, made her unrecognizable. Bella had always had darkness in her, a lazy selfishness that made her mean, and a disdain for the world and its rules that made her wild. But what Ruby saw in her now went far beyond that.

"That's right," Ruby struggled to say, with Bella's grip on her throat. "He's your son."

Gerald grabbed Bella's wrist, tried to pull her off.

Bella ignored him. Stronger than she ought to be, despite the iron that weakened her. But she did release her grip on Ruby.

"Self-righteous cunt," Bella said, sneering. "Always think you're better than me."

Ruby had had enough. As Gerald held up his hands in an attempt to placate them both, she rubbed her throat.

"If this is who you've become," Ruby said, "then I *am* better than you. I don't even know what you are now."

Bella lashed out, grabbed a fistful of Ruby's soaking-wet hair, and punched her hard in the face. Three quick jabs, and then Bella shoved her to the deck and ran toward Mae. Pain exploded in Ruby's nose and mouth, but she scrambled to her feet, swaying, blood dripping from her split lips. She thought she'd have preferred witchcraft over fists and wondered why Bella hadn't tried to infect her with bubonic plague or something. Maybe the weavers couldn't use hexes or whatever they were on one another.

Or maybe she just wanted to make me bleed. Maybe it's as simple as that. It's just personal.

Gerald moved to check on her, but she waved him away.

"I'm fine. Don't let her get the baby."

But it was too late for that. Bella wanted her son.

"Stay back!" Mae said, waving a wicked-looking kitchen cleaver with her free hand.

Though it was still raining, Ruby could tell some of the damp on Mae's face came from tears. Mae shook her head as Bella stalked toward her. She clutched Aiden to her chest and began to back away, still waving that nasty blade. Stumbled, kept going, until she stepped out onto the catwalk that split the floating forest in two. The mangrove trees swayed, and a fresh wave crashed over the side of the *Christabel*, pouring down into the hole in the deck.

"He's mine!" Bella rasped, halfway bent over, stalking, a two-legged predator. Coughing, she followed Mae and Aiden onto the catwalk. "Give him to me!"

"Gerald," Ruby said, turning toward him. "If she gets him—"

"I know," Gerald said, and he started to circle around the edges of the hole in the deck.

Mangrove crabs dropped from the branches. If there were still birds nesting inside the forest, they were quiet at last.

Bella and Mae were face-to-face. Three feet apart. Bella appeared pale and drawn, but Mae looked as if her will had broken, the fear and sadness taking their toll.

"You said you loved me!" Mae cried out, brandishing the cleaver knife.

"I do!" Bella lied. Or perhaps, in some way Ruby could never understand, it was true. "I want this for both of us. She needs us both, now more than ever!"

Mae didn't have to reply. She kept shaking her head, and that said enough.

"He's my child!" Bella screamed, voice ragged.

"He was supposed to be *ours*!"

"Never," Bella replied. "Never ours. He belongs to me. He's mine to give!"

Ruby never would have risked it, there over the hole in the deck, in the midst of the mangroves. But Bella had never known caution, even before she'd become this broken. This mad. This thing.

Instead of fighting Mae for the baby, risking that cleaver, Bella kissed her.

She wrapped her arms around them both and forced her mouth over Mae's. At first, Mae resisted, but then she gave in to the kiss and this fractured family embrace. Just when Mae seemed to melt, days of exhaustion and terror taking their toll, Bella slammed her forehead into Mae's. Their skulls collided hard enough to echo across the deck.

Mae's legs went out from under her. The cleaver clattered to the catwalk and went spinning off into the mangroves, then down into the water sloshing in the guts of the ship. As Mae fell, Bella ripped Aiden from her grasp.

Ruby could never have reached them in time to stop it. She ran onto the catwalk and stood face-to-face with her sister again, but this time Bella had Aiden in her arms. Beyond Bella, discarded, half-conscious, Mae rolled and began to slide beneath the railing, with the water and the heart of the floating forest waiting below.

Then Gerald was there. He had a long kitchen knife of his own. He'd run around to the other side of the catwalk, and now he raced to help Mae, setting down his knife. He held on to her as she regained her senses.

The wind paused, a quiet moment between breaths. The four of them could hear a raging voice, a beast, and the sound of metal on metal. A grinding, and then a hammering. Reluctant as she was to take her eyes off Bella and Aiden, Ruby turned toward the sound.

The view through the open wheelhouse door was like a glimpse into hell. Whatever the poor soul had once looked like, the woman inhabited by the Ur-Witch had changed. Half her face had fallen away or been torn off, and behind it was something hideous, pink and black like raw flesh burnt in places. A wound with sharp teeth.

She had acquired a length of metal, maybe the broken leg of a chair or table from the wheelhouse. Slavering and furious, three candles still burning on that crown of bones, she smashed the metal club against the doorframe and then shook her head as if struck by a minor seizure before trying to scrape at the frame with the club's edge. She tried to use it as a pry bar to break the frame. Mesmerized, Ruby watched for seconds longer than she should have, and then she saw the flicker of flames and remembered the ward Mae had put on the door. It was keeping Stratim inside the wheelhouse, for now.

Ruby nodded to herself. They had time. Not much, but time.

Then she spotted the figure moving behind the Ur-Witch, inside the wheelhouse.

Book. Bloody-faced, moving slowly, he crept up behind her. Ruby wanted to cry out, to warn him not to be a fool, but if she tried that, she would alert the Ur-Witch.

Which was, of course, precisely what Bella did.

Stratim turned just as Book leaped at her, but she wasn't the only one who'd acquired a broken bit of furniture. Book clubbed her in the face, and Stratim reached for her own eyes, shaken by the blow.

Instead of pressing the advantage, Book got the hell out of there. He slammed a shoulder into Stratim, knocked her out of the way, and hurled himself out through the doorway into the storm. On the deck, he staggered and slipped but managed to regain his footing, and then he glanced around in a desperate search, saw them all on the catwalk—Ruby and Bella, Mae and Aiden, and Gerald.

Gerald, who had come to help his friend and surely by now must have wished he had minded his own business.

"Hey!" Gerald called. "Hey, hey, you don't wanna—"

Ruby assumed Gerald was addressing Book, but when she turned toward him, she realized two things. The first was that her sister had made the same assumption and was staring at Book, her back to Mae and Gerald. The second was that she and Bella were both wrong—Gerald hadn't been talking to Book at all. When he said *you don't wanna*, he'd been talking to Mae, and she wasn't listening.

With Aiden in her arms, her focus on Book, Bella didn't see Mae slipping up behind her.

Mae, who had snatched up the knife Gerald had put down in order to keep her from going over the edge.

Mae, who slapped one hand over Bella's mouth, yanked her head back, and drew that serrated blade across Bella's throat with strength and determination enough to cut deep. Arterial blood sprayed across the catwalk and into the mangroves. Bella's arms relaxed, and Aiden began to slide from her grasp, but Mae dragged her backward, dropping the knife as she reached around to keep the baby safe. Blood poured onto Aiden's face, and he screamed and screamed and screamed.

Or maybe that was Ruby herself, who'd just watched her sister die.

But no. Ruby felt ice-cold, paralyzed, hollow with shock. Unable to scream.

So it wasn't only Aiden's voice, but it wasn't Ruby at all.

The other screaming came from the Ur-Witch.

Just inside the wheelhouse door, the monster jerked her head, twisting around, trying to find a way to see the candle flames on her crown. She'd seen Bella die, and maybe she had felt it as well. Felt that candle snuff out.

Only two candle flames remained. Ruby and Mae.

Mae had seen to that.

But Mae wasn't going to make any more decisions tonight. Not if Ruby could stop her.

She hurried to the place where her sister lay, dead and bleeding. Regret and rage churned, so twined together that she would never be able to separate them, but she could not deal with that right now. Ruby stepped over Bella's corpse, looked at Gerald, and he nodded at her. He understood the needs of the moment and meant to be part of it.

Ruby didn't ask. She tore Aiden from Mae's grasp. Mae tried to fight for him, clutched the edge of the blanket she had swaddled him in, clawed Ruby's arm, but Gerald was there. He went down on his knees behind Mae, reached around her and seized both her wrists, knowing what he was risking. Sickness. Death. Mae had proven herself a willing killer.

"No," Gerald said quietly, firmly.

Mae hesitated and then relented. No matter what precautions she had taken, the exposure to so much rust and iron had weakened her, and now she had murdered the woman she had loved. She had nothing left.

Which was when Ruby finally knew, for certain, that whatever evil had rooted itself in this woman's soul, Mae did truly want Aiden to live. She had not been completely sure until then. Mae had killed Bella to save Aiden, and that should have been all the evidence Ruby needed, but even then, she'd feared some other malignant purpose. But no, this was love. Or whatever love a creature like Mae might be capable of.

Leaving Mae and Gerald on the catwalk, Ruby carried Aiden back onto the deck, where Book waited.

"You look like shit," she told him.

Book smiled. Teeth were missing. Blood painted the swollen, bruised left side of his face. "It hasn't been my best night."

Ruby might have replied with something similarly sarcastic.

She never got the chance.

The shrieking sound of tearing metal echoed across the deck. Only then did Ruby realize the hammering had stopped. Book turned to look back at the wheelhouse. Past him, Ruby saw that the Ur-Witch had succeeded in breaking the doorframe. Metal had been bent away from the frame, which meant it wasn't just the frame that was broken but the ward Mae had cast upon it.

Stratim was free.

Running at Book, torn yellow raincoat flapping.

Screaming, two candles burning.

Baring her teeth as she collided with Book, drove him to the deck, and dug her claws into the soft flesh of his throat, drawing blood.

"*Before you take another breath, woman,*" the Ur-Witch said, "*give me that child.*"

38

Even a creature as old as Stratim could be afraid. Book knew he couldn't kill her—the most ancient part of her wasn't even here in this world, existing in whatever spiritual limbo held ghosts and gods. But it had taken her a very long time to reach this point, to gather a circle of weavers strong enough and willing to conceive and bear and murder an infant so that she could be reborn. She didn't want to start again.

Book didn't give a fuck what she wanted.

Her nails were at his throat, drawing blood, but she wanted the baby and thought she could bargain with his life. That meant she would hesitate to kill him until she got what she wanted, and that hesitation was all he needed.

Her eyes were bloody and black, but deeper within, those glittering blue pinpricks remained. He jammed his fingers into them. She drove her nails deeper, puncturing his throat, and blood drooled down his neck as he grabbed hold of one of the horns with a still-burning candle. Book twisted, yanked her head sideways, wrapped his hand around that candle flame. It burned his palm and fingers, but the fire felt brutally cold. Could he do it? Since the moment he had realized one of these flames linked to Ruby's life, he had prayed it wouldn't come to this. Other weavers had died, candles had winked out, but now he was close enough to finish it, and one of those flames could kill Ruby.

He could kill Ruby.

Stratim shrieked as she let go of his throat and reached up to rip his hands away from her horns. The second she released him, he used his grip on her horns to drive her backward. He surged to his feet and shoved her away from him, then turned and lunged across the rain-slicked deck. He couldn't risk it. Could not take the chance he might kill Ruby.

The gun Gerald had brought on board lay a dozen feet away. He'd spotted it moments before the Ur-Witch broke free of the wheelhouse. Now he dove for it, smashed down on his chest, and got his right hand on the grip. Would there be any ammunition left? How many bullets did it hold? Had it been fully loaded at the start?

Ruby screamed his name.

Not his name, really. She cried out the name of the child they'd lost—*Charlie*. The name he refused to ever use again.

Book rolled onto his back. The yellow raincoat flapped in the wind as Stratim came for him, not on foot but in the storm. In the air. Flying.

He pulled the trigger twice, hit her dead center with both shots. The impact did not stop her, but she fell short, crashing to the deck only inches away. Book scrambled backward and lurched to his feet, keeping the gun aimed at her. Luisa's black hair veiled Stratim's face as she rose to her hands and knees, panting, huffing like a bull about to charge.

"Get away from her!" Gerald shouted.

Book wanted to remind him that there was nowhere for him to run. If he went into the wheelhouse, or climbed back down into the roots of the floating forest, or up into the mangrove trees, the Ur-Witch would have him. And jumping overboard would do her dirty work for her. No way could he swim to safety from here.

Ruby kept her distance, and he was glad. She had Aiden in her arms, and protecting him was the key. But Mae stepped past Ruby, gliding slowly toward the creature she had once worshipped.

Stratim raised her head to look at Book. Those two remaining candles still burned. She climbed slowly to her feet and wiped rain off her yellow coat. The coat hung open, and Book could see the holes in her body, black with blood.

"Charlie," Ruby said, her voice steady and calm somehow, as if she could see how this would all end and was resigned to it. "You have to put out all the candles."

Book could see the three of them in his peripheral vision—Mae, Ruby, and Gerald—but he didn't dare look away from Stratim. Those last two candles flickered in the rain, and they all knew what their flames represented. The Ur-Witch knew, as well.

"*Go on, Mr. Book,*" she said. Her voice slurred, until she reached up and peeled away the left side of her mouth, tearing off skin and muscle to expose more of her true face. Very little of Luisa remained now. "*Keep shooting. Let's see if you can snuff me out.*"

The hideous mouth grinned. Those needle teeth made an awful sound when they scraped together. Book felt his skin crawl. He felt filthy, as if he hadn't bathed in months. That was the effect of her presence.

Not just her presence, he thought. *Her regard.* Having her focus on him, being seen by those glittering blue pinpricks, made him feel as if he would never be clean again. But he knew what she wanted, with her taunting and that smile. Stratim thought she could goad him into wasting whatever ammunition remained in the gun, because of course there was no way he could shoot accurately enough to destroy the horns where those last two candles burned. More importantly, she banked on him being unwilling to pay the price of stopping her. If he put out those candles, Ruby and Mae would die.

Her upper lip curled. The true mouth of the Ur-Witch had lips that were purple-black and moved like worms when she spoke.

"Book," Mae called to him.

He'd never know what she was going to say. Book turned and pulled the trigger. The first bullet struck Mae in the abdomen. Ruby screamed, prompting Aiden to join her. Gerald called out to God. Book hoped like hell there was at least one more bullet in the gun because his aim had been off—he hadn't meant for Mae to suffer, but he also couldn't afford for her to linger.

The second bullet struck her in the chest. It knocked her back a step, and then the strength went out of her legs and she plopped down on the deck in the rain, sat there staring at him for a moment, and then toppled over. Dead.

Stratim screamed louder than the rest of them. Her screams were so shrill, so deafening, that even baby Aiden was stunned to silence.

The Ur-Witch came at him, but Book turned the gun on Ruby. Stratim skidded to a halt. The wind whipped her hair in front of that hideous, ruined face, hiding the evil that had taken Luisa's place.

"That's right, Charlie," Ruby said. "Finish it."

"No," Gerald said. "Goddamn it, Book!"

Book hated himself. If he hadn't needed to keep Stratim from killing him, he'd have crumbled. Mae had committed at least one ritual murder and been unrepentant about it. There was no way to tell how many other atrocities she might have committed as part of her circle. But he'd killed her, and telling himself it was necessary didn't make him hate himself any less.

"Back away," he told Stratim. "Give me some space and we'll see if we can't work something out."

He'd lied. But the Ur-Witch's eyes gleamed. Evil would always assume others could be corrupted, mostly because it was so often true.

She smiled so widely that her face split up the middle. For a few heartbeats, he could see what lay behind the ruin of Luisa's face, and beyond the true features of the Ur-Witch, where a void awaited—a bottomless space full of those cold, glittering blue lights, floating like stars in a sea of endless dark, an eternity of uncaring and disdain. Book wanted to scream. Every part of him yearned to look away, but Aiden was a speck of innocence and hope, and he held on to that speck in his mind. He could not flinch. Not now.

Stratim shuffled backward, her smile turning to a sneer. The split in her face resealed wetly, doors closing, and Book stepped over Mae's body, moving away from the Ur-Witch. He noticed the rain sluicing away Mae's blood, but he kept the gun trained on Ruby and Aiden until he was only a few feet from them, and from Gerald.

This was it now. The three of them, the baby, and evil fucking incarnate out on the deck of the *Christabel* in the middle of this storm.

One candle burning.

If only he knew what the hell to do now.

"I think," Ruby said, "it's time to make a deal."

39

Gerald stood in the rain, numb with shock. Book and Ruby were a few feet ahead of him, all of them facing the monster on the deck. The monster in the torn yellow raincoat. The monster wearing what remained of the woman he loved.

Ruby held the baby. Book held the gun. Both had their backs to Gerald, so they didn't notice when he crouched and picked up the knife Mae had used to murder Ruby's sister. The knife Gerald himself had brought on board. He had taken it from Otis Halstead's cottage—Otis, another casualty of this storm, this horror—and now it felt repulsive in his grasp. But he needed it. Wanted it, because it seemed like everyone was doing their share of killing tonight, and Gerald wanted to get off the boat alive.

He held the knife down low. His thoughts blurred. The world had shifted on its axis, and he thought he would be dizzy for as long as he lived. The rain poured down, water ran across the deck, the wind battered him, and he barely noticed. Barely felt any of it.

The Ur-Witch's crown of horns had been ruined. Some of the horns were broken off, leaving sharp edges. Others still had the waxy coating on them that reminded him of antler velvet, but the candles on top of those horns no longer burned. They had all been snuffed out.

All but one, and he had come to realize that last candle belonged to Ruby. Whatever rituals had taken place, whatever the women who'd died on the *Christabel* tonight had done, they'd linked their lives to the flickering flames atop this thing's head, on the bones that had grown out of her skull.

Gerald flexed his fingers on the hilt of the knife and stared at the center of Ruby's back as the truth hit him. All he had to do to stop all of this was plant that knife between her shoulder blades. Kill her, and it was over. He and Book could live. They would let the authorities handle the baby. Even now, he could hear the child whimpering. From his vantage point, he saw the baby's legs kicking and straining at the blanket that swaddled him. Ruby still had her back to him, but the edge of the blanket pushed out to one side, and he could see that the kid was squirming.

Kill Ruby, and the Ur-Witch died.

Book had murdered Mae. The shock of that had been worse than seeing Mae slit Bella's throat. Gerald hadn't known Mae at all, but Book was his colleague and friend, a good man. A good man who'd turned the gun on Mae and killed her, the echo of those gunshots swallowed by the storm.

Gerald couldn't have just shot Mae like that. He had killed tonight, but that had been in self-defense and in defense of his friend. Yes, if he murdered Ruby, this whole thing would be over, but there was no way he could do such a thing.

And yet . . .

These people were monsters inside. Not metaphorically, either. They were actual monsters.

Like Luisa.

The smile on the Ur-Witch's face made him close his eyes, but he could still see it in his mind and knew he always would. The upper part of Luisa's face remained, although her eyes were gone. The Ur-Witch wore the shred of that face like a mask, peering out from behind it. The teeth and the mouth belonged to the Ur-Witch, and hideous skin like the rotten flesh of a pumpkin left too long on the stoop. He had seen the gap that opened in her face when she smiled, and a glimpse of an impossible abyss behind that face.

"*You wanted a bargain, Ruby,*" the Ur-Witch said. "*But here we are, and all I can see is—what would your generation call it?—'mutually assured destruction.' Either we both live or we both die. I can give you dreams you have not yet dared to dream. Delights—*"

"Nah, no, fuck off with that shit," Ruby said.

Gerald flinched. So did the Ur-Witch.

The baby kept kicking. Ruby rocked him back and forth in her arms unconsciously, the way anyone would learn to do if they wanted to soothe an infant.

The Ur-Witch lowered her head, her shoulders curled inward, and she cocked her head, looking for an opening. She thought she would have to attack after all. After Ruby's reply, of course she did.

"Even if you were willing to let me take Aiden and walk away," Ruby said, "I wouldn't ever be able to sleep, knowing you were still out there. Knowing you could come back to kill him anytime you like."

The Ur-Witch sneered and spit, and Gerald could see the animal in her. In her eyes, her very presence, he saw a wildness that redefined that word for him. This was a wildness, a savagery, so old that nobody alive had seen it up close until now. If it still existed at all, it was only at the very fringes of human experience, out in the remotest parts of the world, where people still feared to go and could never survive for long. This was a simmering malevolence that lurked behind what he'd always thought was reality.

"*All right,*" the Ur-Witch said. "*What do you suggest?*"

Book raised the gun. "I suggest I just keep shooting until there's nothing left of you."

The Ur-Witch ran her pink tongue along fat earthworm lips. "*And your lover dies.*"

Ruby shifted Aiden so she could cradle him in one arm, and she reached for Book. "Give me the gun, Charlie."

Book shied from her. "What for?"

Gerald knew what for. He could hear it in Ruby's voice. She had bought them a couple of minutes talking about making a deal with the Ur-Witch, but she had come to the only conclusion. There was no deal to be made. Gerald thought Ruby meant to put a bullet in her own brain.

Book had been slow on the uptake, but he must have seen it in her eyes, for he took a step away from her. "Not a chance."

Standoff. They could end up out there on the deck forever.

Gerald stepped between them and kept going. Book tried to grab his arm, but Gerald shook him off. Ruby said his name, but he shook that off as well. The Ur-Witch hissed at him, grinned, and licked her lips, and Gerald tightened his grip on the knife. He stared at the single candle flame still burning at the tip of one of her horns, a smaller one, that jutted slightly to the left.

He stopped four feet from her, close enough to smell the rot in what was left of Luisa's flesh. The wind gusted that stink into his face, and he forced himself not to be sick.

"*What are you going to do?*" the Ur-Witch asked him. "*You are an intruder here. This does not involve you.*"

Gerald hadn't meant to answer. He'd intended only to drive the knife into her heart, to put an end to this. Ruby didn't really want to die and Book didn't want to let her. That left it to him. But the Ur-Witch told him he didn't belong, and he could not keep silent.

He pointed at her with the tip of the knife. "You're the intruder. On this ship, in this goddamn world, and most importantly, in that *skin*."

The Ur-Witch inhaled deeply, as if catching the scent of his grief. "*Oh, you loved her. Sad little man. It destroys you to see her like this?*"

Gerald had never said it aloud to anyone, knowing it would

change everything. Maybe Luisa would never have fallen in love with him. Maybe he would have had to satisfy himself with what they'd had instead of what he hoped the future might bring. But now he would never know.

"I loved her," he said, breath catching in his throat, fingers clenching the handle of that knife. "She was everything I ever wanted. You killed her . . . and you're wearing what's left of her. You want to know if it rips me apart, seeing what you've done to her?"

Gerald lunged at her, aiming for her throat. He could see that rotting pumpkin skin there. If he could kill her without driving that blade into flesh that had belonged to Luisa, it might haunt him a little less.

The Ur-Witch grabbed the knife, fingers wrapped around the blade, and hissed as momentum brought them face-to-face. He felt the knife cut through skin into tendon and meat.

She ripped the knife from his grasp and shoved him backward. Gerald reeled, hit the deck, and skidded in the rain. He threw his body flat and scrabbled with his palms and the toes of his boots to keep from going over the edge into the hull. Mangrove trees bent in the wind above him. Rusty deck cracked under his knee as he crawled away from the edge. Several mangrove crabs dropped down around him and hurried away, back toward the trees.

"*Worry not, little man*," the Ur-Witch sneered. "*You don't have to see your woman like this anymore.*"

The monster plunged the knife into her own abdomen. "*I have a foothold in this world now, and I won't surrender it so easily. I will build another circle, gather new weavers, but I will not forget this. You will see me again.*"

She ripped the blade side to side to open a wound, and then dragged it upward.

Gerald rose to his feet, staring in breathless silence.

The wind lessened. The rain began to let up.

The Ur-Witch toppled to one side, the knife plunking to the deck.

The baby cried.

For a moment, Gerald thought it was over, but then he saw that the last remaining candle still burned.

40

Book whipped his head back and forth, looking at Stratim and then at Ruby. The deck of the *Christabel* was littered with corpses, but in that moment, the only one that mattered belonged to Luisa. Stratim had cut herself open and fallen, and now she didn't even twitch. It made no sense at all.

"Charlie!" Ruby said, grabbing his arm and tugging him toward her. She tried to push Aiden into his arms. "Take the baby!"

Book found himself accepting the wailing bundle, barely aware of it until he looked down to see Aiden in his arms. Red-faced from crying, Aiden arched his back as if trying to break loose—from the blanket, from a stranger's arms, from the threat all around him. But the threat had ended, hadn't it?

He looked up. "Ruby?"

She stood waiting to die. Her hands were out like she was fighting the swaying of the rusted freighter or expecting an earthquake. Her gaze shifted rapidly, looking at nothing and everything.

"I don't understand," she said. And he knew what she meant. She didn't understand still being alive, sure that Stratim's death would mean her own.

Gerald walked toward the Ur-Witch's stolen body, grieving for the ruins of Luisa that lay before him. This was a funeral walk. He stood over her, looking down. "The candle's still burning."

Book looked at Ruby. "How?"

She shrugged. He knew what was going through her head because it was the same thing going through his. Was there a way for her to survive this? Book looked down at Aiden in his arms, and a warm ripple went through him. *Cry all you like*, he thought.

He looked at Ruby. The edges of his mouth turned upward in the tentative beginning of a smile. Bella and Mae were dead. But if Ruby could make it through, and Aiden . . .

The presence of the Ur-Witch still made his skin crawl. He felt like he'd been injected with a kind of poison that would never leave him. The first finger of his right hand still ached with the weight of the trigger he had pulled and the blood he had spilled. But if they could live, all of this might mean something.

Long seconds passed with only the storm for company. Book, Ruby, and Gerald glanced back and forth among themselves. Aiden had fallen silent, and Book looked down to see that the baby had fallen asleep against his chest, so exhausted from screaming that his body could no longer sustain it.

"Charlie," Ruby said quietly, moving nearer to him, glancing down at her own body as if astounded by her own moving limbs, stunned to be alive.

He realized she'd been calling him *Charlie* for a while now, but he didn't correct her.

Ruby reached out to touch his stubbled face.

Which was when Gerald said, "Jesus Christ. Look at her."

On the deck, Stratim had not moved, but something jerked and twitched in the dark cavity she'd carved into her belly. Where there should have been innards, instead something sharp poked itself out of the papery edges of that wound.

The beak of a bird. It emerged from the shadowed inside of Luisa's stomach, first its head and then its wings. Its feathers were iridescent white, like glittering bone.

It took flight. The wind bore it aloft, and Book stared at the little fire that flickered on its tail feathers, streaking the air with its yellow glow. The bird flew across the deck toward the open water, that flame guttering.

"Gerald, no!" Ruby screamed.

But Gerald could not be stopped. He raced after the bird. As it cleared the railing, Gerald hurled himself after it, right over the side. He reached for the fire-tailed bird, got his hands around it, and pulled it to his chest as he fell.

Book held Aiden tightly as he and Ruby rushed to the railing. They heard the splash of Gerald hitting the water, but by the time they looked over the edge, he'd sunk beneath the churning Gulf, bird and all.

The bone-white bird's tail feathers still burned, even underwater. Gerald had the bird in his hands, and the flame burned his wrists with cold fire. The air in his lungs would not last very long, but he did not try to kick toward the surface. His clothes and boots were heavy with water, dragging him down, but all he cared about was the creature in his hands.

With a fierce twist, he broke its neck. The bird stopped struggling, its wild heart going still, but the flame on its tail still burned. He wrenched and jerked until he tore the bird's head from its body and that little flame winked out, leaving him to drown in utter darkness.

Nearly.

He released a tiny bit of air through his lips and felt bubbles tickle his cheek as they rose toward the surface, and he followed them. When he burst up amid the waves, gasping for air, coughing to clear his lungs, he reached down to unlace his boots and kick them off. On a clear day, well rested, he could have swum to shore from here, but tonight, he had no chance, and even less with those boots on.

Turning, he saw that he was only thirty feet from the floating dock attached to the hull of the *Christabel*, and he struck out for it, thinking he might live to see the sunrise after all. He'd closed within twenty feet when he heard a shriek of stressed metal and looked up to see the whole platform tear loose from the freighter. Their research ship and the boat he'd borrowed to get out here were both tied to the floating dock, but the dock was attached to the permanent platform, and the platform crashed down into the water and sank. He expected the dock to be dragged down with it, or to bob on the surface, anchored there. Instead, the iron rings that kept the dock affixed to the platform slipped up over the tops of the pilings as the platform sank, and the dock began to float away, with those two boats still tied to it.

Gerald looked up at the single flight of fire-escape-style stairs still affixed to the hull, nearly up to the deck, and he knew he could never reach it from the water. He looked at the dock and the boats, floating away, and pictured himself climbing aboard one of them. Surviving.

He thought of Luisa, and he started to swim.

41

The wind died like it had been blown out.

Ruby and Book stood on the deck, alone now except for Aiden and the dead. Just a few feet away, the last candle on Luisa's hollowed remains still burned, but it had begun to flicker. The rain lightened, falling almost as if embarrassed it had made such a fuss. Ruby thought the storm clouds had begun to thin. The influence of the weavers faded.

Book shifted the baby's weight against his chest and reached out his right hand. Ruby took that hand, fingers twining with his, so painfully familiar. So much a part of the past. She would have given anything to go back there.

"This is it," Book said, searching her eyes. "You and me—"

"Shut up, Charlie," Ruby told him.

"I was so stupid."

"You were," she agreed. "But we both were. Dumb and hurting. I couldn't think past what I'd lost, and you were too confused about what you were supposed to feel to see what I needed from you."

"I wasn't mature enough to deal with it."

Ruby smiled. With her free hand, she stroked hair away from Aiden's sleeping face. "Understatement of the century."

She took it all in—this image of the two of them with a newborn, the life they could have had together. The life they should have had.

One reassuring hand on top of the sleeping baby, Ruby rose up on her toes and kissed Book. She let her lips linger, gently brushing his, a kiss full of the love she would always have for this man.

Ruby ran her hand along his arm the way she had one hundred times before, and then she turned and knelt by Luisa's remains. She looked at the tangle of horns on the dead woman's head, then let herself focus on the last remaining candle. Wistful, she reached out and pinched the flame between two fingers.

The candle went out.

Book cried out in wordless sorrow. Ruby's head drooped as her body relaxed. She'd been kneeling, but now she spilled to one side. With Aiden asleep in his arms, he went gently to his knees and for a moment only watched her, waiting for some sign that she had not just snuffed her life along with that candle flame.

"Ruby," he said, those two syllables almost a eulogy.

The rain had stopped. Overhead, the clouds began to thin. Aiden purred in his arms, asleep for now but wrapped in a soaking-wet blanket. He needed to be somewhere warm and dry, needed to be changed and soothed. Aiden needed a parent.

Book balanced the baby against his chest and reached out, still on his knees, to try to brush the heavy, wet hair from Ruby's face. He wondered if it would have come to this if things had been different. If *he* had been different. What would their lives have looked like then?

Her body twitched.

Book jerked his hand back, watching her, wondering if he'd imagined it. But no, there, her chest moved. The shirt clung wetly, but beneath it, her chest rose and fell, and he felt a flutter in his own chest. She was breathing.

But of course she was not.

Something moved under that wet fabric. The sounds that came from Ruby's chest made him shuffle backward, still on his knees. He held Aiden, ready to take the child and run, but when the small beak and flat disk of a face pushed through, Book froze. He'd never seen a red owl before, but the muted hues of its feathers could only be called red. It tore fabric and slipped from Ruby as if being born in that very moment.

He should have felt horror or fear, even disgust. Instead, he exhaled, grieving but relieved to know that she was not entirely gone from this world.

The owl didn't belong out here on the water, and knew it. She took flight, and Book stood to watch her go. He walked to the railing of the *Christabel*, tracking her journey into the thinning clouds. Several stars peeked through, along with patches of indigo sky that suggested dawn was still hours away, but that it would be here soon.

The rumble of a motor reached him, and Book looked down to see a familiar-looking boat arriving. It was *Country Girl*, Steve Orway's restored Chris-Craft, and Book realized it must be the boat Gerald had borrowed to get out to the *Christabel*. The Chris-Craft slowed as it drew alongside the old freighter.

It gladdened Book's heart to see Gerald pop out onto the deck and wave his arms. Gerald called out something that the shushing of the sea erased, but Book got the general idea. The docking platform had torn away from the derelict freighter's hull, and there was no way he and Aiden were getting off the ship until Gerald could reach shore and return with help.

Country Girl's engine growled to life. The boat turned and roared toward Galveston with Gerald at the helm. Book searched the sky for that red owl and was not at all surprised that it had not lingered.

It would be a couple of hours, he suspected, before Gerald returned. Book would take Aiden inside, get both of them warm and dry, and with any luck, they would be napping together by the time rescue arrived.

In Book's arms, Aiden shifted and squirmed. He needed to

sleep, but he was cold and wet, trapped in that blanket now and unable to put those feelings into words.

"I've got you, kid," Charlie Book rasped, wiping at his eyes. "Don't worry about a thing. I've got you."

Acknowledgments

By my count, this is the fourteenth novel I've done with my editor, Michael Homler, with more to come. I'm forever grateful for his faith and support. Thank you, Michael.

My gratitude also to the entire team at St. Martin's, including Madeline Alsup, Allison Ziegler, Hector DeJean, and the extraordinarily talented Jonathan Bush, whose covers make everything better. Thanks as well to my entire team, most especially my agent, Howard Morhaim, and my manager, Peter Donaldson. Thanks to John McIlveen and Roberta Colasanti, who offered me a safe haven when Covid kept me away from home (and where I tried to work on this book during a terrible time).

There are so many others to thank, and I'm grateful to you all, but always first and foremost to my love, my wife, Connie, and the family we've made together.